Maurice Procter and The Murder Room

》》》 This title is part of The Murder Room, our series dedicated to making available out-of-print or hard-to-find titles by classic crime writers.

Crime fiction has always held up a mirror to society. The Victorians were fascinated by sensational murder and the emerging science of detection; now we are obsessed with the forensic detail of violent death. And no other genre has so captivated and enthralled readers.

Vast troves of classic crime writing have for a long time been unavailable to all but the most dedicated frequenters of second-hand bookshops. The advent of digital publishing means that we are now able to bring you the backlists of a huge range of titles by classic and contemporary crime writers, some of which have been out of print for decades.

From the genteel amateur private eyes of the Golden Age and the femmes fatales of pulp fiction, to the morally ambiguous hard-boiled detectives of mid twentieth-century America and their descendants who walk our twenty-first century streets, The Murder Room has it all. 》》》

The Murder Room
Where Criminal Minds Me(

themurderroom.com

T0352075

Maurice Procter 1906–1973

Born in Nelson, Lancashire, Maurice Procter attended the local grammar school and ran away to join the army at the age of fifteen. In 1927 he joined the police in Yorkshire and served in the force for nineteen years before his writing was published and he was able to write full-time. He was credited with an ability to write exciting stories while using his experience to create authentic detail. His procedural novels are set in Granchester, a fictional 1950s Manchester, and he is best known for his series characters, Detective Superintendent Philip Hunter and DCI Harry Martineau. Throughout his career, Procter's novels increased in popularity in both the UK and the US, and in 1960 *Hell is a City* was made into a film starring Stanley Baker and Billie Whitelaw. Procter was married to Winifred, and they had one child, Noel.

Philip Hunter

The Chief Inspector's Statement (1951)
  aka *The Pennycross Murders*
I Will Speak Daggers (1956)
  aka *The Ripper*

Chief Inspector Martineau

Hell is a City (1954)
  aka *Somewhere in This City*
The Midnight Plumber (1957)
Man in Ambush (1958)
Killer at Large (1959)

Devil's Due (1960)
The Devil Was Handsome (1961)
A Body to Spare (1962)
Moonlight Flitting (1963)
  aka *The Graveyard Rolls*
Two Men in Twenty (1964)
Homicide Blonde (1965)
  aka *Death has a Shadow*
His Weight in Gold (1966)
Rogue Running (1966)
Exercise Hoodwink (1967)
Hideaway (1968)

Standalone Novels
Each Man's Destiny (1947)
No Proud Chivalry (1947)
The End of the Street (1949)
Hurry the Darkness (1952)
Rich is the Treasure (1952)
  aka *Diamond Wizard*
The Pub Crawler (1956)
Three at the Angel (1958)
The Spearhead Death (1960)
Devil in Moonlight (1962)
The Dog Man (1969)

Moonlight Flitting

Maurice Procter

An Orion book

Copyright © Maurice Procter 1963

The right of Maurice Procter to be identified as the author of this work
has been asserted in accordance with the Copyright, Designs and Patents
Act 1988.

This edition published by
The Orion Publishing Group Ltd
Orion House
5 Upper St Martin's Lane
London WC2H 9EA

An Hachette UK company
A CIP catalogue record for this book is available from the British Library

ISBN 978 1 4719 0277 2

www.orionbooks.co.uk

Chapter One

At eleven o'clock on the night of Tuesday the twenty-sixth of September, Sam Glover decided to make a telephone call. He made the call, to the A Division headquarters of the Granchester City Police. It concerned his father, Luke Glover. If his father's name had been new to the ears of the police switchboard operator, he would probably have been told to call again when the matter became serious enough to take up a policeman's time. But Luke Glover was a millionaire, as near as made no difference. Furthermore—a matter of importance to the police —he was a city councilor and a member of the Watch Committee. The call was put through to the station sergeant.

"Yes, Mr. Glover," the sergeant answered patiently, when he had listened to the complaint. "Your father did not get home at his usual time of seven o'clock. It is now eleven o'clock, and he has not telephoned or sent word. Very well, I'll have inquiries made."

"You don't seem to be terribly interested," Sam said crisply. "I might save you a bit of time if I tell you about the inquiries I've already made. To start with, my father *never* fails to inform my stepmother when he isn't going to be home for dinner, or when he's going to be late. He hasn't been at his club this evening, and he hasn't been to the Town Hall. He hasn't been seen at any of his favorite restaurants, and he never goes into a pub. In fact, he doesn't seem to have been seen by anybody since he left the club after lunch."

"What time was that, sir?"

"Around half past two."

"Does anybody know where he intended to go from there?"

"Not his immediate destination. I phoned his secretary's home. She didn't see him at all this afternoon, though he'd said he'd be back at the office soon after five. He told her he had a small private matter to attend to after lunch, then he was going to the new factory site at Dodsbury. I phoned Hardwick, the contractor. Hardwick was on the site all afternoon, but he never saw my father, or heard any mention of him. So it's reasonable to assume he wasn't there."

"So he's actually been missing since half past two this afternoon," said the sergeant, very alert now. "I assume he was driving a car?"

"Yes. A sage-green Silver Cloud."

"That's a Rolls-Royce, isn't it?"

"Yes. It's practically new. Only done about a thousand. I don't know the number, but I'll get it for you and ring you back."

"Thank you, Mr. Glover," the sergeant said. "Now will you give me a description of your father and, as far as you know, what clothes he was wearing?"

In this way the search for Luke Glover was taken over by the police. Receptionists at local hospitals heard his name and description, but their replies were negative. Descriptions of the man and his car were given to all members of the Granchester police, and to the county police, and to the police of the boroughs and county boroughs which surrounded the big city. That was all, for the moment. It was generally understood that there was nothing to get excited about. The old fellow would turn up, and then somebody would be in trouble for forgetting to transmit some message he had left.

Jonty Blades first saw the Rolls-Royce at a quarter past four on Tuesday afternoon. It was standing in Grimwood Road, near the front gate of Grimwood Cemetery. He could see that the car was unattended, nor was there any person in sight. He approached, and peered inside. He hoped to see a rich leather briefcase, or some other valuable article, but there was nothing movable except the ignition key. The key was golden, with a golden tag. Noting the immaculate condition of the car, he assumed that the key would be of solid gold. Walking round the vehicle he found that the door beside the driver's seat was not locked. He looked doubtfully at the key and decided not to touch it. It would not be an easy thing to sell.

He looked from the car to the cemetery gate, and saw that it was padlocked, as usual. If the owner of the car was moon-ing about in the cemetery, he must have gone in by the side gate. It was then that Jonty narrowed his keen brown eyes to read the name on the tag of the ignition key. He read it, and whistled, and looked over the locked gate at the roof and chim-neys of Cemetery Lodge.

"Aha," he said to himself. "Trouble, Jonty. He's found out."

As his small, spry legs moved him along the cemetery frontage, he tried to rehearse the role he expected to play. Normally he was capable of simple constructive thought, but by the time he was halfway along the short lane which led to the side gate, his incurable optimism had led him into a dream of sudden af-fluence. "He's a millionaire," he reflected gleefully. "Four or five hundred nicker 'ull be naught ter him."

Though it was a cool, damp afternoon, the back door of Cemetery Lodge stood wide open. But there was no sound of angry voices, and Jonty interpreted that as a good sign. Perhaps the millionaire was a reasonable man. "He can get off wi' payin'," he chuckled.

But there was no stranger in the kitchen of the lodge. The Blades family was at peace. Mrs. Blades was sitting in one of the imitation-leather armchairs, darning a sock. Sitting on the bare boards at her feet little Carrie was childishly engaged with a similar task. Across the hearth from her, Uncle was sound asleep in the other chair, and for a change he was not snoring. The boy Gaylord was sitting on the settee, staring at the log fire; which he frequently did, for long periods. Twenty-two-year-old Ellie, whom Jonty's glance instinctively sought, was standing at the kitchen table, serenely busy with scissors, pattern and material, cutting out a dress.

Jonty was disappointed. "Has nobody been?" he asked.

His wife showed surprise. "Should somebody a-been?" she asked.

"There's a car at front gate."

"Well, nobody's been," she said without ill-humor. "I wish somebody had. I'm fed up wi' t' same owd faces."

Jonty turned and went out of doors. He rounded the house and stood on the straight main drive of the cemetery, and gazed around. He could see no movement among the graves, the ancient graves of people long forgotten. He went to the gate and then he walked the full length of the drive, looking this way and that. He saw nobody. He stared suspiciously at the trees beside the cemetery wall, and then he told himself not to be a fool. The driver of that splendid car outside would not waste his time in watching the half-ruined lodge of a disused graveyard.

In the kitchen again, Jonty grumbled that it was a funny do. There was that posh car outside. There wasn't a Rolls went along Grimwood Road once in a blue moon, let alone one being left there.

4

"It was there just after three," said Ellie calmly, without looking up from her work.

"And was there nobody with it?"

"No, not a soul."

"Were you comin' back from a meetin' wi' yer boy friend?"

"Yes."

"Did he see the car?"

"No. He went the other way."

"On his own?"

"Sure. He's always on his own, isn't he? What on earth is the matter with you?"

"Naught," Jonty replied. "It's a funny do, that's all."

Two hours later Jonty went out of doors again. The Rolls-Royce was still in Grimwood Road, and the ignition key was still in its socket. He returned to the lodge, pondering. There was a chance of profit in reaching the rich man on the telephone and letting him know where his car was to be found. Then, probably, a chauffeur or somebody would be sent, with a tip for Jonty in his pocket. And the chauffeur would keep the tip for himself, as likely as not. Or he might keep four pounds fifteen out of a fiver and part with a dollar. No, that move was no good. Nor would it be wise to drive the car to its owner's residence. He might not like that.

Sitting looking at his family and possessions, Jonty lowered his sights and decided that he would have to be satisfied with a small advantage. The previous day an employee of the City Parks Department had discovered the Blades family in residence at the lodge. Since the building had been condemned as both unsafe and unfit for habitation, he had informed Jonty that he would have him out of there as soon as he could get an eviction order. Fortunately, Jonty had another deserted building in mind, and he had made the usual preparations for a move.

MAURICE PROCTER

He had bought furniture on hire purchase, so that he could vanish into the blue with it before the first monthly installments became due. He would sell it and acquire some more furniture as soon as he became convinced that the credit firm's investigators had ceased to hunt for him. He would not commit a criminal offense until he sold the furniture.

That afternoon Jonty had been to see about the hire of a handcart for Sunday morning, to move his furniture and bedding to the new place. Now, he calculated that the handcart would have to be brought to Grimwood, and used for at least two trips with a full load, and then returned to its owner. It would have to be pushed for at least fifteen miles by the male members of the Blades family. A grim prospect. And suppose it was raining!

Until someone had, apparently, abandoned a big car on his doorstep, Jonty had seen no alternative to this hardship. He could not engage a reputable furniture remover to transport his goods, because credit investigators always went to the removers for information when there had been a moonlight flit. And anyway, he could not bear to think of the cost. But he had looked at the Rolls-Royce and seen that it had wide doors, a large luggage compartment and a sunshine roof. With the roof open, dismembered bedsteads could be carried. The settee could be roped across the open trunk. The armchairs could be taken on a second trip. Mattresses and smaller chairs would go inside the car. The table was one of the recent purchases. It was of the type called "gate-legged." When closed it would go inside the car.

Jonty went out to the car again. Attached to the tag of the ignition key there was a second key, and this fitted the glove compartment and the trunk. He looked up and down the road. There was no one in sight. And soon it would be dark. He got into the driver's seat, started the car and found the reverse

6

gear. Carefully he backed the vehicle to the lane, and along to the side gate of the cemetery.

He returned to the lodge. "All right," he announced. "Yer can all start packin'. We're flittin' tonight."

An hour later, when it was quite dark, Jonty and Gaylord went with the first load of furniture to the new place. Jonty avoided main roads as much as possible, and he instructed his son to have a sharp eye for policemen and police cars.

But he was gleeful. "This'll save us five bob an' a right lot o' leg work," he claimed. "It's just the job, this is."

Gaylord made no reply, and Jonty glanced at him uneasily. The boy enjoyed any unusual activity, and particularly he enjoyed a flitting. But tonight when he had helped Jonty to take down the beds, his mind had obviously been wandering. He had smiled wanly at some of his father's sallies, and some he had not seemed to hear. He was always clumsy, but tonight his hands and feet had seemed to be no part of him. And when not given a specific task, he had stood helpless, as if he did not know what had to be done.

That was strange. Gaylord had flitted before, many a time. As a rule, he knew exactly what to do.

"Yer quiet, lad," Jonty commented. "What ails yer?"

"Naught," Gaylord replied.

"Feelin' poorly?"

"No."

"Look, I know yer liked at cemetery. But this place where we're goin' is better. Plenty firewood fer yer ter chop. Lots an' lots a-trees. Yer can't see t' place fer trees. Yer'll like it all right, an' so will our Carrie an' Uncle. I know yer will."

Gaylord did not reply. Jonty sighed. The boy had always been dreamy and moody. Children like that generally had brains of some sort, but not Gaylord. He was definitely backward.

7

Jonty had to admit it. Gaylord knew that two ha'pennies made a penny, and twelve pennies made a shilling. His ambition in life was to be a firewood dealer, at a time when fewer and fewer people were buying firewood. Ah well, happen he would be able to make some sort of a living.

Chapter Two

The Rolls-Royce was found soon after midnight, by a constable on his beat. It was standing in a side street, in the poor, rough neighborhood of Churlham. The place was central enough to be in A Division. Detective Sergeant Devery, the officer temporarily in charge of A Div. C.I.D., heard the news and considered the significance of a Silver Cloud apparently abandoned in Churlham. The assumption was that the car had been illegally borrowed, used for some purpose and then left in a place convenient for the borrower. If that was the offense which had been committed, it was not really a C.I.D. matter. But Devery was curious, and not too busy. He asked himself why the unlawful taking away of such a valuable car had not been reported by the owner. There was a smell of trouble about every answer which occurred to him. He went to Churlham, taking Detective Constable Hearn with him.

In the ill-lit street of grimy brick houses the Silver Cloud shone with dim resplendence, as incongruous as a crystal chandelier in a cowshed. There was a uniformed constable guarding it. "You found it?" Devery asked.

"That's right. Couldn't miss it, could I?"

"When are you taking it in?"

"Inspector says leave it a while, till we're sure it's been abandoned," the P.C. replied. "He's trying to find out if the owner is still somewhere around here. What a hope! What would Luke Glover be doing around here?"

"You never can tell," said Devery absently. He was looking into the car.

The P.C. said, "Ignition key's still there."

"So it is. That'll be Glover's key. Car thieves don't have spare keys for Rolls-Royces."

"Not made of gold, they don't."

"It's a gold key?"

"Looks like it to me. I've not touched it, mind you."

Hearn said, "It's a wonder somebody else hasn't, in this street."

"Which makes it look as if it hadn't been here a long time when it was found," Devery rejoined. "Was the radiator warm?"

"Eeh, I never noticed," the P.C. said lamely.

The sergeant opened the door beside the driver's seat. The questing beam of his flashlight came to rest on the floor of the car. "Look at this muck," he said to Hearn. "Glover's shoes never left dirt like this. It looks as if a couple of farmers have had their feet in here."

It had been a damp day, with a little rain in the evening. The dirt was not gray and dusty, it was moist and new.

Devery reached for the keys. "Have you looked in the trunk?" he asked.

"Inspector did. Nothing in there."

Devery opened the boot. His light moved around the interior and picked up a glitter of bright metal in a far corner. Hearn saw it too. He leaned forward and reached to secure the gleaming object. He looked at it, and handed it to the sergeant. It was a steel-and-brass castor or runner, of the sort used to give some mobility to armchairs and settees. It seemed to be new.

"If somebody has been using a car like this to move furniture about, he certainly has a nerve," Devery commented. He put the castor in his pocket.

"Oy!" the P.C. protested. "Inspector won't like you taking that away."

Devery replied coolly, "Tell him I'll give him full and frequent reports of the progress of my inquiries."

The two detectives returned to their own car. The P.C. watched them go. He was conscious of missed opportunities. "Bloody C.I.D.," he muttered. "Buttin' in where they're not wanted."

On the morning of Wednesday the twenty-seventh of September, Detective Chief Inspector Martineau rode down to Headquarters in good humor. Things were quiet: not much doing. His department's crime clearance average was unusually high, and the average of property recovered was good. That day there would be no need for him to harass any of his subordinates or be harassed by any superior. With that peaceful prospect he was able to dwell pleasantly on an item of yesterday's news, delivered not by a newsboy but by a copper's nark called Pot Eye Walker. Pot Eye had brought information of a crime. The crime had been committed in Martineau's manor, a part of the city where crime was his immediate responsibility. But this crime was unusual in two important respects: Martineau could laugh about it, and he did not need to bestir himself in the clearance of it. Its details would be filed in his readily evocative memory and nowhere else. Also, through a habit of reticence, he intended to keep those details to himself. It was a good joke which he had no desire to share.

With regard to the crime, he thought now of the excellent cover which so-called legitimate business could give to a thoroughgoing crook. His old enemy Dixie Costello, a rogue who had been successful enough to become a sultan among thieves and swindlers, had been using that sort of cover for years. Patiently and discreetly he had occupied himself in acquiring modest concerns with good reputations, and afterward he had nursed those reputations carefully. He had used nominees like a smoke cloud. Martineau had heard whispers and speculative comment but, until yesterday, he had no real knowledge. He did not know who were Costello's accountants, or his solicitors, or his bankers. He did know, with certainty, that Costello would not cease to be an active criminal until he was put away for a term of years, or laid in a coffin.

He had dwelt wistfully upon Costello's opportunities. The premises of a wholesale tobacconist can be used for the storage and disposal of a million stolen cigarettes. An outwardly respectable wine and spirit business can handle much stolen whisky. Merchants of various sorts can handle ill-gotten goods of the kinds in which they are accustomed to deal. Costello had criminal connections throughout the country, and goods in transit were being stolen every day. The possibilities were endless.

Yesterday Martineau had learned from the reliable Pot Eye that Costello was the owner of a firm called Palmer Radio. The Palmer business consisted of a central warehouse and workshop, and a number of radio and television shops. And Costello had acquired five hundred transistor radios valued at more than twenty pounds each, which had been stolen in Birmingham.

So it seemed that Martineau should have been taking some action about the transistors. But not so. The story had a punch line. Somebody had stolen Costello's stolen transistors. They were in his possession no longer. The whole consignment had been taken.

Martineau wondered which thief or gang of thieves had had the impudence, or the blissful ignorance, to rob Dixie Costello. Of course the goods had been taken when the premises were closed, and apparently nobody had seen the vehicle which had been used. Also, according to Pot Eye, it looked as if it had been a duplicate-key job. This meant that Dixie would now be regarding the staff of Palmer Radio with a very cold eye indeed. Martineau could imagine his wrath. He would calculate his loss not by the price at which he had bought the transistors, but by the selling price. Five hundred at twenty pounds. Ten thousand of the best. What would Costello do for ten thousand pounds? Anything, literally anything. He would seek first to recover the stolen property, using an intelligence system which Martineau knew to be superb. If he found out who had robbed him, and the robbers failed to make good in cash or kind, then somebody would be killed, or blinded, or maimed for life. Death or permanent injury was the price of flouting Dixie Costello.

Martineau had little hope of being informed that Dixie had recovered the transistors. Pot Eye was a brave little man in his way, but he was not a suicidal type. To be the means of sending Dixie to prison was to invite an early and uncomfortable demise. Nevertheless, the chief inspector was pleased with what he had already learned. It might lead to something. This time it had been transistors. Another time it might be television sets.

With that comforting reflection, Martineau walked into Headquarters. In the C.I.D. main office, the first person he saw was Sergeant Devery. "Hello," he said. "What are you doing here at this time? I thought you were on evening duty."

"I am," Devery replied. "I stuck my neck out last night. I've got to get busy as soon as the shops open."

"Tell me about this chance you took."

Devery gave all the information he had about Luke Glover's disappearance, about the Rolls-Royce, about the metal castor. He showed Martineau the castor.

"And Glover is still missing?" came the question.

"I've heard nothing to the contrary."

Martineau looked at his watch. "Luke Glover," he said

thoughtfully. "The boss will be hearing about him any minute now. He'll get into a tizzy. You'd better get cracking with that castor right away. Take a man with you."

Devery nodded, and turned away. Martineau went into his own office. The internal-line telephone buzzed. He picked up the receiver and heard the voice of Chief Superintendent Clay, the head of the Granchester C.I.D.

"Martineau," Clay said. "I want you. Immediately."

Immediately, Martineau went to Clay's office. The stout superintendent was frowning over the call book. "Have you heard about Luke Glover?" he asked.

"Just this minute," his subordinate replied.

"Can you imagine the headlines when the press gets hold of it?"

"Sure, 'Missing Millionaire,' and all that."

"Inspector Bradley has had the job all night. He's still on with it. He's complained to Superintendent Anderson about Sergeant Devery removing some evidence from Glover's car."

"Yes, sir. A castor from a chair or a sofa. It was Devery who found it. He felt justified in removing it in order to make inquiries about it."

"And he's done that?"

"He's doing it now, sir."

"Good enough. I'm going to treat this as partly a C.I.D. matter. I'll see the chief as soon as he comes in and get his word on it. Glover may have lost his memory, or something of the sort, but he's such an important man that all branches of the service must be engaged in finding him. Drop anything you're doing and attend to it. Divisional boundaries don't count. Get hold of Bradley and see what he's done. Then get busy on the Glover family. See the wife first, then the son."

"Yes, sir," said Martineau.

Chapter Three

Taking Detective Constable Cassidy with him, Martineau drove out to Broadhulme, the residential suburb where the Glover house stood. The house had the somewhat unimaginative name of "The Beeches," but it was a beautiful dwelling. Regency, Martineau guessed as he admired its perfect proportions.

At the front door, his pressure on the bell button was answered by a middle-aged housemaid. It could be reasonably assumed that never before had she opened that door to two such visitors. Both were very big men, both obviously very hard men. Martineau was moderately handsome in a craggy sort of way, Cassidy, with his quick eyes, snub nose and long lip, was the Irishman of the type pugilistic. But the maid was a hard case herself. She looked at them severely. They were the sort of people who ought not to be there.

Martineau introduced himself, and asked if he and his companion might see Mrs. Glover. The woman's expression did not soften, but a look of unfriendly satisfaction crept into it. If a policeman had to be admitted to the house, it was right that he should be a policeman of rank. She bade them enter, and without a further word left them standing in the hall while she went into one of the rooms. Martineau looked at Cassidy with raised eyebrows and a faint grin. The Irishman winked solemnly.

The woman returned, leaving the room door open. She indicated that the two men should pass through the doorway. She closed the door behind them and, presumably, went away.

It was a drawing room or lounge, a big room with four tall windows. The chief inspector thought that it was furnished in good taste. He wondered briefly if the taste was that of some interior decorator or of a Glover.

The room had two occupants. A stocky, good-looking young man with crisp dark hair was standing on the hearthrug with his back to the fireplace. Near him, a handsome woman of thirty or so was sitting on the edge of an armchair. The woman rose as the policemen entered. "Is there any news?" she asked.

Martineau shook his head. "No news of Mr. Glover," he said. "We have his car. It seems to be undamaged except for a few scratches on the coachwork. We're working on the car. We think it has been in the possession of someone other than himself."

"You mean somebody stole the car?" the young man asked.

"Borrowed it more likely, since it was found in Churlham. Or else he had passengers for a while," Martineau replied. He looked at the woman. "I presume you're Mrs. Luke Glover?"

"Yes," she replied. "And this is his son, Sam."

"I see," Martineau had his notebook out. He learned that the wife of Luke Glover was called Diana. She was well named. Diana, a huntress, he reflected: a tall, handsome blonde with a perfect figure and glorious coloring. She would do her hunting without moving. When she wanted a man, she would snare him.

"We're doing all we can to find Mr. Glover," he said. "Who was the last member of the family to see him?"

Sam Glover and his stepmother looked at each other. It was a glance without collusion, a glance which could have passed between two people who knew each other only slightly. It carried an unspoken question: who was going to speak first?

"I saw him at breakfast yesterday," Diana Glover said. "I haven't seen him since."

"Did he inform you of the day's intentions?"

"Only that he was having lunch at his club."

"That is the Granchester Club?"

"Yes."

"At breakfast, was he, er, normal?"

"Quite. He was reading the paper. We don't talk much in the morning."

Martineau smiled. "That's about normal for everyone, I think. What time did he leave here?"

"About nine. I didn't notice exactly."

"In the Rolls?"

"Yes. Driving himself."

Martineau looked up quickly. "Isn't that usual?"

"No. He usually has Brown, the chauffeur, drive him to town. Then Brown takes the car in when he wants it."

The chief inspector turned to Sam. "Did you see your father yesterday?"

The young man shook his head. "Sorry. I can't be any help at all. I was in the office early, bang on nine, then straight off to Liverpool. I got back in the middle of the afternoon."

The next question was addressed to both wife and son. "Can you give me any sort of clue? Any little thing might help. For instance, has Mr. Glover been worrying about business?"

"Not to my knowledge," Sam said, and the woman shook her head. Sam added, "Business hasn't been too good lately, but not bad enough to worry anybody."

"I know this may sound a bit dramatic, but did he have an enemy? Was any person likely to do him a physical injury?"

"Not that I know of," said Sam, and again the woman concurred.

"Has he been threatened recently?"

"No."

"Has he ever had a bad lapse of memory?"

"No."

"Has he been deeply worried about anything at all?"

"No."

The questions went on. The sum of the answers was that Luke Glover had been in good health as far as his family knew, and that he had driven away from his club after lunch on the previous day to attend to a "small private matter." From there, nothing but an abandoned car and a chair castor. Martineau's questions about the possibilities of the castor produced only bewilderment.

Finally he checked with the wife the missing man's apparel on the previous day, and departed from there. He went to the head office of Glover Domestic Machinery—known throughout the country as G.D.M.—and saw Luke's secretary. The information she had, had already been given to the police by Sam. She did not change it in any way. He returned to his own office and sent for Sergeant Bird, whose duty it had been to give the Rolls-Royce a thorough examination.

"Well?" he asked.

"Lots of dabs," Bird reported. "There are fingerprints of five different persons. They're all shapes and sizes. None of them in our files. I'm preparing the usual forms for Wakefield and Scotland Yard."

"Mmmm. Not so good. Anything else?"

"I've scraped some of the dirt and grit off the floor of the car to send to the laboratory. And, by the way, the bodywork is knocked and scratched a bit."

"And that's all?"

"There's a sort of negative evidence. The steering wheel, steering column, dashboard in front of the driver's seat, driver's door and driving mirror are all as clean as a whistle. They've been wiped down."

"So the person who drove all the other characters about was

being careful. He didn't want us to find his dabs. He probably has a record."

"That's what it looks like to me," Bird agreed.

As the sergeant was leaving, Devery appeared. His face wore an expression of controlled elation which his colleagues knew quite well. "You've got something," Martineau said.

Devery produced the castor. "I found one concern which uses this type," he said. "There may be others in this town. I got the name and address of the makers."

Martineau waited. Devery was not looking like a dog with two tails because of a routine discovery like that.

"It's that new place, the Pay Tomorrow shop," the sergeant went on. "Non-deposit, a lifetime to pay, all furniture guaranteed not to fall apart in the first fortnight. The manager was cagey. Details of hire-purchase deals were confidential, he said. I pointed out that some customer had done a moonlight flit with some of his furniture. At last it sank into his skull that if we didn't find this customer, he might eventually have to set about the job himself. I assured him of our discretion, and he opened the books."

"He gave names?"

"He gave names, and I wrote them down. When he came to the name of Jonty Blades I told him I'd got enough."

"I think you had. Old Jonty. It must be five years since we heard from him. Nowadays he can only get away with it at a new shop. What address had he given?"

"Cemetery Lodge, Grimwood Road."

"An address which he vacated yesterday, I've no doubt," said Martineau. He took a map from a drawer, and spread it on his desk. "We know that Luke Glover intended to go to Dodsbury," he said. He found the place on the map and said, "If he went through Grimwood to get to Dodsbury he went a damned funny way, or else he came from a most unlikely direction."

"There was a private matter, you said."

Martineau put four fingertips on four adjacent districts on the map. "Luke Glover with *private* business in one of these places?"

Devery shook his head. "It doesn't look like it, does it? But we don't know yet that he ever went near Grimwood. We're making an assumption."

Martineau sat in thought, about Jonty Blades.

Jonty had recently made a purchase of Pay Tomorrow furniture, and Devery had discovered a castor—possibly from Pay Tomorrow furniture—in Luke Glover's Rolls-Royce. That could have been sheer coincidence. But coincidence was something which Martineau always regarded with deep suspicion. When men and events had a connection, he looked for a reason. That they might be connected by chance he would not believe until all search for a reason had been fruitless. He was now looking for the reason for the slightly fantastic discovery of a component of cheap furniture in a new Rolls-Royce. At the moment, the only person he could connect with it—apart from Glover himself—was Jonty Blades, a man who would pick up and appropriate anything which had been left lying around. By his habit of finding things before they were lost, Jonty had earned himself a police record: a comparatively harmless one, but still a record. When investigating an offense, Martineau liked to hear nothing better than the name of a man with a record. There had been an offense, the taking away of a motorcar without the owner's consent. Such an offense was well within Jonty's scope. It put him right in the line of fire.

Could Jonty have moved his sticks of furniture in a Rolls-Royce? Martineau believed he could have done that. It was a big car. Jonty was an inveterate moonlight flitter who was used to making hurried and secret removals in vehicles not built for carrying furniture. He could have done it, all right. But how and where he had got hold of the car was a different story, and one which he would be required to tell at the proper time.

The chief inspector rose, and with a long arm he reached for his hat. "As you suggest, we may be assuming too much," he said. "Let's go see if we can find Jonty."

Chapter Four

While he allowed Devery to drive him along Grimwood Road, Martineau's thoughts again jumped ahead of the known facts of the case. He wondered what could have been in the mind of a man like Luke Glover as he passed through a place like this. The long, dreary length of the railway sidings would offend his sense of order and industrial efficiency, no doubt. He would grumble to himself that it was valuable land being put to only partial use. Then there was the cemetery, consecrated ground where no body had been interred in the last fifty years. Being compelled to build his own new factory away out at Dodsbury, would he regard the cemetery as a dreadful waste of a good site?

Devery stopped the C.I.D. car at the cemetery gate. It was a high gate, securely padlocked. The hinges were sound. "We'll have to find another way in," Martineau said.

They found the little lane which led to the side gate. It ran between the side wall of the cemetery and the brick-built premises of a paint manufacturer. Its surface of cinders on clay was muddy in places, and tire tracks were clearly visible. The cemetery wall on this side was no more than four feet high, but there was a ragged screen of trees, mostly sycamore, on the other side. Perhaps the trees had not been there when the paint manufacturer built his place, because it had its solid brick back turned on the moldering dead. This gave the lane a secluded air. It could be seen only from its own entrance.

The two policemen moved along, pointing out tire tracks to each other. When they had walked a hundred yards they came to the end, which was simply an angle of the cemetery wall with trees beyond. Here on the right there was a wicket gate giving access to a path of black and mossy flagstones. The path went straight among old graves until it reached the cemetery's central drive, the main street of the dead. On the drive, near the front gate, stood Cemetery Lodge: empty, neglected, and condemned as unfit for human habitation.

No smoke came from the chimneys of the lodge, and there was no sign of human tenancy. But the back door had been left unlocked. The policemen entered and stood in the kitchen looking around. There was visible evidence of recent occupation: empty food cartons and tins, a crust of bread, crumbs on the kitchen floor. They sniffed. The odor of cooking was faint but definite.

"Jonty was here, and he skipped," said Martineau. "Have a look round while I go and see if they know anything at the paint works."

To enter the paint works he had to go through a little lobby with an office door and an inquiry window. There was a larger door at the end of the lobby, with a time-card clock beside it. The policeman tapped on the inquiry window. It was opened, and he saw the head and shoulders of a girl.

"Police," he said. "Could I see the manager?"

The girl turned away. A stout man of fifty or so appeared at the window. "Ah, Mr. Martineau," he said. "I've seen your picture in the paper."

"Are you the manager?"

"I'm all the manager there is. I own the place."

"Were you here yesterday afternoon?"

23

"I was here all day, up till half past five."

"Did you have any callers?"

"Only a traveler. Annie, what time did we have Smithson's man? Aye, that's right. About eleven o'clock, Inspector."

"Did you have a caller in the afternoon?"

"No, never a one. Did we, Annie? No, that's right. No callers in the afternoon."

"Do you happen to know Luke Glover?"

"Not to talk to. I've seen his picture in the paper, same as yours. Council affairs and such."

"Would you know him if you saw him?"

"I daresay I would, if I happened to look at him. What's he done?"

"He's got lost. Did you see any strangers at all yesterday?"

"No, I can't say I did. Did you, Annie? No, she didn't."

"Did you see anything at all out of the ordinary?"

"Yes, I did. When I went home I saw a car standing at the front gate of the cemetery. When I drove past it, I noticed it was a Rolls-Royce. A Rolls waiting in Grimwood Road is out of the ordinary, you can take it from me."

"Did you notice the number?"

"No."

"Was anybody with the car?"

"I didn't see anybody. There was nobody sitting in it."

"What color was it?"

"Two tones of green. Sage green and a soft olive. That's definite. I notice color. It's my business."

"Thank you. What do you know about the people who have been living in the cemetery lodge?"

"Nothing. Not a thing. What about you, Annie? No, she didn't know there was anybody in the lodge. Course, Annie and me, and the men here, we just come and go. The lodge is there all the time, but we wouldn't notice if it had fallen down in the night."

"I see. What time did you notice the car?"

"Turned five. Quarter past five, happen."

Martineau thanked him and returned to the lodge. Devery was looking in outhouses. "There's nothing here," he said.

The chief inspector looked toward the front gate. "Nevertheless," he said, "we'll have to get some men and have the whole cemetery searched. Glover's car was standing out there just after five. If Jonty had been using it at that time, he wouldn't have left it there. He'd have left it at this end, or in the lane where we found the tire tracks."

"So do we assume that Glover left it there?"

"No, but he could have done. The Lord knows why, unless he entered the cemetery for some reason. I'll tell you what. Before we send for more men we'll have a preliminary look around."

If Martineau had been alone, he would have traversed the main drive, as Jonty had done the day before. Having Devery with him, he started at the gate and walked along the inside of the wall, while Devery set off in the other direction. By doing so they would be able to look along all the aisles between the graves, whether they ran the length or the width of the cemetery.

Devery's course led him along the four-foot wall beside the little lane, and he found Luke Glover's body close to the inner side of that wall. It was lying among deep, wet weeds. He whistled, and Martineau came.

The cause of death was obvious. There seemed to have been one terrible blow with some sharp, heavy weapon. The wound was nearly horizontal, across the back of the neck. A phrase of criminal argot came into the chief inspector's mind: Luke Glover had taken the chop.

"A messy way to die," he commented. "But he can't have felt much pain after he copped that one."

He considered the small, spare body and wondered if Jonty

Blades—himself a small man—would be strong enough to raise it to a height of four feet and drop it over the wall. He decided that Jonty would be able to do it. Jonty had always been regarded as harmless. He had no violence in his history. Well, he would not be the first harmless-looking murderer.

Whether or not the killer had been Jonty, he had had enough presence of mind to avoid the commission of a capital offense. It was not a hangman's job. The body still had money in its pockets. A watch and other valuable personal articles had not been taken. Apparently it had not been murder in the furtherance of theft.

Devery had vaulted over the wall, and he was looking for footprints in the lane, hoping to find a confused group of such prints which would mark the scene of the attack. On the other side of the lane, close to the wall of the paint factory, small stones and loose cinders had collected where no man trod and no wheel rolled. In one place the stones were unnaturally discolored.

"Blood here," he announced. "This seems to be the spot where he went down."

Martineau went to look. The cinders of the lane's surface were hard and dry just there. There were no footprints.

"Stay with it," he said. "Maybe you can look around for the weapon while I ring it in."

As he walked back to his car he wondered if Devery had indeed found the spot to mark with an X. If Luke Glover had been killed in that little cul-de-sac, what on earth had he been doing there? On his way to look for somebody's grave? On his way to visit Jonty? One possibility was as unlikely as the other.

On the car's radio he broke the news to Headquarters. Then he walked along to the cemetery's main gate, where Glover's car had been standing. There was nothing to see: no marks of any kind. He went further on to the other end of the cemetery's frontage. It extended a considerable distance, and on the other side of the road there was still railway property, bounded by hoardings above a six-foot wall. A very gloomy section of thoroughfare, he decided.

One does not walk very far in the older part of an English town without seeing a public house, whether it calls itself tavern, inn or hotel. Beyond the cemetery there was the Grimwood Inn, and beyond the inn were the rows of old working-class houses whose adult occupants it would serve. Newly painted, and generally well maintained by the brewers who owned it, it was the only bright spot in a drab landscape.

The name of the licensee, George Wensley, was painted on the fanlight above the front door. Martineau looked at his watch. The time was a little after two o'clock. The inn was still open for the midday period. He entered and walked into the bar. It was small, clean and more old-fashioned than modern; and it was deserted. He looked into the taproom, the best room and the snug. There wasn't a customer in the place.

He called, "Shop!" and a man came through a doorway behind the bar.

"You're not very busy," Martineau commented.

"No. It's very quiet today. They've all gone home to their dinners."

"Were you as quiet as this yesterday?"

The man raised his eyebrows. "We was fairly busy, as a matter of fact. What can I get you?"

Martineau shook his head. "Nothing at the moment. I'm a police officer." He showed his warrant card.

"Ah. I thought I knew your face. You're Martineau."

"That is so. Are you the man whose name is over the door?"

"That's me. I'm the boss here—when the wife is out. What can I do for you?"

"Answer a few questions, that's all. There's a body in the graveyard."

"Now you're kiddin'. It's full of bodies."

"This one was left lying on top."

"Oh. Who?"

There was no need to withhold the information. The newspapers would already have it. Martineau replied, "A man called Glover, Luke Glover. According to his driving license."

"Not Luke Glover of G.D.M.!"

"The same."

"Not murdered!"

"Yes. Murdered."

The landlord thought about that, obviously considering his own position, and the effect that Glover's murder might have on himself and his business. Martineau studied him. He was a short, sturdy man, essentially urban, essentially a man of the people, a common man of a common type. He spoke the language of his customers, who, in a place like that, were also common men.

The landlord seemed to decide that a sensation on his doorstep would not be a bad thing for business. His pleasure was obvious, but decently restrained. "Ida," he called.

From the landlord's living quarters a woman appeared. She was the common man's mate: pleasingly plump, quite pretty, capable, sensible and no doubt completely devoid of intellect. When she saw Martineau she knew him to be a policeman. Her face was wooden as she waited for the news.

"There's been a murder in the graveyard," Wensley said. "Councilor Glover, of all people."

He stopped, giving her time to digest the information. Her dismay was obvious, but fleeting. She assessed the position more quickly than he had done. And, typically, she concealed elation behind false sympathy. "Ooh, the poor man!" she said.

Wensley had his cue. Helpful sympathy, that was the line. Reporters would be in here, buying large whiskies and asking questions. They would mention the Grimwood Inn in their articles. The Grimwood Inn might be in the Sunday papers and all. Therefore, it would be necessary to give a good impression: to policemen, reporters, everybody.

So, with sympathy, the landlord asked, "Was it nasty? What was he killed with?"

That too would have to come out. "We think he was killed with an ax," Martineau said. "A big woodman's ax, probably."

Wensley's mouth fell open. His wife's sharp intake of breath was audible. Both of them turned pale. "Ooh, that's awful," the woman said weakly.

"You know something about a woodman's ax?" the chief inspector asked.

The couple looked at each other. Their doubt was plain to see. They were not criminals and they were not actors. Immediately after a shock, they had not the self-composure to dissemble successfully.

"I can see that you know something," the policeman went on. "Better tell me. Better keep your noses clean from the start. It's a murder case, and a big one. For the sake of your license you'd better tell the truth from the beginning."

The man nodded. "Happen we'd better," he said to his wife. "Happen it wasn't ours, anyway. We'll go look."

He came round the bar and beckoned. Martineau followed him to the rear of the premises, through a doorway to the back yard. There were outbuildings, and across the yard there was an outdoor toilet for men only.

Wensley went to the door of a brick-built shed and opened it. "Hold it," said Martineau. "Let me go first."

He stood in the doorway of the shed, looking round. There were two strong trestles which appeared to have been used as chopping blocks. There was a hatchet, and a small pile of firewood. There was a big saw. Four old railway sleepers were propped against the wall.

Wensley peered past the big policeman's shoulder. "Somebody's took the big ax," he said. "Oh, dear."

"What did you use it for?"

"I buy these old sleepers and make my own firewood. It gives me summat to do when things are quiet. I saw 'em into lengths, an' then split 'em with the big ax. Then I make sticks with that there little chopper."

"And the last time you used the ax?"

"Oh, happen a fortnight since. I've still got a few days' supply, you'll notice."

Martineau nodded. He stepped into the shed. The only possible hiding place for an ax was behind the leaning sleepers. He stooped and looked. An ax was there.

Carefully he lifted it out, holding it head downward by the end of the haft. "That was a very childish attempt at concealment, I must say," he remarked.

Wensley was staring in horror at the head of the ax. His face was gray with shock.

"Yes, you're quite right," the detective said coolly. "If that stuff on the blade is paint, somebody is kidding us. This could be the murder weapon."

"Mr. Martineau. I swear I—"

"Hush. Nobody has accused you yet. If you left the ax there in that condition, it was the cheekiest double bluff I ever heard of. That doesn't mean you're right in the clear. We're not at the assizes yet. Everybody is a suspect until the contrary is proved."

"Believe me, I haven't touched that ax since I chopped me last lot of firewood."

"Did you ever lend it to anyone?"

"Yes. Jonty Blades borrowed it once. I didn't like lendin' it to a man of that sort, but you don't like offendin' a customer. That was months ago. He kept it so long I went round to the lodge and collected it. I needed it, see. I haven't lent it him since."

"But he knew where it was kept?"

"Yes. He came in the yard once while I was choppin' wood. That's when he saw it first time."

"Did you ever lock this shed?"

"No. I never thought there was aught worth stealin'. I should a-known better."

"Maybe so. Now will you do something for me? Walk along to the other end of the cemetery. There'll be some bobbies around there by this time. The first one you see, tell him that Chief Inspector Martineau wants him here. Come back with him. We'll put a guard on this shed, and then we'll have a little talk."

Chapter Five

Contrary to the usual practice, Martineau questioned George and Ida Wensley together. He did it in this way because his first questioning of the pair had provided vital evidence, and because he was in a hurry. They were seated in the private parlor of the inn after it had been closed for the afternoon.

As he had expected, the Wensleys were able to give him a number of names for the purpose of proving that neither of them had left the inn, even for a few minutes, between the eleven o'clock opening time on the morning of yesterday, and twenty minutes past three in the afternoon, when the last laggard customer had departed after closing time. For the two hours after that they had no alibi except each other. Both of them said that neither had stepped out of doors during that time. At the five thirty opening time they had had a customer on the doorstep, after which they could provide alibis right through to eleven o'clock.

Taking the names of customers, Martineau demanded to be told of all who had called at the inn the previous day, and particularly of people who had been there between two and three.

He wrote down the names, with as many personal details as he could elicit. The last name on the list made him look up.

"Uncle?" he asked. "Uncle who?"

"Just Uncle," Wensley replied. "I've never known him be called aught else."

"Where does he live?"

"With Jonty at the lodge. Your man will have talked to him already, happen."

"I doubt it. He isn't there. Jonty neither. The whole family has flitted."

"When?"

Martineau hedged. "We don't know for sure."

"Well, Uncle was here yesterday, that's definite."

"What about Jonty?"

"I didn't see Jonty at all," Wensley said, but suddenly both he and his wife looked uneasy.

"Did you see any others of the Blades family?" Martineau probed, and their uneasiness increased.

"We'll have to tell him," the man said almost in apology to his wife. "After the ax, we've got to be dead straight on this thing."

"Yes," the wife agreed. "But I don't want him to start gettin' any wrong ideas about us. We've never allowed anythin' immoral."

"I'm sure you haven't," Martineau interposed smoothly. "What is it you want to tell me?"

"There's a young man been coming here two or three months. He's better off, like. He comes to meet young Ellie Blades, an' we let 'em sit in the parlor, sort of private. Nothin' wrong, mind you."

"This isn't a badhouse," the wife said.

"I'm sure it isn't. What is the young man's name?"

"We don't know. I once asked him, an' he said, 'Call me Jack.' Ellie might know his full name, an' then again she might not. He looks as if he's right well off."

"What's he like?"

The landlord gave a description which might have fitted any

one of ten thousand young men in Granchester. Nevertheless, Martineau solemnly took notes.

"How often do they meet here?"

"Happen once a week, gen'rally on a Tuesday."

"What times?"

"About two as a rule, an' they stay till closin' time."

"Those were the times yesterday?"

"That's right. Happen it were a bit after two when he came."

"He went about ten past three," the landlady volunteered. "I were upstairs an' I happened to look out of the winder. I saw Ellie wavin' him off."

"Oh, he went in a car?"

"Yes. He always comes in his car."

"Would either of you happen to know the number?"

Apparently neither of them did know. But Wensley said, "I don't think you'll have much of a job findin' the car. I've never seen another like it. It's a two-seater, open sports. A twelve-cylinder Ferrari. A real smasher, it is."

"No, there won't be many of those around here," Martineau agreed. He asked the landlady, "You saw him go. Which way did he go?"

"That way. Toward Derbyshire Road," she replied without hesitation.

"You're sure of that?"

"Yes, I'm sure."

Martineau nodded. The circumstances of the young man's departure in a direction away from the cemetery *seemed* to eliminate him as a murder suspect, but of course he would have to be seen and questioned. "What color is the car?" he asked before he changed the subject. Wensley replied that it was black, and a beauty.

"All right. Have I now got the names of all customers yesterday afternoon?"

"No, and I can't give 'em all," the landlord replied. "There was one customer, a complete stranger. I nearly forgot about him."

"What time did he arrive?"

"Some time after two. I couldn't say exackly."

"And when did he leave?"

"Ah, well before closin' time. Happen a quarter to three."

"Which way did *he* go?"

"I'm blessed if I know."

"Did he have a car?"

"I don't know that, either."

"What was he like?"

"A fairly big chap in his thirties. Well built, with a bit of style about him. Good color, light hair, small light mustache. Blue eyes, I think. Bound to have, with that coloring."

"Were you talking to him?"

"No. He stood at the bar. I was up an' down with orders. He had a gin, or he might have had two."

"What was he wearing?"

"A light suit, sort of fawny-gray. It'd be a nice suit when it was new. It was still all right, but it looked as if he'd had it for a year or two."

"He was a stranger, but otherwise not remarkable?"

"That's right."

Martineau thanked the couple and pocketed his notebook. The information he had received would be followed up by his subordinates. They would ask questions and take statements. These were not likely to provide important evidence, unless some customer on his departure from the inn had actually seen Luke Glover.

He returned to the scene of the crime. Men were searching in the cemetery. He did not call off the search because it was routine. Though it was unlikely that it would provide more evidence than the dead body which had already been found, Chief Superintendent Clay would be sure to ask if the cemetery had been searched.

Investigations in the little lane were another matter. Sergeant Bird, the C.I. Department's quasi-scientist, was directing the taking of photographs and impressions of tire tracks. He was also fussing about the spot where Devery had found blood on the stones. He was regretful in saying that there were no good footprints.

Martineau nodded. If Bird had failed to find footprints, then there weren't any. He told the sergeant about the guarded outhouse at the Grimwood Inn, and the bloody exhibit which was inside it. "It's all yours," he said as he turned away.

He returned to Headquarters, taking Devery with him. As he went he thought about another coincidence which had been put before him: the more-or-less simultaneous presence of two of the world's most expensive motorcars in the dingy environment of Grimwood. He had an urgent and delicate task, to inform a wife of her husband's murder. He decided that Devery could sort out the coincidence for him. Before he went to have a brief conference with Clay, he said to the sergeant, "See if you can find out who drives a twelve-cylinder Ferrari, two-seater, black."

Devery rightly assumed that in Granchester Ferrari cars would be just about as common as birds of paradise. He guessed that he would have no difficulty in getting the information he required from a member of the local sports car club, but first he telephoned his friend Larry Feavers at City Motors.

"Ah, hello," Larry said. "What sort of a car can I sell you today?"

Devery replied, "As a matter of fact I could be interested in a twelve-cylinder Ferrari."

"Why not buy two while you're about it? Those things wear out so quickly. Or I could get you three at the dozen price."

"I want just the single one."

"As far as I know, the only Ferrari around these parts belongs to Sam Glover. And a pretty motorcar it is, too."

"What color is it?"

"Black."

"Open two-seater?"

"Correct."

"Thanks, Larry," said Devery.

Martineau returned. "Come along," he said, leading the way to the door. "We've got to go and see Mrs. Glover. Did you do anything about the Ferrari?"

"Yes, sir," the sergeant replied. "It looks as if it belongs to Sam Glover."

Martineau stopped and turned. For a moment he stood in thought. "Father and son, both in Grimwood yesterday afternoon," he said. "That's another coincidence I won't accept. Luke was there because Sam was there. Or maybe it was t'other way round."

Martineau had Devery with him at his second interview with Diana Glover. They were admitted to the house by the middle-aged maid. The chief inspector thought that she looked a little less forbidding when her gaze rested on the handsome young sergeant.

The maid opened the door of the drawing room, announced the visitors and withdrew. Mrs. Glover was alone. As before, her first utterance was a request for news of her husband.

Martineau said, "I'm afraid it's bad news."

"You've found him? Is he hurt?"

"This will be a shock to you. He's dead."

"Oh, dear." On her lips the exclamation did not seem to be inadequate, but the policemen noticed that she had not changed color. "Was it an accident?" she asked.

"No accident. He was murdered."

37

"Oh." Mrs. Glover had been standing. She sat down quickly and now she was pale. Apparently the news of murder affected her more than the news of bereavement. "I don't understand," she said, as shock was followed by seeming bewilderment. "What happened?"

Martineau thought she could stand it. He said, "He was killed with an ax, in a rather lonely place."

She shook her head. Again she said, "I don't understand."

"I don't think anybody understands, yet. It's a very strange affair. That is why I must question you again, if you feel up to it."

She sighed. "I don't know. Couldn't you leave it until later?"

The detective was not prepared to forego any advantage. He had purposely refrained from actually naming the scene of the crime because of the presumption that Sam Glover had been there yesterday. Other members of the Glover family might be involved, too. He needed to get all the information he could, before there was a chance of collusion.

"It's better if I talk to you now," he said gently. "It'll take your mind off things for a while. Help you to get over the shock."

"Oh, very well." A vague wave of her hand included both the policemen. "Won't you sit down?"

They sat. Martineau said, "I've got to ask a number of personal questions. I hope you'll understand that they're just routine, for the record."

She nodded. "I understand."

"How long have you been married to Mr. Glover?"

"Three years. And two months."

"Were you on good terms with him?"

"Very good terms."

"When did you last have a quarrel with him?"

"We never had a real quarrel. The last small disagreement must have been months ago. More than six months, at any rate."

"What was it about?"

"I can't remember."

"For the report, what was the date of your birth, Mrs. Glover?"

She gave a date. He noted it, and made a private calculation. She was thirty-two years old.

"And how old was Mr. Glover? It being understood that we're talking about Mr. Luke Glover."

Mrs. Glover's normal coloring had returned. Now she blushed faintly as she answered, "He was sixty-seven."

"Were you his second wife?"

"Yes. He'd been a widower for ten years when I met him."

"Was he your first husband?"

"Really, is it important for you to know that?"

"I don't know. It's one of the routine questions I've got to ask. And it's so much better for everyone when a witness answers freely."

"Very well. He was my second husband."

"Were you a widow, or is your first husband still alive?"

She hesitated, then she said, "I divorced my first husband four years ago. I haven't seen him since."

"Were you divorced before you met Mr. Glover, or after?"

She frowned. Martineau could not blame her for showing irritation. But he had to get this stuff about a first husband, probably a young or youngish man, still alive. "Sorry," he said. "Do please answer the question."

She said carefully, "I had been living apart from my first husband for two years when I met Mr. Glover. He asked me to get a divorce so that he could marry me."

"And there was no trouble about that?"

"No. There was no defense. I knew at least two women he had lived with."

There was no emotion in her voice. Martineau shrugged mentally. What did the word "love" mean to some people? Did the cutting of the marriage tie leave a scar, or a mere scratch which would quickly heal and leave no mark?

"What was his name?" he said.

"Gordon Barnes."

"Profession?"

"Jack of all trades. You could call him a salesman, I suppose."

"Does he live in Granchester?"

"I don't know. The last I heard of him, he was in Nottingham."

"Thank you," said Martineau. He had the name. Barnes could be located and briefly questioned. Routine.

He changed the subject, and learned that Mrs. Glover had been born Diana Mercer, in Nottingham. After the break-up of her first marriage, in Nottingham, she had moved to Granchester. She had been a sales supervisor in a department store when she met Luke Glover. Both her marriages had been childless.

With regard to the previous day, she stated that she had had lunch with her sister-in-law, Janet Glover, and then had gone with her to a bridge club. She had stayed until six o'clock. She named other members who had been present. She had been home by half past six, as her dour maid would testify. It looked like a good alibi. She was in the clear. Nobody really suspected her anyway. Policemen may be as imaginative as other people, but no Granchester C.I.D. man had yet startled himself with a mental picture of Diana Glover wielding a woodman's ax.

There were questions about life insurance. She mentioned the name of Luke Glover's accountant, and she also referred the police to his solicitor, a man called Anstruther. His physician, she said, had been Dr. Argyll.

It was then that Martineau noticed strain in her voice, and a certain awareness in her expression. She was facing a tall window, and gazing out of it as she spoke. He turned his head, and saw a gray Rover car come to a stop beside his own plain C.I.D. car. A tall young man alighted. He glanced doubtfully at the drawing-room windows and at the police car. He walked round the car, considering it. Presently, if he knew anything about cars, he would notice its duplex radio equipment.

"Devery," Martineau said. "There's a man out front, just arrived. He might change his mind and go away. Dash out there and ask him in."

The sergeant departed with long strides. Diana Glover said, "Really, Inspector!"

"Sorry," was the equable reply. "Who is he?"

"Billy Glover. Luke's nephew."

"His brother's son, then?"

"Yes."

"How many brothers had he?"

"One. Matthew. If he's still alive."

Martineau allowed that cryptic remark to go unquestioned. Outside, Billy Glover had started to go back to his own car. He stopped and turned, looking toward the front door. That would be Devery calling to him. Devery appeared. There was a brief conversation. Billy glanced at the drawing-room windows again; then he shrugged and went with Devery.

When the two men entered the drawing room, Diana said at once, "Billy. Luke is dead. He was murdered."

Billy stopped. He stood quite still, looking at her. There was no doubt that he was surprised. At last he turned to Martineau, and spoke to him. "Murder," he said. "I was beginning to expect something serious. But murder! How?"

"With an ax."

"An ax! Good God! Where?"

"In a most unlikely place. For the time being, I don't want to name it."

"Why? Is it, er, disreputable?"

"No. Your uncle hasn't involved the family in any scandal."

"I see. Well, I expect you have your reasons." Billy turned to his aunt. "This must be awful for you."

"Oh, I'll manage, thank you."

"It'll be tough. There'll be policemen, reporters, God knows what. Shall I get Aunt Janet for you?"

"No, thank you."

"As you wish." Billy took a deep breath. "Poor Uncle Luke."

Martineau said, "Mr. Glover. Purely as a matter of routine, would you tell me what you were doing yesterday?"

"Surely the family isn't involved in this?"

"Routine, I said. We haven't a clue, yet."

"How do you know about the ax, then?"

"You're very sharp. When I mentioned clues, I wasn't speaking literally. Now, your movements yesterday."

"Up at seven thirty. Breakfast with Aunt Janet. I live with her. Straight to G.D.M. There nine fifteen till nearly one. Straight to club for lunch. Straight back to office at two thirty. There two thirty till about five fifteen. Club again till seven. Home to dinner with Aunt Janet. Stayed in after dinner. Bed about eleven thirty. Plenty of witnesses."

"Name a few."

Billy gave names. His day was well covered. If his witnesses were genuine, he could not have been at Grimwood when his uncle was murdered.

"Thank you," said Martineau. He briefly considered the young man. He was a smart one, all right. Good-looking, too. And he could wear a suit of clothes. Debonair was the word for him. There would be women in his life, for sure. "Are you married?" he asked.

"No. Never have been."

"Where will Mr. Sam Glover be about this time?"

"He'll be in his office at G.D.M."

"Thanks. May I use your telephone, Mrs. Glover?"

Chapter Six

Mrs. Glover's telephone was on the hall table outside her drawing-room door. Standing beside it, Martineau said to Devery, "Slip into the kitchen and break the news to the staff, and then follow me to Headquarters. See what you can get out of them. That hard-looking maid might know something about Luke's relations with his wife. See if you can charm her a bit."

Devery went off to the rear of the premises. Martineau phoned G.D.M., and was put in touch with Sam Glover. "Any news?" the young man asked.

"Bad news, I'm afraid. Your father is dead."

There was silence, and then a choked voice demanded, "Dead? How?"

"I'd rather not tell you on the phone. Will you meet me at Police Headquarters straight away? Ask for A Division C.I.D."

"Does Diana—my stepmother—know?"

"Yes, I'm with her now."

"Very well, Inspector. I'll come to the C.I.D. office at once."

That was the end of the talk. Martineau looked at his watch. With rush-hour traffic, Sam's journey to H.Q. would take about fifteen minutes. If he took a much longer time than that, there would be a suspicion that he had stopped somewhere to call his stepmother and learn what he could. Well, unless she had guilty knowledge she could not name the scene of the crime to him. It was undesirable that he should have knowledge of that.

Martineau's own journey took twenty minutes, and at H.Q. he found Sam waiting for him. "Come into my office," he said.

In spite of his obvious distress, Sam looked around curiously as he entered the little office. He saw the big desk and the smaller one, the small bookcase, the worn carpet, the framed picture of a Rugby XV on the wall, and the plain wooden chairs with semicircular backs. He accepted one of the chairs, facing Martineau's across the big desk, and no doubt he found it to be more comfortable than it looked. Martineau's chair was no different, and perhaps he wondered if all office-bound policemen had such Spartan arrangements. He had no means of knowing that Martineau spent as little time as possible in that chair because he hated desk work.

Martineau made a sympathetic opening. "I'm afraid this has been a shock to you," he said.

Sam nodded, as if unable to speak. Apparently sympathy weakened him. There was a glitter of unshed tears in his eyes.

"What was it? How did he die?" he managed to ask.

"He was murdered. That's why you're here, talking to a detective officer."

"Murdered!" Sam was aghast. Martineau had met many consummate natural actors in his time, but now he was inclined to believe that he was looking at a genuinely horrified and bewildered man.

As gently as possible he described the nature of Luke Glover's injuries. Sam was silent and miserable, apparently utterly at a loss to understand how or why such a cruel thing could have happened.

Eventually he asked, "Where was this? Where did you find him?"

Then Martineau spoke very carefully indeed. "You must realize that a policeman has many disagreeable tasks," he said. "This is one of them. Before I tell you where we found your father's body, I want you to tell me all about your movements yesterday. Where you went, whom you met. Believe me, it is necessary for me to know."

Now Sam was shaken by shock of another kind. He stared. "You mean you suspect *me?*"

"No, I don't. But you can believe me when I tell you that you must be completely honest with me. Later, you will understand."

Sam was doubtful. "I don't get it."

The chief inspector shrugged. "You tell me, then I'll tell you."

Sam shrugged in his turn. "I was in Liverpool all morning. I can show you plenty of corroboration on that. Then I came home. I had a quick meal at the Green Dragon on the way home. You know it?"

"The Green Dragon at Kirkston?"

"Yes. The waiters know me. I had lunch there, and came on to Granchester."

"Kirkston isn't far. Why lunch there?"

"The Dragon is a good spot."

"Right. What time did you leave?"

"Oh, about a quarter to two."

"Then you came on to Granchester. Whereabouts in Granchester?"

Sam was silent. Then he said, "I had some private business. It couldn't possibly have had anything to do with my father."

Martineau shook his head. "When it's a murder job, nobody's business is private."

"I called at a little pub, the Grimwood Inn. That would be a little after two."

"And you stayed how long?"

"About an hour."

"Did you leave the premises during that hour?"

"No. I think I can prove I didn't, if that is necessary."

45

"It might be. From the inn, where did you go?"

"Straight on to Derbyshire Road, and into town. I walked into the office about half past three. The commissionaire will bear witness to that. My secretary too."

Martineau asked for names and wrote them down. After his arrival at the office, Sam had not been alone for more than a few minutes at a time until he had left his club at nine o'clock. At half past nine his stepmother had telephoned to express her concern about his father.

"Very good," said Martineau. "Some of this has already been verified. Assuming that you were driving your own Ferrari car, I knew that you were at Grimwood yesterday. We believe that Grimwood was the scene of the crime. We found your father's body in the cemetery."

Sam looked sick. "My father at Grimwood?" he whispered.

"Yes. I don't need to tell you what is in my mind. I don't believe in coincidence. You were there, he was there. You had a reason, he had a reason."

"I can give you my reason. Will the press get it?"

"Not from me, they won't."

Sam gave his reason, the girl Ellie Blades. He had met her, he said, some few months earlier as he was driving in pouring rain on his way from the Northern Steel Corporation to Granchester Sheet Metal. The girl had been the only person in sight, a lonely figure in the rain. He had stopped, and asked if he could help. She had been so wet, and so cheerful with it, that he had taken her to the inn and bought her a drink. He found her attractive and amusing, and he had arranged to meet her again. He had become quite fond of her, but not fond enough to tell her his name. "She calls me Jack," he said.

"Have you ever met her father?" Martineau asked.

"No. She barely mentions him."

"The entire family probably knows quite well who you are. Have you given her money?"

46

"I have, as a matter of fact. But always simply as a gift. She hasn't been selling anything."

"Fair enough. What would your father have said if he'd known?"

"He'd have gone up in the air. He was very fond of my fiancée, and her father was an associate and a friend. He didn't want anything to go wrong there. Thank the Lord she's away on a world cruise with her mother. The old lady has had a bad illness."

"I see. Well, I think somebody must have told your father about Grimwood. I suspect that his reason for being there was to surprise you with the girl. Would he be capable of doing that?"

"Yes. He'd want to see for himself. If it was serious, he'd try to frighten off the girl, or buy her off."

"Who could have told him, do you think?"

"I don't know. It's a puzzle to me. I never told anybody."

"Well, apparently he knew where to go, and what time. That last meeting with the Blades girl, when was it arranged?"

"The week before. I simply said, 'See you next Tuesday maybe.' I drove past the cemetery and gave three toots on my horn, and went into the pub. Ellie joined me there in a few minutes."

"It might be better if I knew your exact relations with the girl. That is, if you don't mind telling me."

"I don't mind. This is one instance where the lady's honor is in no danger. When I first met Ellie I thought she would be easy. I gave her little presents and money. But she always holds me off when I start getting too affectionate. And the devil of it is, I like her better for it. I'm getting much too fond of her. It won't do. I suppose I ought to have stopped it long ago."

"What about the girl's feeling for yourself? Have you any clue?"

"Not really. I never know whether or not she's kidding. She's a wise little beggar, you know."

"Yes, I can imagine. Well, it's my opinion that you and she were the lure which drew your father to Grimwood. There doesn't seem to be any other reason, and I refuse to believe he was there by accident."

"You mean somebody planned to kill my father, and used me as a sort of bait? That's horrible, man."

"I allowed you to draw the inference. Horrible things do happen, you know. Now we'll have to find out who set the trap, if it was a trap; who told your father where to find you."

"If I can get the slightest clue, I'll let you know," Sam said earnestly.

"Thanks. By the way, have you any idea where Ellie is now?"

"No. We have an arrangement to meet next Tuesday, same place, same time."

"If she gets in touch before then, will you inform me? I must find the family."

"I'll keep you fully informed of everything, Inspector," Sam promised grimly.

"You were fond of your father?"

"It's something I never thought about. I realize now that I was."

"Did you quarrel much?"

"We had a bit of a squabble once in a while. The last one would be two or three months ago, soon after I met Ellie."

"Was it a family quarrel?"

"Good Lord, no. We never had a family quarrel. It was a business do, and a fairly typical one. It was a certain American, coming over here. Very important business; I can't tell you more than that. Father wanted me to meet him in London and show him a good time before bringing him up here. I said why couldn't Billy go? I said Billy was sales and public relations, and a better entertainer. Billy can get on with anybody. Father said, 'This is big business. If I can't meet this man myself I must do him the courtesy of sending my own son. You're going to London. If you refuse, I'll see that you're thrown off the board and out of the firm.' "

"So you went?"

"Yes. Father was the boss."

"Would he have thrown you out?"

"I don't know. He was a very hard case. I've known him to do some hard things."

"Did Billy mind you taking on a job which should have been his?"

"Billy? No, he wouldn't mind. He's all right."

"How many more Glovers are there?"

"Only one more. My Aunt Janet, Father's sister."

"She's a spinster?"

"Yes. She's all right, too."

Martineau said, "But of course." He reflected that Aunt Janet would be the one who could give him the family history, if it became necessary to learn the family history.

Chapter Seven

While the search for Jonty Blades and his family became more
persistent, over a widening area, Martineau and a few detectives
busied themselves with the routine inquiries which served the
purpose of cutting off loose ends and getting the case into some
sort of shape.

Part of the routine was a talk with Luke Glover's solicitor.
Though the news of the murder had not been released in time
to appear in the evening newspapers, there was no doubt that
it would soon be known at his club and at the Town Hall,
and from those two hives of gossip it would spread rapidly.

Martineau decided not to wait until morning. At seven
o'clock, at the first available moment, he telephoned the lawyer's
home. He was informed that Mr. Anstruther was not at home,
and he had to overcome a certain resistance in order to learn
that the man was still in his office, working late on an urgent
and important matter.

He telephoned the office and introduced himself to Anstruther. "It's important I should see you," he said. "I'll be with
you in ten minutes. Don't go away."

Devery drove him the short distance to the solicitor's office,
and on the way they discussed the possibility that its occupant
might not yet have heard of the murder.

"I don't suppose it matters, anyway," was the sergeant's

opinion. "You've got to give a lawyer an awful big surprise before he lets anything slip."

Anstruther was alone in the office. As he answered the bell and let them in, Martineau studied him. He was a smooth-faced, youngish man whose clothes were still immaculate at the end of the working day. In speech he was leisured and exact, with an accent noticeably haw-haw. It was a reasonable guess that the accent had been acquired at a public school, and not a minor one. School would have been followed by an unhurried qualification in law at Oxford or Cambridge, and a laid-on partnership in a firm which was particular about its clientele. It was safe to assume that Gerald Anstruther had never soiled his hands with a police-court case.

The visitors were shown into a private office, seated, offered cigarettes. Anstruther spoke from behind a desk littered with documents. "Now, Inspector. What is all this urgency? Do you bring me news?"

"If you haven't already heard, we do."

"Concerning?"

"Concerning Luke Glover."

"Yes?"

"He's been found dead."

Anstruther raised his eyebrows slightly. "I understand he was murdered."

"You knew?"

The lawyer smiled. "I knew that he was missing, of course. When you said you were coming here, I rang up Mrs. Glover, asking for news. She told me."

"Were you shocked?"

"Surprised is the word. Luke Glover was a client, not a friend. One expresses a decent sorrow to the widow, of course. And to any other relations one meets."

You're a cool hand, said Martineau, but he said it to himself. Aloud he asked, "What about Glover's will?"

51

"My firm has the will."

"For the record, I want to know its terms."

"It would be irregular for me to tell you, I think."

"This is a murder case."

"It's a murder investigation. As yet there has been no arrest, no trial. I shall not disclose the terms of the will until I have consulted the trustees and made arrangements with the family. The police *may* be allowed to sit in when the will is read, if none of the family objects."

Martineau said, "You're not very helpful, but I don't suppose the will is important, anyway. Widow and son will get most of what there is, I suppose?"

"One is always at liberty to guess."

"Won't you tell me anything?"

Anstruther smiled and shrugged. "Not until after consultation."

Martineau rose and picked up his hat. "I'll be doing a bit of consulting myself," he said. He turned away with an unsmiling promise. "I'll be after you tomorrow."

Devery also had risen, and Anstruther stood up politely, though he stayed behind the desk. When the two policemen were at the door he said casually, "There'll be a post-mortem examination, I suppose?"

"After a murder, there usually is," Martineau growled, with sarcasm. He said, "Good night," and departed with his colleague. Outside, he said, "That was a damn fool question, 'Will there be a post-mortem?'"

"He's one of those lawyers who has never had to bother with common things like murders and suicides," was Devery's reply. "He's a lucky boy and a wise guy."

"He certainly is discreet," Martineau admitted. And with a change of tone he added, "Let's go see if the doctor is any help."

Dr. Argyll was a general practitioner, and a good one, with a mixed suburban practice. He was a canny and careful man who had somehow managed to acquire a don't-give-a-damn reputation. He was immensely popular. His patients were flattered and relieved to be treated with skillful care and gruff sympathy by a man who so obviously didn't give a damn. Martineau and Devery slipped into his surgery just before he let out the last of his evening patients. He frowned when he saw them. "What the devil do you fellows want?" he demanded, strictly in character.

His visitors were not offended. "You should know," Martineau retorted mildly. "You've heard about Luke Glover."

The doctor nodded, and looked rather sad, in a devil-may-care sort of way. "Shocking thing," he said. "What do you want from me? You don't need the medical history of a man who's had his head cut off."

"Ah, but we do. Recent medical history, at any rate. Have you treated him recently?"

"He came to me with a belly ache about five weeks ago. I gave him something. He hasn't been back since."

"And did he otherwise seem to be in good health?"

Argyll coughed. "I think so."

"What about his mental or nervous condition? Would you say he was normal?"

The doctor's frown became quite fierce. "This word 'normal'!" he said. "His temperature was normal! With regard to his nerves, I didn't detect any illness. And he seemed to be as much in his right mind as anybody I ever met."

Martineau looked shrewdly at the doctor. He detected worry. There was something which had not been told.

"Odd, wasn't it?" he asked. "A man like Glover coming here to see you? I'd have thought he was more likely to send for you, even if it was only a bit of tummy trouble."

"Well, he came here."

"What was the cause of the trouble?"

Argyll shrugged. "Something he'd eaten, no doubt."

Martineau grinned. "It usually is, isn't it? Did he think something had poisoned him?"

"What do you mean?"

"Shellfish, or something of the sort."

"No. He never mentioned shellfish."

"What did he mention?"

"Nothing specifically."

"You haven't answered the question, Doctor. Did he think he'd been poisoned?"

"He had none of the signs and symptoms of poisoning. He hadn't been poisoned."

"But he thought he might have been poisoned? Is that it?"

"He didn't say he thought he'd been poisoned."

"Did he mention poison at all?"

The doctor sighed. "He did mention poison. I told him he hadn't been poisoned."

"Did he name any particular poison?"

"He mentioned arsenic in a vague sort of way. I said it was nonsense."

"And could you be sure?"

"I told him to get in touch with me again if there wasn't an immediate improvement, and to get in touch with me at once if there was a recurrence of the trouble after an improvement."

"You played it safe, eh?"

"I don't take chances with the health of my patients."

"How long have you known Luke Glover?"

"Thirty years. Ever since I took this practice. That is to say, he was a patient of mine, though I didn't see much of him. He was not a poorly sort. I didn't really get to know him till he became a member of my club."

"He was not a hypochondriac?"

"No."

"To your knowledge, did he ever have delusions of any kind?"

"No. He always seemed to be a very sane and sensible fellow, though not an entirely likable one. He wasn't awfully popular."

"But he mentioned arsenic. Did any other person's name come up in that connection?"

"No. No names mentioned."

"Did he ever mention poison to you before, at any time?"

"No, never."

"Did you ask him what had put the idea into his head?"

"I did not. If he had wanted to confide in me, he would have done so."

"Perhaps he would. Thank you, Doctor. We have to ask questions, you know."

"No doubt. But the way Glover was killed seems to be a very far cry from a vague suspicion of arsenic. I don't see how there could be a connection. You've got the information out of me, but I don't see what good it will be."

Martineau nodded absently. The doctor's view was an outsider's. Such a murder in such a place seemed unlikely to be a family affair. And yet there had been a member of the family near the scene of the crime, while now there was talk of poisoning, the most intimate and domestic of murder methods. Jonty Blades would have to answer some searching questions when he was found, but in the meantime an investigation of the murdered man's relations was not entirely an irrelevant activity.

At ten o'clock that night Sam Glover was alone in his flat when the telephone rang. He picked up the receiver and gave his number.

"Mr. Sam Glover?" he was asked.

"Yes?"

"This is Jonty Blades, Ellie's father. Yer know Ellie."

Sam made a face. He had wondered if he would have trouble with Ellie's father, and if so, when and how. Well, here it was, and not at a good time.

"Yes, I know Ellie, Mr. Blades," he said, at his most suave.

"I'm glad to hear from you. But this is an odd time, and there's been a death in the family. I don't really feel like talking to anybody. Ring me again in a day or two, will you?"

"Don't cut me off, Mr. Glover," Jonty said in some agitation. "I ought to see yer tonight. It's summat what concerns yer fam'ly more nor mine."

"Really?" Sam was remembering that Jonty had recently been living at the scene of his father's death. The police would be seeking him. "Where are you?"

"I'm in the phone booth just round the corner from yer flat."

Sam had half a mind to ring off and call the police. And what would little Ellie think of that when she heard? Not much. "All right," he said. "Come up, will you?"

Jonty arrived, and entered the flat cap in hand. He trod carefully on the thick carpet, and sat down gingerly when invited to do so. Sam was surprised to find that he had seen this little man before, several times. The man had passed him at the entrance to the Grimwood Inn. He had even passed when Sam had been talking to Ellie outside the inn just before driving away. He had never given a sign that he was Ellie's father, or that he knew her.

"Would you like a drink?" Sam asked, and Jonty replied that a drop of whiskey was a good thing on a cold night.

When the drinks had been poured, Sam lit a cigarette and said, "I know you've seen me with Ellie, but how did you know my name?"

"I've known that fer some time, sir. When a young spark is courtin' yer daughter, at least yer want ter know who he is."

Sam grinned. "Fair enough. What can I do for you?"

"Well, it's yer cousin I've been after, but I've not been able ter get hold on him. But it concerns yer an' all. Yer see, I've just found yer Uncle Matthew. I mean, I've just found out he *is* yer uncle."

"Really?" Sam put down his glass. "You're certain?"

"I'm certain enough. I wouldn't a-come ter yer if I'd not been."

"Who is he?"

"He's a man who's been livin' wi' my fam'ly fer years. We never knew his name."

"You mean Uncle? Ellie has mentioned Uncle. I believe I've seen him a time or two, at a distance."

"Yers, it's Uncle. I were right surprised when I found out."

Sam looked at him keenly. "I'll bet you were. *How* did you find out?"

"I just happened ter be sayin' summat ter my missis, an' Uncle sort o' half heard it. He said, 'Matt Glover? That name rings a bell.' Well, I hadn't said Matt Glover at all, but Glover's a name in this town, an' I started wonderin'. I thought there were just a chance as Uncle might once a-been somebody important enough ter know somebody in the Glover fam'ly. I started nosin' around, an' bit by bit I found out."

"Assuming you're right, are you now telling me that Uncle has been hiding his light under a bushel?"

"No. He's not been hidin' nothin'. He doesn't know. He doesn't know his name."

"Are you sure of that?"

"Well, he always acted as if he didn't know."

"You haven't told him, then?"

"No. I'm lettin' somebody else tell him."

Sam had learned something of Jonty's character and way of life from Ellie. Also, it sounded a lame sort of tale to him.

"What makes you so sure?" he asked shrewdly. "Has somebody identified him for you?"

"No, but I'm sure. Yer can have him identified, an' yer'll find I'm right."

"Obviously you didn't know Matthew Glover in the old days.

I'd like you to tell me how you know him now. I want some evidence before I start raising the hopes of my cousin and my aunt."

"Take it from me. What I'm tellin' yer is right."

"Does anybody else know?"

"No," Jonty replied after a very brief hesitation.

"You're not convincing me," Sam said bluntly. "There's more to it than that. You couldn't be so sure, simply by guesswork. If you weren't Ellie's father I'd call the police and let them straighten this out. I'm not sure it wouldn't be the best thing to do in any case."

"Don't do that. Don't call the police."

"Why not? They won't hurt you if you've done nothing wrong."

"Callin' the police 'ud be a big mistake."

"I don't see it. You may be able to give some information on another matter. Did you know my father was missing?"

"Yers, I knew that."

"Did you know he'd been found?"

"No."

"He was found dead. Murdered. In Grimwood Cemetery. What do *you* know about it?"

"Nothin'. Listen, don't go into that. It'll only mean more grief fer yerself."

"There can't be any more grief. My father is dead. And you know something about it, I can tell. I'm going to call the police."

"No no!" Jonty was alarmed. "Don't do it. Yer father can't be brought back."

"No. But the man who killed him can be hanged."

"That's just it. That's where yer'll make a lot more grief for the 'ole fam'ly."

Sam stared. His eyes narrowed. "Some member of *my* family is involved?"

Jonty made a regretful noise. It was more than a sigh and less than a groan. "Yer see? I told yer ter leave it alone."

"And now are you telling me that the man you call Uncle was the man who killed my father?"

"Yer forcin' me ter say stuff I never intended."

"You bet I am. You can tell me all of it before I call the police."

"Yer'd set the police on yer own uncle?"

"Why not, if he killed my father? I don't know the man anyway."

"But what about the disgrace? An' yer cousin? An' yer aunt?"

Sam rose from his chair. He paced about in thought. He sat down again.

"Tell me about it," he said.

"Well, yusterday afternoon Uncle come out o' the pub a minute or two before closin'. He were drunk more or less, but he remembered seemin'ly he'd promised my lad Gaylord he'd bring the big ax. He went out the back way an' borrered the ax from the shed, an' walked on home wi' it. Gaylord were in the cemetery, an' he saw Uncle pass the front gate. He run ter the gate ter see if he were sober. He saw this Rolls-Royce come along an' pass Uncle, an' then stop. A little owd man got out an' went runnin' after Uncle. Accordin' ter Gaylord, he were callin' out, 'Matthew. Matt, me boy,' but Uncle didn't seem ter hear. Uncle turned in at the lane an' the owd chap follered him, an' Gaylord went hoppin' over graves ter see what were goin' ter happen. Well, the owd chap kept callin', but Uncle never took no notice. He'd had a lot ter drink, understand, but he weren't staggerin'. The owd chap caught up wi' him an' grabbed his arm, and' he stopped an' turned round. What happened then beats cockfightin'. When Uncle saw the owd chap his eyes fair blazed, an' he up wi' the ax an' swung. The owd man must a-been took by surprise. He ducked away, but the ax caught him across the back of the neck. What Uncle did that for God only knows, but seemin'ly he did. Our Gaylord stood petrified watchin' behind a tree. He saw Uncle chuck the ax over t'wall among graves, an' then go pick the poor owd man up an' drop him over t'wall an' all. Then he looked round as if he were wonderin' what he'd forgot, an' then he turned an' went home ter his dinner. Gaylord ses he never even looked back."

"Oh, dear." The story had distressed Sam. "Is Gaylord a truthful boy?"

"He's sixteen year old, an' I wouldn't call him a liar. For why would he lie over summat like that? He's real upset is the lad. He thinks the world o' Uncle."

"Did he come and tell you straightaway?"

"No. He said naught ter nobody. All he did were look ter see if he could do aught for the owd man, an' he found him dead enough, so he said. Then he found the ax an' went an' put it back in the woodshed at pub."

"When did you find out?"

"Late last night, the same night. Yer see, I were out in Mossbank when all this happened. When I got home I sees the Rolls at the front gate. I had a look at it, an' saw yer dad's name on the ignition key. Well, I thought he'd found summat out, an' come ter see Ellie about you an' her. But she were at home an' he hadn't been ter see her, an' he didn't seem ter be nowhere about. It were a proper mystery. Anyway, I knew we were goin' ter be kicked out o' the lodge nearly any day—a Corporation man had found us there, yer see—an' when the Rolls were still there after dark I used it ter flit us all ter another place I'd had in mind. Then I dumped it in a street in Churlham."

"And then did Gaylord tell you?"

"Not right then. Yer see, he had ter help ter flit, but I could see his heart weren't in it. I wondered what were up wi' him, an' I thought happen he knew more about that Rolls-Royce nor I did. When we flitted in at a new place we just put beds up an' we didn't bother wi' much else, but still it were lateish-on afore we could sit down to a bit of supper. After supper I heard Gaylord tellin' his mother he didn't want ter sleep with Uncle, which he did as a rule. He were frightened, yer see. His mother said he could have a couple o' blankets an' sleep on settee."

"And did that make you more than ever suspicious of him?"

"Bless yer, I weren't suspicious o' the lad. But I guessed summat had happened, an' I wanted ter know what it were. So after we'd gone ter bed an' all were quiet I nipped out an' found him wide awake. I ast him what were the matter, an' after a while he tol' me."

"Will he tell anyone else?"

"No. He's all right now he's got me wi' him, sort o'. He won't tell. He doesn't want aught ter happen ter Uncle."

"What will he say when Uncle is arrested?"

"He'll be sickened. But I'm hopin' it'll never come ter that."

"The police will find out eventually, you know."

"They might, they won't find out through me an' Gaylord. He's terrified o' police. Terrified. When they get hold on him I know what he'll do. He'll belt up an' he won't say a word. An' they won't knock it out o' a lad. I've never known police be rough, but I've heard they can be. But they wouldn't play it rough wi' a lad."

"What about you?"

"Me? It's me they'll be lookin' fer this minute. An' when they find me they'll get a suck. I were miles away when it happened, an' I can prove it. So I know naught about it, see?"

"You're quite sure nobody else knows about this? Not Ellie or her mother?"

"I'm dead sure nobody knows."

"Why did you come and tell me?"

"I didn't come an' tell yer. It were forced out. I just come ter tell yer I'd found Matthew Glover. I thought there might be summat in it fer a poor man like me."

"I see." Sam was thoughtful. "You got the name Matthew

from Gaylord. How did that lead you to Matthew Glover?"

"Simple. Uncle an' yer dad must have been middlin' close at one time, fer him ter run callin' after him like that. An' Uncle had said the name Matt Glover rung a bell wi' him."

"Is that all?"

Jonty's brown eyes were limpid and innocent. "That's all," he said. "Enough, isn't it?"

"But you must have heard somewhere that there was a missing brother."

"I got that today wi' listenin' around an' sayin' naught. Folk were talkin' about the missin' millionaire. Somebody remembered his brother were once missin' an' all, an' he'd advertised a reward."

Sam was satisfied. Jonty's motive was clear. "And you thought you might get the reward even though my father was dead?"

"I thought I might get a bit o' summat."

There was a long silence while Sam pondered the matter. At last he spoke. "So neither you nor Gaylord wants Uncle to be arrested," he said. "And, after some reflection, neither do I. My father is dead, and nothing can bring him back. The reason why he was killed is a long story and an old one. It must have preyed on Uncle's mind, and at the least he must be slightly insane. But if it comes out that it was a case of brother killing brother, it will bring great sorrow to Billy and my Aunt Janet."

"An' disgrace ter the fam'ly," Jonty said.

"And disgrace to the family. It's quite likely that the police will find out anyway, but at least they won't have the backing of Gaylord's evidence. They may never be able to bring a charge. Here."

Sam fished small change and a few crumpled notes from a pocket of his trousers. He sorted the notes from the change. He said, "I don't have much money with me right now, but you can take these to be going on with."

Jonty took the money. "Aren't we sayin' aught ter yer cousin, then?"

Sam considered the question. Some thought brought a glint to his eyes. "Is Uncle still drunk?" he asked.

"Aye. He's on a rant. He'll be drunk again tomorrow, likely enough."

Sam spoke almost to himself. "It might not be a bad idea to let Billy see his father." He got up and went to where the telephone stood on a table. "We'll see if we can get him to come over, shall we? But we won't tell him what his father did to my father."

Chapter Eight

The following morning—Thursday—there was a reply to a routine inquiry which had been sent to the Nottingham City Police. It concerned Gordon Barnes, ex-husband of Diana Glover, and it brought the interesting news that Barnes had a criminal record. Twice in his working life he had succumbed to the temptation which besets a salesman and fraudulently used his employer's money for his own purposes. Also, he was an undischarged bankrupt, an indication that at one time he had had enough ambition to go into business on his own account. Some Nottingham police officer had taken the trouble to seek Barnes at his last known address. Barnes had gone away, and the information was that he had left town.

Martineau looked at the set of photographs which had been supplied. At full length G. Barnes was a stalwart lad who wore his clothes with an air. In profile he was presentable, with perhaps a little too much flesh under the chin. In full face he was handsome, and he looked at the camera with an insouciant grin.

"Impenitent," Devery said as he looked over the chief inspector's shoulder. "A cheeky chappie."

"A good-looking boy," came the comment. "I can understand how Diana Glover would go for him."

"And lots more of the girls, I'll bet."

"Yes but he married the fair Diana. That was more than a

passing fancy. They'd make a handsome couple."

"Both tall, both fair."

"Yes." Martineau was thoughtful. He was remembering a description given by the landlord of the Grimwood Inn. "A fairly big chap . . . well-built, with a bit of style about him . . . good color, light hair, small light mustache . . ." It seemed like a long chance, but he said to Devery, "Put this picture in the book. Take the book to Mr. and Mrs. Wensley at the Grimwood Inn. Let them turn over a few pages and see if they pick this one out."

The sergeant departed. The chief inspector went to confer with the head of the C.I.D. There he learned that more men would now be engaged in the hunt for the Blades family. Jonty's presumably fortuitous success in eluding the hunters was an irritating hitch. "He isn't all that clever," Clay said. "I wonder where the little scrounger could have got to. We can't really get on with anything till we've found him."

Martineau's own recent inquiries were discussed. Clay was much more interested in Jonty, but he admitted that Dr. Argyll's reluctant statement had revealed an aspect of the case which required attention. "Of course we must get to know the terms of the will," he said. "Get after that lawyer."

So Martineau returned to his own office to go after Gerald Anstruther. On the telephone, the solicitor was reasonable. "I'm trying to arrange it," he said. "Give me another hour."

"Right," the policeman said. "I'll be with you in an hour's time."

He filled in the time with desk work, which he greatly disliked. But before he was ready to go and see Anstruther, Devery returned.

"Bang on, sir," the sergeant said. "Both the mister and the missus looked at the picture. Separately. They both spotted Barnes. They're quite certain."

"He was in the bar of the Grimwood Inn on Tuesday after-noon, between two and three?"

"That's right."

"It hardly seems credible."

"There's no doubt about it unless somebody is trying to frame the man. They couldn't have picked him out from dozens more, if they hadn't recognized him."

"Luke Glover, his son and now his wife's ex-husband. All at Grimwood together. Put out the word on Barnes, to All Districts. Wanted for interview in connection with the murder of Luke Glover. You'll want more pictures. See that the press gets pictures. I'll have a word with Mr. Barnes. And if he tells me his visit to Grimwood was just a coincidence, I'll thump him."

"The Glover family is being very helpful about this, In-spector," Gerald Anstruther said. "They made no objection at all. You will be the first person outside this office to know the terms of Luke's will."

"The family doesn't know yet, then?"

"No. They'll know this afternoon."

"What are the terms?"

The solicitor picked up a document and handed it over.

"This is it?" Martineau asked.

"That is Luke Glover's will."

"Not a very long one," the detective commented, as he began to read.

"No. Only four legatees. Nothing to charity."

"Two thousand to Hannah Styles. That's the maid, isn't it? She's an old retainer. We can't get a word out of her, yet."

"I always thought she was a very nice person."

"She would be, to you. You're one of the aristocracy. What's this? Five thousand to Diana Glover. That's not much for a rich man's wife."

66

Martineau looked up as he spoke. Anstruther met his gaze without expression, nor did he comment.

The policeman returned his glance to the will. The next bequest was a sum of ten thousand pounds to Matthew Glover, together with 10 percent of Luke's holding in Glover Domestic Machinery and 70 percent of his holding in Glover Carburetors, Ltd. In the event of Matthew's dying before Luke, the whole of the bequest was to go to Matthew's only son, William Glover.

"What about this Matthew Glover? Is he retired and living in Eastbourne, or what?" Martineau demanded.

"As far as my knowledge goes, nobody knows where Matthew is. But don't quote me. You'd better ask the family."

"How long has he been missing?"

"Years. I don't know how many."

"When I was asking, yesterday, who were the members of the family my informant quite forgot to mention Matthew. Is it generally assumed that he's dead?"

"That seems to be the general idea. Nothing is proven."

"H'm," said Martineau. He returned his attention to the will. After the three bequests, the residue of Luke's wealth and property was left to his son Samuel.

"Nothing to Luke's sister, Janet," the reader observed.

"No," Anstruther agreed. Then he volunteered, "I wouldn't jump to any conclusions about that. She's a wealthy woman."

Martineau nodded, and went on reading. His eyes widened suddenly. He read the final clause with an expression almost of consternation.

"What's this?" he burst out. "He insists on an autopsy after his death, whether or not the doctor has certified death by natural causes! So that's why you asked me last night if there'd be a p.m."

Anstruther smiled slightly. "It was one way of getting to know."

"What's the date of this?" Martineau demanded in some excitement. He looked and saw the date. "Why, this was signed less than five weeks ago!"

"Quite true. Luke came in and dictated the terms of a new will."

"Was it much different from the old one?"

"Considerably."

"Did he give you a reason for changing his will?"

"No. I started to give him some advice. He shut me up. Said if he wanted advice he'd ask for it and pay for it."

Recollection of the industrialist's bluntness had made the lawyer color a little. Martineau remembered now that he had been surprised but not grieved to hear of the man's violent death.

"What were the terms of the old will?" he asked.

"My partners have agreed that I should tell you. The legacy to Hannah Styles was five hundred. The residue was divided equally between Diana, Sam and Matthew. There was no clause about post-mortem examination."

"You still have a copy of that will?"

"Of course,"

"Don't lose it."

"We don't lose wills, though I don't see how it would matter much in this case. In other circumstance the changes might be interesting to a policeman, I can see that."

"They're interesting now," said Martineau. "Though I agree with you that they might be misleading in this instance. There is evidence to suggest that Luke expected an attempt on his life, but I don't think he expected the sort of attempt which finished him. If there was any foundation to his suspicions, there must have been more than one person who wanted to kill him."

"Well, there it is," said Anstruther, and he sounded relieved when he added, "I don't think *I* shall have to give evidence in your murder case. It isn't a family affair."

Martineau let that pass without comment. "I'd like to know more about brother Matthew," he said.

"You'll have to inquire elsewhere," replied the lawyer, somewhat shortly.

"Is there no Mrs. Matthew, then?"

"No. She died. And Billy is the only child."

"If they can't find Matthew, I suppose Billy will get busy right away, trying to establish his death. Has nothing been heard of him for more than seven years?"

"I don't know." Anstruther made a gesture of looking at his watch.

Martineau rose from his chair and looked around for his hat. "Your time is valuable," he said dryly.

"I have to earn my living. There are no fees for talking to policemen."

"You could charge it to the estate," retorted Martineau on his way out.

On his return to the C.I.D. he reported to Clay. "I may be getting a lot of material which has nothing to do with the actual murder," he said, "but I'm convinced now that there was something wrong in the Glover family." He went on to tell the chief superintendent about Luke's will.

"Yes, there seems to be something queer," the senior man agreed. "And the trouble seems to have been between Luke and his wife. From a man as rich as he must have been, five thousand pounds to his wife is an insult. And the autopsy clause seems to be aimed directly at her."

Martineau nodded. "It certainly doesn't seem to be aimed at the maid. It looks as if Luke increased her legacy from five hundred to two thousand in order to make that clear."

"Could be. What about the cook? She would have the opportunity to give him poison."

"I sent Devery to see the staff. The cook is new. Mrs. Glover gave her the job. At the time of Luke's visit to the doctor she'd been working for him a fortnight, but she hadn't even set eyes on him. And she's a stranger to the town. She's Welsh, from Cardiff."

"You'll make the usual inquiries into her background, of course. You've checked the dates of the visit to the doctor and the visit to the lawyer?"

"Yes. He went to the doctor first. The doctor told him he had *not* been poisoned. But that didn't stop him from changing his will and dictating the autopsy clause."

"When are you going to talk to Mrs. Glover again?"

"I'm in no hurry. It's evident that she lied to me when she said she was on good terms with her husband, but that won't matter if Jonty Blades is our man."

"She might not have lied. If Luke had suspicions, he might have thought it was good tactics to keep them to himself."

"Possibly. But I don't see him as a dissembler. If there was something like that on his mind I think she'd be sharp enough to spot it."

"Not unless there was some foundation to Luke's suspicions. If she was trying to poison him she'd be watching for reactions. But according to the doctor, nobody had been trying to poison him. That being the case, she might have noticed a slight strangeness in his manner and put it down to any cause except the right one."

"She said there was *no* strangeness in his manner. He was absolutely normal, she said."

Clay shrugged. "If he'd been a bit quiet or sulky she probably wouldn't think it worth mentioning. She'd think of it as ordinary bad temper. We must remember that he wasn't a very nice fellow. But this is a waste of time. When we get hold of Jonty Blades and make him cough, the job will be cleared, and Glover's will and Glover's belly ache won't matter a damn."

"I hope you're right," said Martineau. He spoke sincerely, but that did not prevent him from being doubtful. Somebody had *arranged* for Luke Glover to be at Grimwood on Tuesday afternoon, by telling him that he would find Sam and Ellie Blades together. The chief inspector intended to learn the name of that informant. Such knowledge was relevant to the case, whether or not the murder had been committed by one or several of the Blades family.

Chapter Nine

On that same Thursday, a little after two o'clock in the afternoon, two detective officers named Robieson and Brabant were in Wales Road, visiting shops and salerooms where second-hand furniture was bought and sold. Wales Road was a thoroughfare lined with establishments which catered to the needs of workers of the poorer sort. At the crossroads made by Wales Road and two less important roads, they climbed the stairs of Joy's Emporium, a business which occupied one big room over four shops of modest size.

They entered the Emporium, and they were immediately seen by Mr. Joy, who was not busy. He watched them from his little spider's web of an office, in the darkest corner of the room. He was not hopeful of doing business with them. He knew a copper when he saw one, and two together he recognized twice as quick.

The detectives looked around, but they did not see the furniture they sought. They went to the office. Joy met them at the doorway.

"Is this all the furniture you've got?" Robieson wanted to know.

"Sure, isn't it enough for you?" the man retorted. "I could furnish Buckin'ham Palace with the stuff I've got here."

"We're looking for an imitation leather suite, dark brown."

"Well, if it's been half-inched you won't find it here. This is all straight stuff what's been paid for. I'm very pertic'ler."

"The best of us can be diddled," Robieson persisted, but Brabant appeared to lose interest in the talk. He wandered away and stood staring out of a window.

Robieson soon found that he had no more questions to ask. He was ready to depart. But Joy had become curious. Robieson explained that a man called Jonty Blades, wanted for interview in the Glover murder, might try to dispose of the furniture. "If he comes here, try and keep him here while you get on the phone. Dial Central one-two, one-two or nine-nine-nine," he advised.

Talking, the two men moved to the door. Brabant joined them there. He pointed his thumb over his shoulder, toward the window. "What's that place across the road, among the trees?" he asked.

"Holly Lodge, you mean?" Joy laughed. "That's a real white elephant, that is. Old man Markham lived there on his own for donkey's years. Lived in one little room, I believe. When he died he left the place to the nation."

"Not to the city?"

"No, the nation." The man laughed. "Only the nation don't seem to want it. The Corporation did some work on it, 'cause the nation was goin' to hand it over. Then summat went wrong an' the thing fell through. Ever since then the place has been locked up, goin' to rack an' ruin."

"H'm. It seems a pity," Brabant commented without much interest. "You'd think they could do something with it."

The two policemen went down the stairs. When they were in the street, Brabant halted and gazed at the tall trees behind the wall of Holly Lodge, which stood diagonally opposite on the other side of the crossroads. Because of the trees, no part of the house could be seen from street level.

"What's on your mind?" Robieson wanted to know.

"You can see the tops of the chimneys from up there in the saleroom."

"You mean—you saw smoke?"

"That's it, boy. One of the chimneys is smoking. Somebody is in there."

"Glover's Rolls was left in Churlham. That's only a tuppenny bus ride from here."

"Yes. It makes you think. Let's go look."

They waited for the traffic lights to change and crossed the road. They walked fifty yards along Holly Road to the high front gate of the lodge. It was padlocked. The lock was rusty but strong. "You don't need a key to open that," Robieson observed. "You need a hacksaw."

"Let's go round to the back," was his colleague's reply.

At the end of the front wall there was a leafy alley, over-hung with trees, between the lodge and a block of stone houses. A little distance along the alley there was another gate to Holly Lodge. It was of solid wood, more than six feet high. In each leaf of the gate there was a square hole for a chain. The chain was there, and the padlock. "Another hacksaw job," said Robieson.

"All the same, there's somebody inside," Brabant muttered.

Robieson moved to one of the stone gateposts and peered into the crack between the post and the gate. He put both hands on the gate and pushed. The gate did not move. He tried the other side, and the gate moved a little. He was able to get his fingers between the stone and the wood and grasp the edge of the gate. He lifted it forward, making an opening wide enough for him to edge through. Grinning, he looked back through the opening. "It's off the hinges at this side," he said.

Brabant followed him through the opening. They were in a cobbled back yard. On one side were a potting shed and green-houses with every pane of glass broken. On the other side were stables and a coach house, with doors hanging open. The potting shed door had lost some of its boards, and at least one of the boards had been taken quite recently.

Before them was the house, with the kitchen door standing wide open. A woman's voice could be heard, calling someone.

"They're at home, whoever they are," Brabant said dryly. "Let's invite ourselves in."

He went forward, and climbed two steps to enter the kitchen. He went in quietly, without knocking. Robieson followed. They stood watching just inside the door. It was a big kitchen, with a big fireplace and a big old-fashioned stove. A heap of dead twigs and small logs beside the stove indicated that the tangled, overgrown grounds of the house had provided the fuel. Logs smoldered in the fireplace, and there was a fire in the stove. Around the fireplace a small settee and two chairs were arranged. They were covered in brown material which had the appearance of leather. In one of the chairs a large, elderly man was sleeping noisily, with his mouth open.

In the middle of the room was a gate-leg table, and around the table were four dining chairs. They looked new. Evidently Jonty Blades had recently done business with some furniture firm other than the Pay Tomorrow. The two detectives were quite sure that they had found Jonty.

Between the stove and the table a woman stood. She had her back to the door, and she had not heard the policemen enter. She poured tea into two cups which were on the table, and put the hot teapot down on the polished wood.

"Jonty!" she yelled. "I poured yer a cup!"

"Righto!" came a reply from elsewhere in the house, and the sound of boots on boards could be heard.

The woman picked up a cup of tea and went to sit by the fire. As she rounded the settee she became aware of the two men standing near the door. She was a small woman of forty or so. Her proportions were still good, and when she turned it could be seen that her face still had a certain pudgy prettiness.

And, the men noticed with surprise, the face was clean, with a clear healthy pallor. Her hair was dark, curly and plentiful. She stared open-mouthed at the intruders; then she said in deep disgust, "Hell fire! The above have arrived."

The tramp of boots drew nearer, and the door to the back hall was opened. The man in the doorway was small and dark. The policemen recognized him as Jonty Blades. They looked at each other and smiled. Still smiling, Brabant said, "All right, Jonty. Come and get your cup of tea."

Jonty moved into the room. His manner was defiant, yet somehow furtive. "Yer can't touch me," he said. "I've not sold a stick o' that furniture."

"You borrowed a Rolls-Royce, I think," Brabant said.

"Yer can't prove it."

The policeman walked to the fireplace and looked at the imitation leather suite. One rear corner of an armchair was supported by a piece of one-inch board, in place of a castor. He tilted the chair forward and removed the castor from the other rear corner. He showed it to Jonty before he put it in his pocket. "This matches the one we found in the Rolls," he said.

"It were naught," Jonty said. "I did no damage."

"You think that's what we want you for?" Robieson asked in surprise. "Don't you ever read a newspaper?"

"I've not seen a paper since we moved into this place. Been too busy settlin' in."

"Ah. You can tell that to Mr. Martineau."

"Martineau? He's a top copper. What does he want wi' me?"

"He wants to know who murdered the owner of the car you borrowed."

Jonty did not flinch. It was possible that he did not appreciate the implication of the remark. "Well, it weren't none o' us," he said.

The big man still slept soundly before the fire. "Who's that?" Brabant asked.

76

"That's Uncle."

"And are you Mrs. Blades?"

"I am," the woman said with emphasis. "Properly married an' all."

"Where is the rest of the family?"

"You're a detective, aren't yer? Yer'd better find 'em."

Brabant ignored that piece of impudence. He muttered to his colleague, "I'll go and ring in."

Robieson nodded. That was fair. Brabant was the man who had noticed the smoking chimney and appreciated its significance. He was the one to take the credit.

Brabant departed. Mrs. Blades said roughly to Robieson, "You'd better sit down an' have a cupper tea."

Robieson sat, on the chair nearest the door. "How many *are* there in the family?" he asked.

"There'd a-been more if Jonty hadn't gone an' got mumps," the woman replied enigmatically.

"That had naught ter do wi' it," Jonty protested warmly. "It were you."

"Ah, but it weren't," she answered serenely. "Yer'd know different if I'd not been faithful."

While Robieson asked questions and received wantonly evasive replies. Brabant was in contact with A Division C.I.D. On the telephone, he asked to speak to Martineau. The chief inspector listened to his story with satisfaction, but without surprise. After all, it was high time somebody picked up Jonty Blades.

"Well done," he said. "Have you got all the family there?"

"There's Jonty, his wife and the fellow called Uncle."

"Ah. We want Ellie, the daughter. And I'm sure there are more of them. Go back there and hunt around. I'll send you some help, and the van. I want the whole family brought in for interrogation. And don't give them the chance to talk among themselves."

Brabant returned to Holly Lodge. The position was the same, with Uncle snoring and Jonty and his wife using Robieson's questions as matter for amicable bickering. He left them to it and went on a tour of the house. Three more rooms on the ground floor were being used by the Bladeses. Two big front reception rooms and a room which might have been a study were being used as bedrooms. The bedsteads looked like salvage from a scrap heap, and the other bedroom furniture was home made, from packing cases. Apparently Jonty had been unable to furnish his bedrooms through hire purchase, probably because he lacked the money to make further initial deposits.

The rest of the house was quite bare. Having looked over it, Brabant went outside. He walked round the house and stood at the head of the drive. On one side there was an expanse of tall grass and weeds which had once been a lawn; on the other side there was shrubbery which had become a little jungle. Beyond the lawn, there was more jungle near the perimeter wall.

Standing there, the detective heard the crack of a breaking stick in the shrubbery. He made his way in that direction and found a narrow path. As he walked along the path he heard the breaking of another stick, and then another. He discerned a boy of sixteen or so, and a girl a few years younger. They were among the trees a few yards from the path, and they seemed to be collecting firewood.

"Hey!" he called. "Come out, you two."

They turned and saw him, and then without further delay the youth fled, plunging noisily through the thicket. Given an example, the girl panicked too, and fled after him. Brabant did not follow. He ran along the path and round to the front of the shrubbery. When the boy emerged, the policeman was only a few yards away from him. The chase was brief. It was a good runner, twenty-five years old, chasing a coltish lad in big boots.

"Now then," said Brabant not unkindly, as he held the boy by the shoulder. "What did you run away for?"

The boy was speechless, cowering in palpitating fear like a trapped animal. His wild eyes would not meet his captor's, and indeed his whole expression was withdrawn. Knowing that it was useless to ask any more questions at that time, Brabant looked him up and down, from his mop of uncombed black hair to his oversize boots. His hands and face had been blackened by sooty twigs and foliage. His blue dungarees were faded and dirty, and his blue jersey was frayed at the neck; but his shirt was clean, and he was wearing a lumber jacket which was almost new.

"You could do with a haircut," said Brabant humorously.

He took the boy home. The girl was already there, and there was a pretty young woman who was undoubtedly Ellie Blades. Apparently she had just arrived. She was holding a folded newspaper and she seemed to be breathless.

"You've flayed that lad," Jonty accused Brabant. "He can't do wi' bein' flayed."

"On the contrary, he frightened himself," the policeman denied. "I haven't said a cross word to him." Then he asked, "Have we got all the family here now?"

"Aye, this is the lot," Jonty admitted.

"All right, we'll just wait till the van comes."

"What! You're not takin' all on us?"

"We are, for the time being."

"What about all this stuff, an' no lock on the door?"

"Don't worry," Brabant assured him. "It'll be guarded, most carefully guarded. It might produce some evidence."

Chapter Ten

Martineau decided to question Jonty Blades in the windowless Interrogation Room. The prisoner waited for him there, seated at a central table under a strong light, and the contents of his pockets lay before him on the table. At another table in the corner a clerk was ready to record the conversation. Beside the door, on chairs against the wall, Robieson and Brabant were seated.

The chief inspector entered the room, and the metal door closed solidly and inexorably behind him like a prison gate. He took a seat across the table from Jonty and studied him in silence. Jonty stared back innocently, with big brown eyes. Martineau was not impressed by the stare. He had known some shocking liars with eyes like that.

He looked at Jonty's personal property. Nothing remarkable there. He noted that the man had had nine pounds in notes and some change in his pockets when he was arrested.

"All right," he said at last. "What have you got to say for yourself?"

"About what?"

"About that Rolls-Royce, for a start. We'll begin at the beginning."

"I don't know anythin' about no Rolls-Royce."

"Oh, you wiped off your dabs, all right. But the rest of the family left theirs. If you make us prove it through them you'll cause us a lot of trouble. That'll make it twice as bad for you."

Jonty thought about that. "Well, it were left there, right by the cemetery gate," he said. "Door unlocked, ignition key there, nobody about. That was a gold key. If anybody stole it, it weren't me."

"Nobody stole it. When did you first notice the car?"

"I saw it about a quarter past four, when I were comin' home. I mentioned it when I got in. Our Ellie said she'd seen it just after three."

"Where had you been?"

"I'd been to see Tommy Cross, to fix up about borrerin' his handcart. It's a good big 'un. I can flit in two trips wi' it."

"Did you make the arrangement?"

"Yers. I found Tommy in Mossbank, on 'is fruit round. He said I could borrer t'cart Sunday mornin'."

"What time did you meet Cross?"

"It'd be about three, 'cause when I left him I nipped in t' Raven for half o'common. Landlord wouldn't serve me, 'cause it'd gone time."

"Does the landlord know you?"

"Yers, he knows me. He said he were sorry, but he weren't goin' ter risk his license fer half o'common."

"Quite right, too. What were you doing between two and three?"

"Walkin' round Mossbank, lookin' fer Tommy."

"Did you see anyone you knew?"

"No. I ast a few folk if they'd seen a feller sellin' fruit from a handcart. Women."

"And had they?"

"No. None on 'em. But I were there. I found Tommy, didn't I?"

"We shall check on what you say, of course," Martineau said.

"Yer can check. I've spoke the truth."

"You can afford to keep on speaking the truth. It'll serve you better, as you know. So you were going to flit on Sunday morning. What made you change your mind?"

"The Rolls, standin' there. I thought I'd use that. Tommy charges five shillin' fer t'cart."

"What made you so urgent about wanting to move from the cemetery? Your furniture payments weren't due."

"A Corporation man found us there. I said we weren't doin' any harm, but yer know what they are. He said we'd be kicked outer there soon enough, so I ast him ter give us a week. He said he wouldn't give us a day as soon as he got the order, then he softened a bit an' said it might take a week."

"So you had to find another place to go?"

"I allus have another place ter go. Holly Lodge were next on me list."

"How did you come to know of it?"

"Two fellers in a pub. A coupler tatters I know. One said what about gettin' the lead pipes outer Holly Lodge. T'other chap was one o' these wise guys. He said he'd got all the lead outer there years since. I thought I'd have a look round there, just in case. I found I could manage t'back gate."

"How did you go on for water, if there was no plumbing?"

"Rain water. A big butt back o' t' greenhouse."

"H'm. How long is it since you borrowed Wensley's ax?"

"Oh, a long while since. We found a dead tree. Good firewood. I cut it down an' lopped main branches, then left it fer t' childer an' Uncle ter cut. Then Wensley come an' took th' ax back."

"Has your son, Gaylord, ever borrowed the ax?"

"Not as I know of."

"Has Uncle?"

"No. Not ter my knowledge."

"Did either of them know where it was kept?"

"I daresay both on 'em did, but I can't be sure. Yer'll have ter ask 'em. What about th' ax?"

"That was the murder weapon."

"Yer don't say! Well, none o' them two 'ud murder anybody. It had naught ter do with us Blades."

"That remains to be seen. How long have you known Uncle?"

"Twenty year, I should think. I found him in a owd stable in Boyton. A nice dry stable it were, an' we were just movin' in. But Uncle were sleepin' in there wet through as if e'd been lyin' in t' rain. Sleepin' in 'is sodden clo's. He'd bumped his head somewhere an' he were in a proper bad way. Well, we looked after him fer two or three weeks, happen. But it weren't so good. 'E were proper dim. No sense at all, an' didn't know nothin'. I'm wonderin' how long I'm goin' to keep feedin' him when he walked out an' vanished. I didn't set eyes on him again fer happen fourteen year."

"Fourteen years!"

"That 'ud be about it."

"Didn't you ever know his name?"

"No. Never at no time. I ast him, an' he said he didn't know. Our Ellie were a babby at that time, so we just called him Uncle."

"How did you come to meet again, after fourteen years?"

"We met in Lacy Street. I said, 'Hello Uncle,' an' he said, 'You know me?' So I said, 'I knew yer years since.' Then he, 'Let's go have a drink.' An' I said, 'No, thanks.' He said, 'Yer teetotal?' An' I said, 'No. Hard up.' So he laughed an' took me by the arm an' we went into the nearest taproom."

"Did you tell him about your first meeting?"

"Yers. He looked a bit thoughtful, an' then he said, 'So this is where I come from.' Then he ast me if I knew his name, an' I said I'd never known it. An' he said he didn't know it either. But he were a different man. A lot brighter. He were livin' in a doss house an' he didn't like it, so I took him home wi' me, to the place where we were livin' then, an' he's been wi' us ever since."

"He drinks, I gather."

"Yers. But he never makes any trouble. He's bright fer about a week an' then he gets moody an' proper dull. Then he brings out his little cash reserve an' goes on the rant. After he gets over that he's all right fer a bit; then he starts all over again."

"Where does he get his money?"

"Oh, we're in business together, me an' him."

"Doing what?"

"He's a inventor. He's clever, is Uncle, when he's in his better mood. He's invented some real nobby little gadgets fer sellin' door ter door. To t' women, yer know. He invents 'em an' I sell 'em, an' our Gaylord is th' errand lad. He does the runnin' about."

"Are they patented?"

"No. We don't bother wi' patents."

Martineau looked at the money on the table. "What invention are you selling just now?" he asked.

"Oh, it's a good 'un. The Magnetic Door Sneck. It's just two little plates o' metal, magnetized, see? It holds the door shut. When yer want ter open it, all yer do is push."

"What happens when the plates lose their magnetism?"

Jonty looked vague. "Happen they can have 'em remagnetized," he said. "I don't know. Yer see, we never work the same area twice. That way, we don't get any complaints."

"There are worse ways of keeping out of trouble," Martineau agreed. He was patient, hoping that Jonty would eventually tell him something really definitive about Uncle. "Who makes the things for you?"

Jonty looked even more vague. "We have a good man. He's reasonable. But we don't mention his name. We don't want everybody buttin' in, yer know."

"I won't interfere in your business. You can tell me."

"No. Not till I've ast Uncle."

Martineau nodded, as if that were a matter of no importance. He continued to be curious about Uncle's inventive talent, and he was told of the Everlasting Tap Washer, the Sanitary Pipe Scourer and other small productions which had served their turn, each being cast aside as a new idea was developed. While defensively pointing out the merits of each item, Jonty let slip the name of one Ben Chase. Chase, it appeared, had a small engineering shop in Sawford.

"He works fer hisself," Jonty volunteered, now that the name was out. "He can make aught, or mend aught."

"Who knew him, in the first place?"

"Well, it weren't me. It musta been Uncle knew him, or he knew Uncle."

Martineau made a note of the name. At last, he thought, there might be a man who knew Uncle's name and some of his past.

"There's just one other thing," he said. "Your daughter Ellie was doing a bit of courting at Grimwood."

"Aye, that's right. A lad wi' a fancy car. Jack, she said they called him."

"Didn't you ask her his full name?"

"Yers. She wouldn't tell me."

"Weren't you worried, your daughter being courted by an obviously rich young man who wasn't likely to marry her?"

"No. Why should I a-been? If she's goin' to get wed, a rich lad is better nor a poor 'un. If she's simply goin' to get put in the fam'ly way, it's better a rich lad nor a poor 'un. If naught like that is goin' ter happen ter her, there's no harm done."

"Didn't you take any precautions?"

Jonty allowed himself a grin. "I had the number o' the car, just in case. An' there's not many cars like that in Granchester."

"And you left it at that?"

"Yers. I'm a busy man."

85

Martineau sighed. "So am I," he said. "I shall want to talk to you again, but just now one of these officers is going to take you down and charge you with taking away a motor vehicle without the owner's permission. And if you think that isn't a serious offense, you're kidding yourself."

"I didn't do any harm," Jonty replied. He was taken away, protesting that he had never done any harm in his life.

Martineau left the room, and went to the corner of the main C.I.D. office where Devery was trying to interrogate Uncle. He drew the sergeant aside. "What does he say?" he asked.

"Nothing," was the disgusted reply. "Tuesday afternoon he was drunk and he doesn't remember anything. He seems to have been fairly well oiled ever since. I've had his coat off and looked at it under a glass. Plenty of spots, but nothing which could be blood."

Martineau nodded, and went to where Cassidy was trying to coax answers out of the boy Gaylord. At his approach, the Irishman looked up, shook his head and shrugged. "Not a word, sir," he said. "Neither Yes, No nor kiss my backside." He lowered his voice. "I'm thinking he's a bit dotty."

"Backward, possibly," Martineau admitted. "You mean he hasn't said anything at all?"

"Not one solitary word. He just looks at me, and I haven't the heart to bang his head against the wall."

"Never do that," said Martineau, who had done it many a time, but not to a reluctant witness. "I wonder if his mother could get him to talk."

He spoke to the boy. He was answered by the beseeching stare of a spaniel. Gaylord had his father's eyes. The policeman was doubtful. Jonty could lie until the cock crowed. This attitude of tongue-tied fear could be an act of deception.

He sent for the mother. She came, and spoke rapidly and quietly to the boy. The policemen did not try to listen. They waited, and at last the boy answered in a whisper. The woman turned and spoke. "He doesn't know aught," she said. "He knows naught about it, an' he's flayed to death."

Martineau questioned her briefly. She professed to have as little knowledge of murder as the boy, though she was obviously not afraid. He moved across to the detective who had been speaking to Caroline Blades, the younger daughter. "I got her talking," the man said. "I don't think she knows anything at all."

The chief inspector sighed. He looked at another corner of the room where Ellie Blades was sitting, under the eye of a C.I.D. clerk who was getting on with his work. "Bring her into my office," he said to the clerk.

When the girl sat facing him across his desk he studied her briefly, and decided that she was not the type he had expected. His knowledge of Jonty led him to assume that Jonty's daughter would be pert, ignorant and dishonest. Sam Glover's assertion that she was at least prudent in her love affairs had not affected his prejudice. Now, he formed the opinion that he had been wrong. This girl looked all right. She even looked intelligent. She was more than pretty, and her brown hair was neat and clean. Her dress and her short suède coat were a quite tasteful casual ensemble. She was pale, and probably scared, but she looked her inquisitor squarely in the eye.

"Your full name is Eleanor Blades?" he asked.

"Yes," she replied.

"How old are you?"

"Twenty-two."

"What do you do for a living?"

"I sign on at the Labour Exchange. I'm out of work."

"How long have you been out of work?"

"Oh, a few months now."

"You haven't been trying to find work?"

"No," she admitted.

"How did you come to know Sam Glover?"

She told him. Her story corroborated Sam's.

"You say he called himself Jack," Martineau pursued. "But you knew who he was?"

"Yes."

"How?"

She told how Sam had taken his coat off in the Grimwood Inn one day during the warmest month of the summer. He had been called aside by the landlord over some small matter. She had looked at the tailor's label inside a pocket of the coat.

"Did you tell him what you'd done?" Martineau asked.

"No."

"Did you give his real name to anybody?"

"No."

"Not to your father or your mother?"

"No. My mother was a big nosy about it, but I didn't tell her anything."

"Were you quite content to go drifting along, meeting Sam once a week or so?"

The girl was silent.

Martineau went on, "Let us put it this way. Were you trying to make him fall seriously in love with you, as any girl might do with a young man?"

"I suppose so."

"Now please don't be offended. Was it because he had money?"

"Any girl likes to marry somebody with money, but I think it was more because I liked him. I still like him. You're talking as if it's all over. Has he done something wrong?"

"There is no evidence that he has done wrong. Now, let us go back to last Tuesday afternoon. What time did you meet Sam?"

She told him. Again her story corroborated Sam's.

"And when Sam had gone, what did you do?"

"I walked on home."

"To Cemetery Lodge?"

"Yes."

"On the way, did you see anybody?"

"No. Nobody."

"Did you notice anything unusual?"

"Yes. The Rolls-Royce car near the cemetery gate. There was nobody in it, and there was nobody about."

"What did you think?"

"I thought it must be somebody coming looking for an old grave."

"Ah. You thought that the driver of the car must be in the cemetery?"

"That's right."

"Did you see anyone in the cemetery?"

"No."

"Who was at home when you arrived?"

"Everybody except Dad."

"What were they doing?"

The girl pondered. "Uncle was having his dinner, and slobbering over it. My mother was nattering at him for being late. Carrie was just sitting and listening, and I can't remember what Gaylord was doing. I think he was listening, too."

"What was Uncle's condition?"

"He was drunk. It was one of his bad days. After he'd had his dinner he fell asleep in front of the fire. He's on a rant. He hasn't been really sober since."

He continued to question her. She told him how Jonty had come home and mentioned the Rolls-Royce at the gate, how he had become excited when he found it still there at nightfall, how he had reversed it into the lane, as far as the wicket gate.

"Did you help with the flitting?" Martineau asked.

"Oh, yes, we all helped. Was that wrong?"

"Yes, but we won't discuss that just now. Did you at any time see anybody near the cemetery while you were loading up and driving off?"

"No. Not a soul."

Martineau smiled ruefully. "You haven't told me a lot," he said, "but it seems to be all you know. Will you be seeing Sam again?"

"I hope so."

That was the end of the interrogation. The Blades family, who were to have been so important, had added practically nothing to the sum of the evidence. Martineau was not satisfied with the reactions of Uncle and Gaylord to police questioning, but it seemed that nothing more could be done with them at the moment. They could go home to Holly Lodge. With the exception of Jonty, the whole family could go home. Martineau had other work to do.

A detective had telephoned from the central employment exchange. Eight weeks ago Gordon Barnes had started work as a salesman at Palmer Radio, and he had given an address in Rubber Street, Granchester. Martineau had already sent men to pick him up.

Chapter Eleven

"This is the place," said Detective Sergeant Devery. "Anvil Yard."

In company with Detective Constable Cassidy, he was driving a C.I.D. car along a shabby section of one of the city's main streets. He slowed the car and drove it through an archway between two shops whose windows were packed with gaudy wares. Beyond the archway was a cobbled space with the back yards of the shops on one side. On the remaining three sides were two-story buildings with unpainted doors, dirty windows and outside stairways of rough unpainted wood. It was a place symbolic of the everlasting optimism of private enterprise. Every establishment was a workshop of some kind. Great companies of the future were having their beginnings in Anvil Yard; less ambitious ones were steadily making a living there; unlucky or inefficient ones were dying there.

The two men alighted and looked around. "There it is," Cassidy said. He pointed. Above a big sliding door there was a faded sign: BEN CHASE. ENGINEER.

Though it was after six o'clock in the evening, someone was still at work. The sliding door was half open, and as the policemen approached they heard the hum of running machinery. They stopped in the doorway and looked into a room about forty feet square, well lighted by big windows at the rear. Most of the floor space was taken up by machine tools. They seemed to be modern tools, in good condition. While Mr. Chase's business might not have a great future, very obviously it was not dying.

There was a man working at a lathe. He was about fifty years of age, tall and thin, gray of hair and of face. He wore a dingy gray overall coat. The two big men filling the doorway may have caused a change of light on the spinning metal under his eye. He turned and looked at them, nodded to them and went on with his work. They waited.

Quite soon Chase stopped the lathe. Wiping his hands on a rag, he moved to the door. His colorless face was saturnine, but by no means humorless. He said, "I don't think your business is going to be any good to me, whatever it is."

"We're from Police Headquarters," Devery said. "Are you Ben Chase?"

"That's my name."

"We're seeking information about a man called Jonty Blades. Do you know him?"

"Yes, I know Jonty."

"I understand you've done some work for him."

Chase's features contorted themselves into an expression of sour indulgence. "I've helped him out occasionally. I make his little gadgets when I have the time. There's no profit in it for me."

"Why do you do it, then? What's your angle?"

Chase was hurt. "Does there have to be an angle? Have you never heard of the milk of human kindness?"

"You do it out of friendship, then?"

"Out of good nature, perhaps."

"Who do you feel good-natured to? Jonty, or Uncle?"

"Well, both. Jonty is a likable rascal. Uncle is a nice chap when he's sober."

"You know it's Uncle who invents the gadgets?"

"Of course."

"What's his name?"

Chase shrugged. "Nobody seems to know that."

"Do *you* know?"

"No."

"How long have you known him?"

"Oh, years."

"How many years?"

"Seven or eight."

"I think it might be longer than that. It was Uncle who first came to you with something to be made, not Jonty."

"Well, why not? Lots of people come to me. I can make anything so long as it isn't too big to go through this door. You bring me the drawings and I'll make you your machine, and I work sixty minutes to the hour."

"But when Uncle first came to you with one of his little inventions, you already knew him, didn't you?"

"No, I can't say I did."

"Well, I'll be checking. Uncle is involved in the murder of Luke Glover."

"Is he really?" Chase's astonishment could have been genuine.

"Yes, and we want to know who he is."

"Well, I hope you find out. The poor fellow will be glad to know himself."

"It's quite likely that he was born and bred in this town. *Somebody* ought to know him."

Chase shrugged. "It's a big town. You may know a man, but you can go twenty years without seeing him if his way of life differs from yours."

Devery looked at him shrewdly. "You've met Uncle when he was sober. What sort of a man is he?"

"He's all right. Just an ordinary sort of fellow with a small inventive talent."

"Does he talk like an educated man?"

"If you mean does he speak with a B.B.C. accent, well, he

doesn't. He speaks as badly as Jonty. But that doesn't mean he isn't educated. I don't judge a man's learning by his accent, but by the sum of his knowledge."

"Well, what is the sum of Uncle's knowledge?"

"I don't know. I've never been in debate with him."

"You're a bit of a homespun philosopher, aren't you?"

Faint color came into the gray face. "I'm an engineer in a small way of business, but that doesn't mean I have to be an ignoramus. I like to seek the knowledge I can find in books, and I do it in my spare time instead of gaping at the idiot's lantern."

Devery grinned. "That puts me in my place," he said. "Now open up and tell me about Uncle."

"I've told all I'm going to tell you."

"I don't think you have, somehow. I've got a feeling you know more."

"I'm not interested in your feelings." the man said, and with that he returned to his lathe. Devery retired, temporarily defeated, and got into the car.

Cassidy climbed in beside him. "You got his dander up," he commented. "He don't like you."

"I'll admit I was a bit cheeky," the sergeant said. "Most fellows would have laughed it off, but not that one. He didn't like that homespun philosopher crack."

"Happen you should've apologized."

"Not me. If he can't take a bit of kidding, that's his lookout. The trouble with that type of would-be intellectual is that they think nobody else knows anything. He mentioned the word ignoramus. He didn't like being kidded by an ignoramus, because that's what he thought I was."

"Maybe he was right."

Devery laughed. "Maybe he was."

"I'll tell you what I think," said Cassidy sagely. "At some time or other he missed the main chance. He thinks he should be a lot better off than he is now. It sort of colors his outlook.

He thinks he's really better than ordinary men like Jonty and Uncle and you and me."

"No. It's intellectual snobbery, I'm sure."

"Well, I don't. Him and his milk of human kindness. He's taking the trouble to do Uncle's manufacturing because he knows none of those little inventions are ever patented. He's looking forward to the time when Uncle brings him something really good, then *he'll* patent it, and to hell with Uncle. He's still looking for the main chance."

"He knows something, I'm sure of that. I'm going to do some research on that bird."

"What satisfaction will you get? We'll know Uncle's identity before you can get going."

"I'll have the satisfaction of knowing."

Looking across the table in the "grill room," Martineau studied Gordon Barnes. The man's shabby condition did not justify his air of insouciance. One side of his face was puffed, and he had winced slightly as he had taken his seat. The face looked as if it had been slapped repeatedly. The careful movements and apparent soreness of body indicated that Barnes had recently taken a beating. Martineau remembered that Barnes worked for Palmer Radio, owned by Dixie Costello. The Palmer Radio firm had recently been robbed of five hundred transistor sets. Evidently Dixie, or his emissaries, had been interrogating the staff with some violence.

"What's the matter with your face?" the chief inspector asked.

Barnes answered without hesitation. "I've had an abscess on a tooth. It's getting better."

The policeman nodded. He did not intend to let Barnes know that he was aware of the transistor theft. It had no bearing on the present case, anyway. He started his interrogation. "I'm interested in what you were doing on Tuesday afternoon."

"Why?" The question was blunt.

"Because you have a sort of connection with a man who has been murdered."

"You mean Luke Glover, of course. I know nothing about that. I didn't know the man."

"Nevertheless, he married your ex-wife. I've got to check on you."

Barnes made a good show of being cheerful. "Routine inquiries, eh? Well, let me see, Tuesday afternoon. I can't exactly tell you till I get my journey book."

"Where is it?"

"In my drawer at the shop."

"If I send a man, will you give him written authority to collect it and bring it here to you?"

"Sure," Barnes said. Then he grinned. "What's the use? I haven't written anything in that damned book for a week."

"Why?"

"Willful neglect. Every once in a while I write it up from memory. Real and imaginary calls. You've got to account for your time, you know."

"Precisely. Now account for your time to me, leaving out the imaginary calls. I'll look at the book later."

"All right. Now, Tuesday . . ."

"Start at lunchtime. Where did you have a meal?"

"Tuesday? The Lacy Arms, I think. I had a wedge of pork pie and a sandwich, with a pint of ale."

"What time would this be?"

"About one. I stayed till about two, having another pint."

"Then where did you go?"

"Now you're asking me something I can't remember."

"All right, I'll try to jog your memory. Did you go anywhere near Grimwood?"

"Ah, now I remember. I went to Buckover. I passed through Grimwood."

"Did you stop anywhere on the way?"

"Yes. I found I was a bit early for my appointment, so I stopped at a pub."

"What was the name of the pub?"

"I never noticed. It wasn't a bad little pub."

"Was it anywhere near Grimwood Cemetery?"

"Yes. Quite near."

"Was it the Grimwood Inn?"

"Now you mention it, I believe it was."

"What made you choose that particular boozer?"

"Pure chance, I suppose. It was there, so I stopped."

Martineau's fist came down on the table with sufficient noise and force to make the other man's nerves jump. He stared open-mouthed.

The policeman controlled himself. "I'm being very patient with you," he said. "You won't make me believe that you called at the Grimwood Inn by chance. If you tell me any more lies like that, you'll be deeper in trouble than you are already. You were once married to Glover's wife. The jealousy of an ex-husband is the best motive I've found so far. It's good enough for me."

Barnes turned pale. "You think I did it?"

"Why not? If you want me to think otherwise, you'll have to convince me."

Barnes recovered some of his poise while he considered his next statement. Obviously, at the mention of Grimwood, he had realized that it was dangerous to deny having been there on Tuesday, because it would have been a simple matter for Martineau to have him identified by the landlord and his wife. Now, he was undoubtedly wondering if Martineau had been playing a cat-and-mouse game with him, knowing all the time that he had been at Grimwood. He was beginning to understand that his position was indeed dangerous.

"I can see I'd better tell you everything," he said. "I did have a reason for going to Grimwood. I followed Sam Glover there."

"Why?"

"General reasons. To see what he was up to. I was trying to get a line on the Glover family."

"You mean, for blackmail purposes?"

"Not exactly. Put it this way. I'm hard up, they've got plenty. I have a connection with the family. I was trying to get to know Sam. He's Diana's stepson. She's a handsome woman, but she's also going to cut into his inheritance. He might dislike her a lot, or he might like her too much. There seemed to be a chance for me to horn in somewhere. God knows, I need the money."

"Where did you pick him up?"

"In Lacy Street. I spotted the Ferrari. I managed to keep on his tail with my heap of old iron. I followed him to Grimwood. He put the Ferrari behind the pub, and I left my car at the front. I went in and looked in all the public rooms, but I couldn't see Sam. I went out into the back yard, and the car was there, right enough. I went back into the bar and ordered a drink. A young wench came in and went into a room behind the bar, and in a little while the landlord took two drinks in there. I asked him if that was the snug behind the bar, and he said it was his private parlor. So I guessed Sam was in there with the girl."

"You thought you were on to something?"

"Yes, sort of. The more I could get to know, the better. I think I had two drinks in there; then I went out and drove my car some way toward Derbyshire Road. I left it and climbed over the wall of the railway property. I made my way along till I could watch the pub from the sidings, looking under the hoardings. It was between five past and ten past three when I got into position. I remember the time because I was wondering if I'd missed Sam and the girl. In a few minutes the girl came round from the back of the pub, and Sam drove his car out. She waved him off and went the other way, toward the cemetery. I followed her, on the other side of the wall. She turned along the little lane beside the cemetery and went in through a gate. I assumed she lived at the house there."

"Did you see anyone else?"

"Not a soul. All the other customers must have gone home before I got into position. Or else they came out of the pub later, when I'd cleared off."

"Did you notice anything unusual?"

"Yes. I saw the Rolls-Royce that was mentioned in the papers. Luke Glover's car. I wondered what it was doing there, but I never dreamed it was Glover's. I hadn't got around to the job of finding out things about him."

"H'm. What did you do then?"

"I went back to my car, and called it a day as regards the Glover family. I had to make a show of doing some work."

"If you wanted money, why didn't you approach your ex-wife directly? You've revealed enough of your character to convince me you wouldn't be too proud to do that."

"Oh, I approached her all right, as soon as I found out."

"Found out what?"

"Who she was married to. You don't know our dear Diana, and you don't know the Mercer family. There I was living in Nottingham, without the faintest idea she was married to a millionaire."

"Well, her family would know."

"That's what you think. She was married quietly. Her brother, Roy Mercer, is still a bit of a pal of mine. He thought she'd married some character who didn't have two ha'pennies for a penny. Coo, Roy'll go stark staring mad when he finds out she was living on the milk an' honey while he was sweating his guts out trying to sell second-hand cars."

"How did she conceal the milk and honey?"

"She was always quietly dressed when she visited Nottingham. No mink, no diamonds, third class on the train. Said she didn't want anybody to visit her in Granchester till she and her husband had got a decent home instead of living in rooms. Oh, she kidded 'em all right. She knows the Mercers. They'd have been round like a flock of crows if they'd known."

"How did you get to know the truth?"

"I got this job with Palmer Radio in Granchester. I thought I'd get in touch with Diana for old times' sake. I was a bit lonely, you see. I knew she was married to a man called Glover, so I started on the Glovers in the phone book. There aren't so many. I found her all right, and talked to her on the phone. She said she didn't want to see me, and hung up on me."

"And is that all the contact you had with her?"

"You're dead right it is. I copied the address and went to look at the house. I knew then she was in the money, the crafty bitch. I called, but got no further than the doorstep. So I started making inquiries about this Luke Glover. I soon found out who he was. So there you are."

"You started prying, to see if you could work your way in somehow."

"That's about it," Barnes admitted. "I thought I might find a way to make some of that money rub off on me. You never know your luck. After all, I have a sort of connection with the family. So now you know just what I was doing at Grimwood Tuesday afternoon."

"You never tried to get in touch with Luke Glover?"

"No, but I knew him by sight, though I didn't know his car. I know Sam too, *and* his car. And the nephew, Billy. But I've never exchanged a word with any one of 'em."

"How long have you been at this game of nosing around after the Glovers?"

"Oh, a few weeks. Five or six."

"Will you be giving it up now?"

"I suppose so. But now that Diana's a widow there's no harm in me trying to get in touch with her again, is there?"

"Not if your intentions are honest."

Barnes was now confident enough to venture a grin. "Oh, they're honest enough. I'll marry her again if I get the chance. She's rich."

Martineau reflected that the man might be a rogue, but he was not a hypocrite. He wondered if he had had anything to do with the transistor robbery. He could have fingered the job for a team of out-of-town thieves. Nottingham men, probably. Well, that possibility would not have escaped the notice of Dixie Costello. Discreet but none the less intensive inquiries were no doubt being whispered around Nottingham at that moment.

Was there any point in attaching a tail to Barnes? Not on the evidence, he decided. He said, "The clerk will put your story in the form of a statement. When you've signed it, you can go. Don't leave this city without letting me know."

Barnes raised his head in the manner of a man about to make a truculent reply, then changed his mind and said, "Very well, Inspector. I'll be a good boy."

"All right then. Oh, by the way, what was the situation between yourself and your wife as regards alimony?"

The man shrugged. "I never paid any."

"None at all?"

"None. Right from the start. I told her she couldn't get money from a man who had nothing; I wasn't making enough to keep myself. So she never set the law on me."

"Happen she was glad to get rid of you at any price?"

Barnes grinned. "But of course. At the time, I thought it was because she still liked me a bit. Now I know different. She was moving in with the money, and she didn't want any bother. What was my humble contribution compared to Glover's millions?"

Chapter Twelve

For Friday morning Martineau had a schedule like a professional man: four interviews, and a fifth and sixth if time permitted. First of all he had to report to Clay, then go with Clay to talk to the chief constable. Then he had to see Diana Glover. Afterward he would go to see Janet Glover, and in his opinion that was an interview which was overdue. From Janet he would go to Uncle, to see if he were sober. After that, if possible, he would try to get a statement from Gaylord Blades. It had occurred to him that in familiar surroundings both Uncle and Gaylord might talk more freely than they would in a police station.

The first two interviews were routine. Clay was still of the opinion that some member of the Blades household would provide the solution to the murder, but he was in favor of leaving Uncle and Gaylord alone for a little while longer. "Let 'em think they've got away with it, then pounce," he advised.

Nevertheless, he agreed that Martineau had discovered some disturbing facts in connection with the Glover family. The report of the interview with Gordon Barnes made him look very thoughtful. "I'd have that bird watched if I were you," he said.

Of course that was an order. Martineau said that he would arrange for Barnes to be kept under observation. The night before, he had given a lot of thought to the matter of Diana and Gordon Barnes. He remembered having once been told that a woman always had a tender feeling for her first lover, no matter how badly he had subsequently treated her. Assuming that Barnes had indeed been Diana's first lover, he wondered if she would lose her will power in his presence, hunger for his caresses or soften to his entreaties. He asked himself if she had already done so. He also asked himself if Luke Glover had known or suspected something of it. That would account for the provisions of the new will.

The chief inspector had checked the timing of events prior to the murder. Gordon Barnes had arrived in Granchester eight weeks before. He had sought his ex-wife, and he had not been long in finding her. His statement that she had refused to see him could have been a lie. He could have seen her, and she, married to an old man, could have succumbed to his advances. All that could have happened in a fortnight. By that time, Luke could already have been suspicious of his wife. At any rate he had shown a fear of poisoning, and his feelings had been strong enough to make him change his will and insert the post-mortem clause.

Assuming that Diana had fallen in love with Barnes all over again, she might have wished to get rid of Luke. Barnes would want that too, but possibly more than she he would want her to inherit a large part of Luke's wealth. This could have led to a discussion of ways and means to bring about Luke's death. This *could* have led to a halfhearted attempt at poisoning. Also it could have caused Barnes to start spying on Sam Glover, in the hope of learning something about him, by means of which he could have been made to "take the rap" for Luke's murder. Weeks ago Barnes could have learned about Sam's secret love affair. He could have told Diana. She could have been the one who had sent Luke to Grimwood, to catch Sam with his sweetheart. She might even have given Luke an exact time, say five or ten minutes to three. Barnes had left the inn a good while before three. He had had time to intercept Luke, and time to kill him.

Martineau had mused over these possibilities without really believing in them. There were too many snags. Would Barnes have appeared at the inn if he had intended to kill Luke? How on earth had he induced Luke to leave his car and walk to the scene of the murder? If he were the murderer, why had he taken the trouble to return the bloodstained ax to the inn?

Still, the statements of Barnes and his ex-wife were disparate in the matter of his alleged attempts to get in touch with her. She had not mentioned them. Also, the new will was like a weapon aimed at her. And it was probable that she had been lying about her good relations with Luke. It was time for her to answer a few more questions.

At his request she came to see him in his office, braving the cameras of the newspapermen who were waiting about at the front entrance. The morning was sunny but cool, and she wore a mink stole over a neat black suit. A smart black hat rested on her bright hair. She made a picture which he mentally captioned: BLONDE IN MOURNING.

In manner she was composed. She accepted a seat and a cigarette. Martineau knew that she had already been told of the miserable five thousand pounds which her husband had left to her. She was taking a big disappointment without showing signs of worry. She was taking it quite as well as she had taken the possibly less grievous news of her bereavement. She was a woman of character, good or bad.

"I'm sorry to have to bring you to this place," he said. "I get busier every day."

"I quite understand," she replied. "You have your work to do."

"There's a clause in your late husband's will which is bothering me. The clause regarding a post-mortem examination. Apparently he thought that someone might poison him. Can you think of anyone who might try to do that?"

"I can't. My domestic staff saw so little of him, they hardly knew he existed. They wouldn't do such a thing, anyway. Away from home he ate fairly regularly at his club, and of course in restaurants too. He did occasionally have a meal at G.D.M., and you could try and find out if anybody there had a reason to hate him. About once a week he called and had lunch with his sister Janet, but of course she's out of the question. She was very fond of him."

"Evidently you've given some thought to this."

"I have indeed. Wouldn't anybody? If Luke and I had been on bad terms, I'd say it was a deliberate insult. As it is, I don't know what to think."

"Evidently you have perceived that the post-mortem clause seems to point a finger at you."

"I suppose it does, and I don't understand. Couldn't it be somebody at G.D.M.?"

"I've given attention to that angle. I have men working on it now. We'll leave that and return to the relations between your husband and yourself. Obviously they could not have been as harmonious as I was given to understand. The new will is evidence of that."

The woman's composure had left her. Deep and bitter feeling was showing. "Everything was all right, I tell you. We never had a wrong word."

"Could he have been jealous?"

"He gave no sign of it."

"Can you think of anybody of whom he might have been secretly jealous?"

"No. I took care to give him no cause for jealousy. And anyway, that wouldn't account for the post-mortem thing."

"It might, if he thought you were infatuated with another man."

"Well, I wasn't. There was no other man."

"Any charming young man with whom you were on friendly terms? Someone whom you found amusing?"

"No."

"What about your ex-husband, Gordon Barnes? He has been in Granchester for the last couple of months."

Mrs. Glover showed no surprise, but the mention of Barnes seemed to sting her. "What has that got to do with anything?" she demanded. "I told you I hadn't seen him for years."

"He tells a different story."

"Then he's lying."

"Haven't you been in touch with him at all? Recently, I mean."

"No. He phoned me one day and asked me to meet him. I knew then he'd found out that I'd married somebody with money. I told him I didn't want to have anything to do with him, and I left instructions with the maids that if a Gordon Barnes should call, he was not to be admitted under any circumstances. That's how much I've been in touch with him."

"He didn't have the opportunity to ask for money?"

"No. And I had no money to give him. Luke was stingy with pocket money. I could get nearly anything I liked on account, except jewelry, but I saw very little actual cash. His excuse was that women were always losing things. He didn't want me to carry much money."

"You didn't have a bank account of your own?"

"Yes, of course. I had a deposit account of my own when we were married. Not much, just a hundred or two. It's still there in the bank. You don't think I'd be married to Luke Glover and spend my own savings, do you?"

"No, I don't think that. The first time we talked, you told me that when Luke left for the office on Tuesday morning you had no knowledge of his appointments for that day. Do you wish to change that story?"

"No. Why should I? It's the truth."

"Do you now know why he went to Grimwood?"

"No, I don't. Can you tell me?"

Martineau shook his head. If Sam had not told his stepmother about his presence at Grimwood, there was no need for a policeman to tell her. Not yet, at any rate.

He opened a drawer and brought out the pictures of Barnes. He showed them to her.

"Just to be sure, tell me who this is," he said.

"Oh, that's Gordon all right," she answered at once. "As large as life and twice as conceited."

Then she looked up sharply. "This looks as if it's come from the Rogues' Gallery. Is he a criminal now?"

"Perhaps. Some men are inclined to slip when they're tempted. I think he's one of those. Real criminals are a different sort of animal. It remains to be seen whether or not he has become one of that species."

She sighed. "Poor Gordon. All his swans turn out to be geese. I don't think he's really bad. Just vain and weak."

The soft spot, Martineau thought. The tender feeling for the first lover. It was partly maternal, distantly akin to a woman's forgiving attitude toward her only son. And yet—assuming, until the contrary was proved, that she was telling the truth—she had refused to see Barnes. Had she been afraid that she would weaken? She seemed to have a strong character. Did she also have strong emotions, and was she aware of the fact? A strong woman with strong emotions was capable of almost anything. She might not sever a man's spinal column with an ax, but she might arrange for it to happen. From the beginning, Mrs. Glover's statements had contained only one small inconsistency, but that untruth had been a part of the only piece of information she had given, her statement concerning her ex-husband. Martineau did not trust her at all.

There was a knock on the door, and Brabant's face appeared. "Could I have a word with you, sir?"

Martineau rose. "Excuse me, Mrs. Glover, I won't be a moment," he said.

He went out to Brabant. The young detective said, "Jonty was remanded on bail, sir. Until the Quarter Sessions."

Martineau nodded. So Jonty would be at liberty until his trial. Well, he would not run away. He would not get the chance to do another moonlight flit.

"I saw that man who was here yesterday," Brabant went on. "He was sitting in the back of the court. I pretended I hadn't seen him."

"You mean the Nottingham chap with the record? Barnes?"

"Yes, sir. I'm quite sure it was him."

The chief inspector looked thoughtful. Apparently Barnes was still interested in the Grimwood case, still trying to put a finger in the pie. But what interest could he possibly have in the affairs of Jonty Blades? Did Jonty really know something about the murder after all? Did Barnes know that Jonty knew? It did seem that Clay had been right in giving the order for Barnes to be watched. Would there be any advantage in watching Jonty, too?

Martineau returned to his office. "Now, Mrs. Glover, we'll just go over one or two things again," he said. "I'd like to know more about yourself and your late husband, and, if possible, more about yourself and your ex-husband."

Chapter Thirteen

Janet Glover's house was a Victorian Gothic pile in the oldest residential suburb of the city. Her drawing room was large, with furniture old-fashioned but not antique. She herself was a large, expensively dowdy woman in her late fifties. Her face was plain and round, but it was made likeable by a pleasant expression and twinkling eyes. Martineau reflected that she and little dapper Luke had been as physically unlike as brother and sister could be.

"Sit down and have a smoke if you want," she said hospitably. "There'll be some coffee in a minute."

Martineau thanked her, hoping that this mood would survive the interview. He chose an armchair, so that he could rest his open notebook on the arm. Devery took a smaller chair beside the door.

"I don't know what you want from me," Miss Glover went on. "I told your detective what little there was to tell."

"I'm in need of some family background," the chief inspector said. "Also, there are certain aspects of your brother's will which make me curious. Professionally curious, I mean."

At once the lady began to look worried, but she said, "I can't say I blame you. That certainly was a funny will."

"Can you give me any explanation for it?"

"I can't except that he seems to have been mad at Diana about something."

"Was he often mad at her?"

"No. She usually took care not to irritate him. This must have been something special."

"Can't you think what it could be?"

"No, and I'm biased. I don't like her, but I've kept on terms with her for Luke's sake. I suspect she doesn't like me, either, and I suppose *she's* been nice to *me* because of Luke. But I must admit that as far as I know, since she married him she hasn't put a foot wrong. If she's done anything she shouldn't do, she's been very discreet about it."

"How does she get on with her stepson?"

"All right. There doesn't seem to be any ill-feeling on either side. Of course, I don't know how she feels since the new will was read. I've kept out of her way, and she hasn't approached me."

"You were present when the will was read?"

"Yes. Her face was like a stone. Good self-control. Come to think of it, we all had poker faces. Flabbergasted, and trying to hide it. I got out as quick as I could, and so did Billy."

"It seems like a good will for him. How does he get on with Diana?"

"Oh, very well. He's been out at the house much more often than Sam. He's taken care to keep well in with his uncle, partly by showing friendliness to Diana. I can't say I blame him, since he's only a nephew and not a son."

"Was Luke fond of him?"

"I think so. He's a good boy."

"Luke seems to have been extraordinarily fond of his long-lost brother Matthew, to leave him an equal heir to Sam. I want to hear the story of Matthew. I thought you would be the best person to tell me."

Janet Glover looked doubtful. She asked, "What do the police do when they unearth a family skeleton?"

Martineau shrugged. "Unless the skeleton has some connection with a crime, the police decently bury it again and keep quiet about it."

"I don't see how this particular skeleton can have anything to do with Luke's death. That can't be a family matter at all."

"There's just a possibility that some member of the family is involved," the chief inspector replied. "Luke was not robbed. The only motive I've discovered, so far, has a connection with the family."

The woman stared at him. Then she looked down at her large, useful-looking hands. After sitting in thought for a while she said, "Well, thank goodness I haven't said anything wrong about anybody. It just shows, you can't be too careful."

"Everything you tell me is in confidence."

"But surely you must put something in your report?"

"Only that I have interviewed you. You'll be asked to make a statement, if anything you tell me requires to go into the file. If your statement contains some evidence, it will be you, not I, who repeats it elsewhere."

"I see. Well, it's obvious that you intend to get the story from somebody, so perhaps it's better for you to get it from me. At least I can give you the truth of it. Oh, dear, it was a sad, sad affair. Men are so headstrong."

"There was a quarrel?"

"You could call it that," the woman answered with a wry smile. "Money. My two brothers and I came from a thrifty working-class family. Money was important to us."

"It's important to anybody. It's important to Sam, and Billy, and Diana."

"Maybe, but I don't think they'll quarrel in the way my brothers did. Luke treated Matthew shamefully, but he did it

111

partly in anger. At least, I think anger enabled him to justify his actions to himself. I suppose the new will was a very late attempt to make amends."

"Is that in character for him?"

"It must be, though I wouldn't have thought so. He was the type who would hate a man more after doing him an injury."

"H'm. What happened?"

"Matthew was of an inventive turn, even when he was quite a boy. He was always making things, and sometimes they worked. But he never followed things up. After he'd made something, he'd lose interest in it and start thinking about something else. Well, we grew up. I worked at the public library, Luke was an accountant and Matt was a draughtsman. Each of us came into five hundred pounds from our grandfather as we reached twenty-one. I put mine in the bank, Luke put his in stocks and shares, and Matt spent most of his, then used the remainder to get married. He drank, you know. Fairly heavily. He quarreled with my father about that."

"So Luke would be the good boy of the family?"

"Yes. Steady and thrifty, but not afraid to risk his money when he thought he was on a good thing. He got married too. The only daughter—only child—of a provision merchant in a good way of business. Matt married a girl who hadn't a penny."

"Typical, you'd say?"

"Quite typical. But Matt started getting serious about his inventions, and at last he made something really worthwhile. It was an electric washing machine, very efficient and yet simple enough to be made cheaply. It was built around two patents. Luke saw to the patents, and he also made sure that Matt's employers wouldn't have any claim on them. I suppose he could smell money.

"Anyway, Matt made the washers in his spare time and sold them to the neighbors, and talked about getting his firm interested in them. But Luke said, 'Why not go into business ourselves? We can raise enough money to get started.' And eventually that is what happened. We formed a company. Matt had no money at all, I put in five hundred and Luke put in a thousand. Father wouldn't invest money in anything of Matt's, and Luke didn't want his own father-in-law in the business at all. So we managed on fifteen hundred pounds. It was enough. Everything went well, and we prospered. Matt had forty percent of the shares, Luke had forty and I had twenty. Matt worked full time at the plant, with four men for a start, while Luke and I did the office work in our spare time."

"And that was the beginning of Glover Domestic Machinery," Martineau said lightly. But he was attending to every word, sitting bolt upright in an attitude which he had assumed at the first mention of Matthew Glover's boyhood. Devery also was still, listening intently.

"Yes," Miss Glover replied gravely. "In a year we had sixty men and girls, and a regular office staff, with Luke in charge. He was a first-class businessman, you know."

"And you?"

"Father was mad with himself for not having put in any money. He said it was all a flash in the pan, and he wouldn't allow me to give up my job at the library. It wasn't worth a family quarrel. I stayed away from the plant, and left the boys to get on with it."

"And something went wrong?"

"Matthew bought himself a car, and I never saw it when it wasn't in pieces. He became exclusively interested in cars. He was always talking about improving suspension, and doing away with valves, and things like that. His work suffered, but Luke was patient. He said he'd get over it."

"And did he?"

"Quite the opposite. He made the Glover Carburetor."

"Ah," breathed Martineau.

"You may well say 'Ah.' Now you can see the way things

were going. Matt wanted to turn half the plant over to the manufacture of his patent carburetor. Luke showed a blind spot there, but you can't really blame him. He wanted all available cash, assets, labor and space to go into the development of the washer business. It was booming, you know. But Matt was so determined to make the carburetor that he said he'd go into business on his own. He wanted to sell his G.D.M. shares, so Father, Luke and I bought him out, to keep the shares in the family.

"Matt found a place of his own, and started making carburetors. He was no businessman, but he was a good engineer. And he was an excellent salesman without knowing anything at all about salesmanship. People liked him. He found a smart young man to look after production, and he went out and sold carburetors. After a little while they sold themselves. Because he wanted to play with other ideas he made his manager into a partner, and then he started to do very well indeed. That was when Luke began to realize the commercial value of a good carburetor. So of course he wanted it, and he took it."

"Phew! Just like that?"

"Well, not quite. Legally, the thing belonged to G.D.M. Matt had designed it and patented it while he was a salaried servant of G.D.M. Luke had seen to it that there was a clause in the original contract to cover other inventions and developments. So G.D.M. owned Matt's carburetor, and Matt no longer had any shares in G.D.M."

"Couldn't there have been a compromise?"

"Yes. Royalties perhaps. Or some sort of a merger. Luke went to see Matt with something like that in mind. Matt was so amazed and disgusted that he lost his temper and took hold of Luke and threw him out into the street. Luke was wild. He told the firm's lawyers to get on with the job. They did. There was no court action. I think an action would have cost Matt more money than he had. I was sickened about it all, as you may suppose. But Luke and Father outvoted me. There was nothing I could do but keep quiet and hope to make amends in other ways.

"The loss of the carburetor ruined Matt in more ways than one. He didn't stop having inventive ideas, but they didn't seem to be very good ones. Not all his ideas were money makers. He had no capital reserve, so he had to warn his men that he would soon be reducing staff. He started drinking really heavily. He'd go on the rant, as they used to call it, doing nothing but drink for days on end and getting absolutely sodden with liquor. His men left him just as fast as they could get jobs elsewhere. One day he sold most of his machines for cash and walked out with the money in his pocket. He just vanished. At first it was thought he'd gone on a rant, but he might have gone to Australia or anywhere. We looked for him. We told the police and we employed private detectives. They didn't find a trace of him. We came to the conclusion that he'd gone overseas somewhere."

"What about his wife and child?"

"Oh, they were looked after. But Alice was very bitter. She hated Father and Luke so much it preyed on her mind. I think she died of it. Poor thing."

"And Billy?"

"Luke could afford to give Billy the best, and he did. Sam was away at a public school, Billy was sent to the same school. At home, he lived at Luke's house, because I didn't have a home of my own at that time. He was treated equally with Sam. When he left school, he was given the choice of entering the firm or going to a university. He chose the firm. Sam entered the firm too, of course. He wasn't given a choice."

Martineau wondered if the treatment of the two young men had been the same since they joined G.D.M. Sam's story of the tiff about the trip to London indicated that this was not so.

Sam was the son, Billy was merely the nephew. And Billy was aware of the difference. He had taken pains to keep "well in" with his uncle.

The policeman looked at Janet Glover's large, plain, distressed face and tried to imagine it bloated with liquor and slack with irresponsibility. He had been trying to do that for some time. Janet was the image of Uncle. Uncle was an inventor of sorts, and a man who did not know his own name. It was just possible that there had been yet another member of the Glover family at Grimwood last Tuesday. If it were so, it was indeed a coincidence.

"Does anybody have a photograph of Matthew?" came the rather wistful question.

"Not to my knowledge" was Janet's reply. "I can never remember him having his picture taken."

Chapter Fourteen

"So now do we go after Uncle?" Devery asked as he took the wheel of the C.I.D. car.

"You bet. Straight to Holly Lodge. You got it, of course?"

"Sure. Uncle invents. He's a drunk. He's the spit'n' image of Auntie Janet."

"Yes. And he was at the scene of the crime at the right time. But let's not get ahead of ourselves. For a start, we'll pull him in and see if Janet identifies him as Matthew Glover."

"There's one thing. If he can't remember his own name—"

"Hearsay, though it *could* be true. The only thing we can be fairly certain about is that he was drunk. I sent Cassidy to verify that. The landlord of the Grimwood Inn said Uncle had a right lot of beer Tuesday lunchtime. At least eight pints, and maybe more. He was drunk, all right. He's been drunk ever since. It could be that he doesn't intend to be in a condition to answer questions. But we'll fix that. We'll leave him in a cell till he dries out; then we'll see what he has to say for himself."

Devery cut across the city, avoiding its busy center. He entered Wales Road and drove toward Holly Lodge. As he turned left into Holly Road he remarked, "Looks like an accident further on. A crowd of people with a bobby's helmet sticking up in the middle."

"I saw it," Martineau replied. "Glad it's none of our business.

Of all the wearisome jobs for a policeman, I think a serious motor accident is the worst."

Devery remembered that Martineau hated paper work. "First aid, ambulance, witnesses, particulars, measurements, plans, statements, reports," he intoned. "Give me a nice simple murder anytime."

He waited to turn the car into the shady lane which ran along the side wall of Holly Lodge. He left the car at the entrance to the lane, and he and Martineau walked along to the wooden gate. They entered the grounds of the lodge, and saw that the back door of the house was open. They walked into the kitchen, and into a redolence of frying bacon. Mrs. Blades was at the stove.

"Good morning," said Martineau. "Where's Jonty?"

"He slipped out for some cigs, when he found I'd none to give him. He'll be back by the time his breakfast is ready."

"Wasn't a prisoner's breakfast good enough for him?"

" 'Not good enough, and not enough,' he said."

"Ah. Where's Uncle?"

"Out."

"Where?"

Mrs. Blades became bitter. "The pubs are open. You didn't expect to find him at home, did you? I'm gettin' proper fed up of Uncle, I am. He can flit someplace else."

"Which pub is he using now?" the chief inspector wanted to know.

The woman gave the information contemptuously, without turning her head. "The nearest, an' that's the Throstle Nest."

The Throstle Nest Inn was in Wales Road. It was as homely as its name, and a place of refreshment for homely people. "Let's go," Martineau said.

As their car turned from Holly Road into Wales Road, the two detectives saw that there was still a crowd at the scene of the accident, but it had been shepherded into some sort of order, and most of the road was clear. Now the tops of three policemen's helmets could be seen, and a police Area Patrol car stood at the curb nearby.

"They've soon got the cars away," Devery commented.

"If there were any to move," Martineau replied, and suddenly he looked anxious. "Stop just beyond the A.P. car and we'll see what it is."

Though they were in plain clothes, their physique and air of authority made them obviously policemen, and the crowd made way for them. In the clear space in the middle of the crowd they saw a sergeant in uniform kneeling and supporting the head and shoulders of a twelve-year-old boy. The boy was pale and undoubtedly in pain. There were tears in his eyes but they had not yet overflowed. He was a stranger to Martineau.

The sergeant looked up. "I'm just telling this brave lad we'll have him as good as new in a month or two," he said cheerfully. Then he added as an aside, "Simple fracture of the femur, I think. The wing caught him and threw him against the wall."

Martineau nodded, and looked at another figure which lay on the ground. It was covered entirely by a policeman's cape. He took a stride, stooped to raise a corner of the cape and looked down into the dead blue eyes of Uncle.

Anger was his chief emotion. He had been robbed of a prisoner. He was sure of it. He stood upright and demanded abruptly, "Where's the car?"

"It didn't stop," the sergeant replied. "According to the witnesses, it mounted the pavement and knocked this boy out of the way, then mowed the man down and kept going. It was accelerating all the way."

Martineau stood in thought. Apparently this was another murder case. Who had so badly wanted to be rid of Uncle? *Why* had this person wanted to be rid of him? Had Uncle been killed because he had killed Luke, or had he been killed because he was known to be Matthew Glover? Who could have known that? And how long had it been known?

The string of mute questions was cut short by the voice of the uniformed sergeant. "Davidson," he was saying to a constable. "Get on the phone again and find out if the ambulance driver has been given a wrong direction. He's had time to go to Hellifield and back."

Martineau asked the man, "What have you done so far?"

"When I got here, Davidson had sent for the ambulance, and he was getting witnesses. I got a rough description of the car from the boy here, and when the A.P. car arrived I put it on the air right away. It'll be damaged. Somebody might pick it up."

"What sort of a car was it?"

"The boy says it was a dark green sedan about as big as a Ford Consul. That should be good enough to get it picked up, if the damage is plain to see."

"Did you ask about the driver?"

"The boy didn't see him at all, sir. You might try some of the witnesses."

Martineau nodded, and spoke to Devery, "Stay here, and see if there's more to be got. About the car and the driver. And get the names of all the witnesses there are, whether they seem to know a lot or a little. I'm going back to see Jonty."

Jonty had eaten his bacon and eggs. He belched contentedly as Martineau walked into the kitchen of Holly Lodge, and then he took a swig from a pint mug of strong tea.

"Ah," he said, and as he became aware of the policeman, "Hello. I thought yer'd gone after Uncle."

"I did. I found him, too."

"Havin' a pint?"

"Not on this earth. He's just been murdered."

Martineau could have said that Uncle had been killed by a

car but he chose to announce the death as brutally as he could. He watched the effect of the news. Slowly, as it took effect, he saw Jonty turn pale: far paler than his wife, who gave a little scream and stood with her mouth open as she waited for details. He guessed then that it was not merely bereavement which had shocked Jonty. That person was staring more in fright than dismay.

As Martineau waited for a revealing exclamation, the sound of hobnailed boots could be heard on the boards of the kitchen passage. The sound of boots came nearer, and the boy Gaylord appeared. He saw the detective and halted in the doorway. He looked ill and childishly apprehensive.

Martineau was missing nothing. He saw Jonty look at his wife and put out a hand to her, speechlessly imploring silence. But she was looking at Gaylord. "Poor Uncle's been murdered," she cried, and burst into tears.

The boy looked sick. He leaned against the door jamb, then fainted. His knees buckled and he collapsed in a heap.

"Damn and blast!" shouted Jonty in deepest chagrin. In the circumstances it was a rather strange outburst, and one which Martineau would not fail to remember.

Her tears forgotten, the mother ran to Gaylord. Martineau went to her assistance. Jonty remained in his chair, staring glumly at his empty plate.

The policeman gently pushed Mrs. Blades aside. He raised the boy and held him from behind with an arm around his waist, allowing his head and body to droop forward. When they did not droop enough, he pushed the head down. "He'll be all right," he said. "Is he subject to fainting fits?"

"No, he's not," the woman replied. "He's a healthy lad, but all this bother has upset him. He's hardly ate aught this last two days."

Martineau nodded. He raised Gaylord's head. The face was still deathly pale, but the eyelids fluttered. He picked the lad up and carried him to the settee, and laid him flat, with his feet resting on the arm.

The eyes opened and saw Martineau. They closed again. "All right, Gaylord," the detective said. "Just stay there awhile and don't be afraid. Nobody's going to hurt you."

There were no smelling salts on the premises, but Jonty stirred himself and found a few drops of whisky in the bottom of a bottle. The mother raised the boy's head and fed him the whisky with a teaspoon. Soon he was able to sit up.

"Good," said Martineau. And to Mrs. Blades, "Don't let him move for a while. I'll get a car and we'll let a doctor look at him, just to be on the safe side. Come along, Jonty."

"I'll stay here with the lad," Jonty replied.

"You'll come with me," the detective answered firmly. "You're not getting at that boy any more till I've had a word with him. And I'm not letting you out of my sight till I've had a word with *you*. Come on!"

Chapter Fifteen

At Headquarters, a call from Devery demanded Martineau's attention. He put Gaylord in Cassidy's care, and left Jonty in the front office under the station sergeant's eye.

"Now," he said on the phone to Devery, "what's this about the car?"

"One of the witnesses is certain it was a three-liter Rover. Another witness says he was going to take the number, but there was a duster or a wash leather hung over the rear number plate."

"Billy Glover's car is a gray Rover, isn't it?"

"Yes. That's why I rang in. I've already put it on the air, for both Billy and the car. Though it might not be his, of course."

"What is the rest of it?"

"The accident, if you can call it that, was within a minute or two of midday, one way or the other. The victims were walking along Wales Road, away from the corner of Holly Road, and the car came up behind them. Uncle was about five yards in front of the boy, William Bates, and he was walking nearer to the curb than the boy. The car mounted the curb at the corner, at high speed. It struck the boy a glancing blow and hit Uncle full in the back. Uncle was sent flying. He hit that high wall there, and bounced off. The car went on, driven dangerously at an increasing speed. At no time, before or after the accident, did the driver use his horn. There was no sound of brakes or tires. There were no tire marks to show that brakes were used."

The crisp narration of facts went on, with Martineau listening in silence. There were four eyewitnesses to the incident. All four were in agreement about the color of the car and its approximate size, but not one of them had seen the driver's face clearly. Apparently he had been hunched over the wheel with an oversize hat pulled down over his forehead.

"Have you made any attempt to get in touch with Billy?" Martineau finally asked.

"I phoned both G.D.M. and G. Carb. He isn't at either place. He went out about eleven, without saying where he was going. He isn't at his club, either."

"Right. Try all the places you can think of. I want him found as soon as possible. It seems crazy for a man to use his own car on a stunt like that, but he may have thought he could get away with it by covering the number plate."

"I'll do my best to find him. What are you doing, sir?"

"I'm just going to chat with Gaylord. I think he's ready to talk."

With that, Martineau put down the receiver and sent for Gaylord. Cassidy brought him in. The big Irishman was good with children, and compared with some of the sixteen-year-old boys with whom the police had to deal, Gaylord Blades seemed to be still a child.

Resting a friendly hand on the boy's shoulder Cassidy said, "This young lad has had a bad time, sir. He's ready to tell you all about it, and I've told him you won't be mad at him."

"Have you ever seen me get mad at anybody, Officer?" Martineau asked. Then he said, "Sit down there, Gaylord, and tell me what's troubling you. All I want to do is to help you."

Gaylord took the seat across the desk from Martineau. Cassidy sat where the boy could see him and be reassured. The girl clerk in the corner was still and quiet. A girl had been brought in specially, also for Gaylord's reassurance.

"You're not *compelled* to tell me anything, you know," Martineau said kindly, "But I think it will be a lot better for you and all of us if you do. The young lady will write it all down, so that we get it right. It might be needed for evidence, you see."

The young lady smiled at Gaylord. He wanly returned the smile, and immediately seemed to be more at ease.

Cassidy said, "Start with you in the cemetery, when you saw Uncle pass the gate."

So, occasionally encouraged but never led, Gaylord told the story which Sam Glover had heard from Jonty. When he had heard it, Martineau sat in thought. Even in the light of his knowledge of the old quarrel between two brothers, the tale seemed to be barely credible. But the murder of Luke was itself incredible, and it was a fact. And what else but the sight of someone long sought would have caused him to leave his car so hurriedly and enter that little lane? If he had been visiting that shabby and unfamiliar place for some other reason—say, for instance, to see Ellie and buy her off—he would probably have locked his car and he would at least have removed the ignition key. And if he had not uttered Matthew's name, how else could Gaylord have known it? If Gaylord *had* previously known Matthew's name, how could he have guessed that an elderly stranger *with a Rolls-Royce car* should have known it. Luke must have called Matthew's name. Undoubtedly he had seen and recognized his brother.

One thing was certain. If Gaylord stuck to his story, and if no evidence was found to upset it, then the story would have to be accepted. If the man known as Uncle had not killed Luke Glover, then Gaylord had, and Gaylord as a murderer was even less credible than Uncle. Uncle was now unable to refute any statement which Gaylord might make, but the probability was that the boy had spoken the truth, and had felt able to do so because the news of the second murder had relieved him of the obligation to be silent. His friend Uncle was now safe from the police.

There was one more question to be asked: "Gaylord. Did you tell your father the name which the stranger called Uncle?"

"Yer mean 'Matthew'? Yers, I told him."

"All right. That will be all for now. Not so bad, was it?"

"No. Can I go home now?"

"I'm afraid not. You did wrong when you took the ax back to the shed. But don't worry about it too much. Mr. Cassidy will take you for something to eat. Then he'll find you some books to read."

"I can't read," the boy said miserably.

The girl in the corner answered him. "Never mind," she said, smiling again. "I know where there are some nice jigsaw puzzles."

Sitting alone, Martineau reflected on coincidence. Up to the present he had been able to prove to his own satisfaction that none of the happenings in the case had been fortuitous. Every participant had had a reason for being where he had been, and a motive for doing what he had done. But now he was faced by the facts of an occurrence which did indeed seem to have been brought about by sheer chance. For years two brothers had moved, each in his orbit, within a few miles of each other. At last they had met, when one of them was carrying an ax, in a place so secluded that murder was possible. One of them had been anxious to make amends and be forgiven, the other had forgotten his own name. But, if Gaylord's story was true, at the moment of encounter there must have been recognition by the one with the faulty memory. It might have been only partial and only temporary. But it had aroused feelings of the strongest kind. Matthew Glover's eyes had "fair blazed." Such an expression suggested anger rather than fear. But the two emotions were related. Matthew had at least recognized the man who accosted him as a dangerous enemy. The sense of danger had roused him to instant action. Obviously he had not had a strong hold on sanity, and in any case he had been drunk. In fear and loathing he had struck with the weapon in his hand, as a man with a fear of reptiles might strike at a harmless grass snake.

After the killing, had the incident been forgotten through a relapse of memory or through drunkenness? Or had it been recalled, causing the need to drown the memory with more drink? Perhaps the truth of that would never be known. Either alternative was possible. Martineau had handled a number of drunks in his time, and he could remember some quite stirring fights put up by men who had no recollection of them on the following day. Matthew had thrown the ax away; then he had made the place tidy by dropping the body over the wall. Had that been a conscious attempt to delay the finding of the body, or had it merely been done to remove a hateful object from everybody's sight? Let the psychiatrists sort it out. As far as evidence went, when Matthew had looked around and failed to see the ax anywhere, he had been unable to remember what he had done with it, and then he had forgotten the whole affair. His demeanor during the subsequent inquiry had been that of a man with nothing on his conscience.

Matthew had dropped out of his family's sight twenty years ago, and he had met Jonty. Then he had gone away somewhere for twelve or thirteen years, and on his return he had met Jonty again. Then for seven years he had lived with Jonty in and around Granchester without being recognized by anyone who had known him in the past.

At first sight that did not seem feasible. Why had Matthew met Jonty so soon after his return to the city? Perhaps it was because he had become used to living the same sort of life as Jonty. He had been living in a common lodging house when they met. Doss house vagrants were akin to Jonty. They lived in the same shiftless way, talked the same language, frequented the same taverns in the same districts. So the two had met and renewed acquaintance. All right. Accepted as reasonable.

If the Matthew-Jonty contact was reasonable, so was the lack of contact with others from the past. Matthew's relations and former friends were seldom seen against the background which had become normal to him. They did not enter rough taverns in rough districts. But what about the ordinary workers who had known Matthew when he was an employer? Dozens or hundreds of them! Had none of them seen him? It was possible, quite possible. Respectable workers of the skilled and semiskilled sort did not mix with the dregs, either. They lived away out on council estates, or bought through the building societies better houses than they had known in other days. They were not likely to have met Matthew.

After all, there were a million people in the city, and three or four million in the industrial area closely surrounding it. It was no marvel when old friends lost sight of each other.

Martineau began to recall old acquaintances of his own, whom he believed to be still living in or near Granchester. Bill Bromwich. What had happened to him? It must be ten years. Jack Parlance. Why, he was still on the force, out at Brackenhill. Martineau hadn't seen him for ages. Bert Rush. Bert was around somewhere, living in Highfield. Somebody must have seen him lately.

The chief inspector went to the door and looked out at the long main office of the C.I.D. He counted half a dozen men there: detectives who got around the city and kept their eyes open. He raised his voice: "Has anybody seen Bert Rush lately?"

The men stopped their various tasks and looked at him, but none answered.

"Do you all know him?"

There was a chorus. "Sure. Yes, sir."

"Have any of you seen him in the last five years?"

Two or three men shook their heads, otherwise there was no answer. Martineau returned to his own office. He remembered that Fred North was the duty inspector. Fred and Bert had been close friends. He spoke on the internal-line telephone, and was connected with the inspector.

"Fred," he said. "Have you seen anything of Bert Rush lately?"

"Well, no, I haven't. Bert and me have right lost touch. It must be four or five years."

"He's still living in Highfield, isn't he?"

"Yes, I think he is. But since he got wed again he's sort of changed his ways, or she's changed 'em for him. I never see him at all. And I haven't heard anybody mention seeing him either."

"Thanks, Fred," said Martineau.

So there it was. A change in circumstances, a change in habits, a change in habitat, could make a man drop out of sight. And he did not need to have lost his memory. Martineau was prepared to believe that Matthew Glover could have lived unrecognized in Granchester for seven years, until the attraction of a girl drew first his nephew and then his brother out of their orbits and into his. That was the coincidence, the one which had to be accepted.

But Luke had uttered the name Matthew in the hearing of Gaylord, and Gaylord had repeated it to Jonty. Half a day before anyone else had known it, Jonty had known that Luke had been murdered. And, very likely, he had read the murdered man's full name on the tab of his ignition key. He had had the morning and afternoon of Wednesday to make his inquiries, before the evening papers had put Luke's name in headlines. Where would a man with a background like Jonty's go to find out something about a man with a background like Luke Glover's?

Martineau tried to put himself in Jonty's place, to imagine what the man would do that Wednesday morning. Whether he would be honestly concerned about Uncle, or whether he would seek to profit from the situation, was a matter of conjecture. In any case he would want to know the identity of the man he now knew to be called Matthew. He would assume that Matthew had been quite close to Luke at one time, as a member of the family or as an associate. He would try the family angle first, because he would know where to go.

Having come to that conclusion, Martineau picked up the telephone, and soon he was in conversation with the local registrar.

"Matthew Glover or Luke Glover?" the man said. "Wednesday morning? Hold the line."

Martineau waited, jotting down a list of inquiries which would soon be overdue. He knew quite well that he did not delegate enough of his work. He had a number of good men, but he was best satisfied with a job when he had done it himself. "Big head," he muttered.

The registrar came on the line again. "One of my clerks, Miss Travis," he announced, and then there was the musical voice of a girl.

"Mr. Martineau? I did have a man asking about the Glover family. He said he'd met a man who claimed to be one of the G.D.M. Glovers, and he had his doubts. He said it was important for him to be sure, because there was money involved. I suggested he should ask Luke Glover himself, but he said he was afraid of queering the deal. These were his actual words. Anyway, I found out for him that Luke Glover had a brother called Matthew. He seemed satisfied with that. He paid the fee and off he went."

"Did he look like a businessman?"

The girl laughed. "There are all sorts of businessmen. He could have been a scrap iron merchant, or a rag-bone man. At that time I didn't know about Luke Glover being missing, or I'd have taken more notice of him."

"What name did he give?"

"Brown. Abel Brown."

"Would you describe him?"

The girl obliged with a rough description of a man who could have been Jonty.

"Would you know him again?" Martineau asked.

"Oh, yes. I'd know him anywhere."

"Thank you, Miss Travis."

Martineau smiled grimly as he put down the telephone. Jonty had assured himself of the existence of a Matthew Glover at the first attempt, and in doing so he had left a trail like a fifty-ton tank. "He should have stuck to Larceny Simple," the policeman thought.

He reflected that if Jonty had been solely interested in keeping Uncle out of trouble, he would have remained very quiet indeed about the man's real identity. But he had been seeking to establish that identity, to his own satisfaction at least. And it did seem that he could have had only one object in doing that. He had been trying to work himself into a position where he could get some money from somebody, either by selling information or withholding it.

Chapter Sixteen

Billy Glover and his car were seen by a policeman on the beat while the car was stopped at some traffic lights. The P.C. climbed into the car and instructed the surprised driver to take him to Police Headquarters. Billy appeared to be bewildered and annoyed. He questioned the constable's authority at some length, but he received only one answer "They want you at H.Q.," the P.C. said.

"What *is* all this?" Billy demanded, when the P.C. brought him to Martineau.

"Please sit down. You'll know in a minute," the chief inspector replied. He addressed the constable. "Where did you find this man?"

"At the junction of Bridge Street and Foresters Road, sir. He was stopped at the lights."

"What time was this?"

"Twelve fifty-five, sir."

"Did he make any statement while you were with him?"

"No, sir. He wanted to know what it was all about. I just told him he was wanted."

"Very good. What about the car?"

"Damaged front, toward the near side, sir. Headlight smashed, hood buckled and wing bulged and dented."

"Right. You've done well. Go and make out your report."

The P.C. departed. Billy said, "Has there been a hit-and-run or something? If there has, it wasn't my car."

"Why wasn't it?"

"Because it was parked outside my Uncle Luke's house from a quarter past eleven till ten minutes to one."

"By the front door?"

"No. Outside in the road."

"Why in the road?"

"Well, I dropped in to see Diana—my aunt. I've been in the habit of leaving the car outside when I've called to see her during working hours. It's the maid, Styles. She's nosy."

"In the past, you've been afraid she might tell your uncle?"

"Not exactly afraid. But the less Styles sees, the less she can talk about."

"As far as the police are concerned, up to now she's done a very successful job of *not* talking. But why did you have to conceal your visits from your uncle?"

"He might have thought I was dodging the column at work."

"He wouldn't have thought so today. He's dead."

"Yes. I left it outside out of habit."

"You didn't leave it outside out of habit Wednesday afternoon when you called. You drove up to the door."

"That was an official visit. Uncle Luke was missing, and I was calling to express my sympathy and offer my help, and so forth. I hadn't been able to get there sooner."

Martineau felt the need for a little break while he took stock of his impressions. He brought out cigarettes and offered them. While he was giving Billy a light he again took note of his good looks. When not under stress, as he was now to some extent, he would be debonair and charming. He was taller and more handsome than his cousin Sam, who was himself handsome enough. His clean-cut nose and jaw were quite unlike the pudgy features of his father and his Aunt Janet. Nor was he anything like his Uncle Luke. Apparently he had taken his looks from his mother's family.

"Isn't it time you told me what all this is about?" Billy asked.

"It's about your car. When the policeman stopped you, did you already know it was damaged?"

"I certainly did. I saw the damage right away when I came out to it, and I was damned annoyed. Some idiot must have bumped me and cleared off without saying anything."

"The damage is on the near side."

"I was parked facing the wrong way. The man who hit me was driving on his own side of the road."

"The headlight is smashed. Was there any broken glass about?"

"I never noticed. There will be, probably."

"An officer will go out there with you, and he'll look. But I think we shall already have found that broken glass in Wales Road."

"Wales Road? Something has happened in Wales Road?"

"Yes. Does that alarm you?"

"No, but it's on odd coincidence. What *is* this all about?"

"Just one more question, and I'll tell you. Is there a hat in your car?"

"Yes. Or at least there should be. It's in the back somewhere. On the floor, maybe. I haven't worn it for ages."

"What size is it?"

"Seven and a half."

"Rather a large size."

"I have a deceptively big head. What has the hat got to do with anything?"

"At about twelve noon today a gray Rover car killed a man in Wales Road and went on without stopping. The rear number plate was covered by a cloth of some sort. The driver had a hat pulled down over his forehead. You have a gray Rover car, and it's damaged in the right places."

"But I've told you where I was at twelve o'clock."

"The man who was killed is believed to have been your father, Matthew Glover."

Billy stared. "My father," he whispered. "Oh, hell, what a mess."

"The mention of your father doesn't seem to surprise you as much as I expected. When did you last see him?"

"Less than twenty-four hours ago. I saw him coming out of a pub in Wales Road yesterday afternoon about two o'clock. At least it was supposed to have been my father. I was going to let Aunt Janet have a look at him when—when it was convenient."

" 'When he was sober,' you were going to say?"

"Yes. He was in a state."

"Well, I'm afraid he's sober enough now."

Billy was silent for a little while; then he said, "The poor old boy. Just when there might have been a chance for him."

"Yes, it's a pity."

"I'll be honest with you, I don't feel heartbroken. Up to yesterday I hadn't seen my father since I was a kid. And yesterday he didn't look terribly attractive."

"Was it Jonty Blades who showed him to you?"

"Yes, that was the name. Sam phoned me Wednesday night, saying he had Blades there with a tale that he'd found my father. He said it was more my affair than his, and would I go over? I went, and met this little man. I took him home in my car and arranged for him to show me my father the day after. I wasn't entirely convinced by him, but the least I could do was have a look."

"I suppose he told you all about this man he called Uncle."

"Yes. How they'd met, and so on."

"Did he mention Uncle in connection with Luke Glover?"

"No. You mean about the old quarrel? I don't suppose he knows anything about that."

"Did he mention Luke *at all?*"

"No. Not at all."

Martineau nodded. He said, "Excuse me a moment," and went and looked out into the main C.I.D. office. Devery had come in. Martineau beckoned and went forward to meet the sergeant. He told him about the alibi which Billy claimed. "Go and check with Diana, will you?" he said.

"At once," Devery replied, and Martineau returned to Billy.

That young man, left alone for a moment, had been considering his predicament. His first words were, "You'd better talk to Diana. She'll tell you I was with her."

"That is being attended to. It would be better for you if someone else had seen you, too. Didn't you see Styles at all?"

"No. And I don't think she saw me. I don't think anybody saw me."

"Didn't you have coffee?"

"No. We had a couple of drinks. Diana got them herself. The stuff was there in the lounge."

"Mmmm. I'm afraid we're going to prove it was your car killed your father."

"Well, you can't prove I was driving it. If it was my car somebody must have taken it away and brought it back."

"We shall have to impound it, you know. You'll have to get along without that particular car for a week or two."

"I'm not going to drive about in a car which is supposed to have killed my father. I'll get a new one."

"Ah, I forgot. You're going to be a rich man."

"I suppose you've seen Uncle Luke's will."

"The will won't be much good to you if you're convicted of killing your father."

"I've already told you I didn't do it," Billy said. And then quite suddenly he looked extremely anxious. "I hope Diana doesn't take the attitude that the police have no right to pry into her affairs. Suppose she denies I've been there?"

"Then you or she will be lying. And your alibi will be up the creek."

"You'll ask around? Somebody might have seen my car there at the right time."

Martineau's voice was cold. "All possible inquiries will be made," he said. "But nobody can have seen your car out at Broadhulme when it was in Wales Road. And if somebody did take your car away from there and bring it back, it could have been you."

Billy was silent. Martineau considered him, reflecting on the thin possibility that somebody had indeed borrowed Billy's car to commit a homicide. He knew what Chief Superintendent Clay would make of that. Devious murderers had no place in Clay's long memory and wide experience. He believed in going after the obvious suspect, and ninety-nine times in a hundred he would be right. He would scoff at Billy's story, and try his level best to break an alibi which he believed to be false.

Clay would have no difficulty in satisfying himself about motive. Here, he would say, you have a young man who, on the death of his uncle, suddenly finds himself on the brink of unexpected prosperity. All he has to do is establish the death of a father who has been missing for twenty years. Then, even more unexpectedly, he finds that his father is very much alive. Moreover, this father is a drunken old scamp. This presumably unpredictable person, for whom he has little or no filial feeling, stands between him and a fortune. Also, this person has grown attached to another family during recent years. He might make a will in favor of them, leaving a pittance to his son. Is that son going to sit biting his nails while a fortune is snatched away from him? Of course not. He decides that his inconvenient father will have to die suddenly, or be killed in an accident.

Then, Clay would say, you have a young woman married to a rich old man who *does* die suddenly. Naturally she also sees a vision of wealth. But when the will is read she finds that she isn't rich at all. However, she is involved in some sort of a love affair with the aformentioned young man, whom she now believes to be rich. So it is natural for her to hope that the affair will continue, and perhaps become permanent. Therefore, she is quite ready to provide the young man with an alibi after he has rashly gone out and killed his father. When she has saved his neck he will be grateful. He'll have to be grateful. She'll have him in the hollow of her hand.

Why, Clay would say, the young woman might even be something more than an accessory after the fact of murder. The young man might have told her about his drunken father, and she might have urged him to go out and save his fortune so that she can save his skin. The hasty deed did seem to have some of the impulsiveness which is so often associated with women. Yes of course, and so on and so forth.

It was Martineau's clear duty to test the alibi in every possible way, and it was good policy for him to anticipate Clay's questions and comments. Here duty and policy went hand in hand. He began to probe. "This thing about you and Diana doesn't sound too good," he said. "It looks as if you've been fooling around with your uncle's wife. I can't see any reason for this secrecy about your visits."

"There's been nothing wrong," Billy protested.

"Of course you've got to say that. If it's proved you've been lovers, it'll weaken that alibi."

Billy sighed. "It doesn't seem to be any use talking to you."

Martineau wondered if the knowledge that his father's murder had been futile would help to break down this suspect. He decided to see what effect it did have. He said, "I don't see what chance you have of inheriting under your uncle's will anyway."

Billy became very alert indeed. "Why?" he demanded.

"I presume you know that a person cannot benefit under the will of a person he has murdered?"

"Yes. But you've got to prove I murdered my father before I can be cut out of his estate."

"That's one thing we might prove. But even if we don't, your father might have no estate."

"What do you mean? You've read Uncle Luke's will."

"There is evidence indicating that it was your father who killed Luke. If that evidence stands up, then he disinherited himself, and consequently you as well."

Billy was staring. "What's this you're saying?"

"You heard me, and I think you understood. It looks as if you killed your father for nothing."

Billy did not react to that remark. His gaze was fixed as he digested the news. There was no doubt that he had received a great shock.

Martineau waited, and at last Billy spoke. "How strong is this evidence against my father?" he asked.

"It's direct and definite, and we haven't found anything to upset it yet."

"You're trying to upset it?"

"I wouldn't say that. We always try to discover the whole truth, whether it upsets evidence or strengthens it."

"My father is no longer alive to deny it, is he? Could he have been a witness on his own behalf?"

"Of course. But I don't think his evidence would have carried much weight. There are independent witnesses who can prove that he'd had a great deal to drink at the time of the murder."

"All the same, there's a motive for somebody besides myself to have killed him, isn't there? So that he could be the what-you-call-it, the fall guy."

Increasingly aware of Billy's perspicacity, Martineau thought about other interested parties. If Gaylord's evidence was false, then he or Jonty had a motive for killing Matthew Glover. But

139

neither could have done it. Holly Lodge was too far away from Broadhulme for either of them to have replaced the murder car and returned to be discovered at home. Who else could have had a motive? Sam Glover? He would be questioned of course, and no doubt he would be able to give a satisfactory account of his movements. In any case, Martineau failed to see how Sam could have had a strong motive for murder. It *was* murder, with its consequence of a death sentence or a life sentence. Sam might have been annoyed by this drunken old fellow turning up at this time to menace the good management of Glover Carburetors—assuming that such a man would be allowed to be a menace—but any annoyance of that sort could hardly be called a motive for murder. As Sam was reported to have said, Billy's father was Billy's affair. It certainly looked as if Billy had attended to that affair, with determination if not with prudence.

With regard to that, Martineau reminded himself of Billy's obvious intelligence. Well, there was nothing out of character. Billy wouldn't be the first intelligent man to have been forced into committing a foolhardy deed by the oppressive feeling that quick action was essential. It did look as if Billy was guilty of the Wales Road murder, and was now using his brains to try and avoid the consequences.

Billy was also trying to avoid the consequences of his father's crime. "*Why* was he supposed to have killed Uncle Luke?" he wanted to know.

"That will come out at the inquest."

"You won't give me the details?"

"Sorry, no."

"I can't see it arising out of a quarrel. Uncle Luke wanted to make amends."

"After his death, at any rate. His will showed that."

"Was it premeditated, or could it have been manslaughter?"

"It doesn't seem to have been premeditated. That much I can tell you."

"What about the question of inheritance if it should turn out to be manslaughter and not murder?"

"I don't know. That's a legal thing outside my sphere. As yet I haven't had time to get a ruling on it."

"You said the evidence was direct. That means an eyewitness, doesn't it? Is this man Blades the eyewitness?"

"No, he is not. I don't think it's wise for me to give you the witness's name."

The telephone rang. The caller was Devery. He said, "Diana Glover is prepared to swear that Billy was with her at the Beeches continuously from about eleven fifteen to about twelve forty-five. She is quite definite about it. She says he arrived soon after she had got back from town, after her interview with you."

"And the staff?"

"None of them has seen Billy today. The maid Styles acts as if she could say a lot about Diana and Billy if she had a mind to. You know, disapproving like. I tried to get her going but she won't talk."

"All right," said Martineau. "Leave that. Have a look round outside the gate. See if there's any broken glass or other signs of an accident. I'm going to send Billy up there to you."

He put down the receiver and turned to Billy. "Your alibi is good, so far. One of my men will drive you out to Broadhulme, and you can point to the place where you claim to have parked your car."

"And what then? Am I under arrest, or anything?"

"No," said Martineau. "Not yet."

Chapter Seventeen

Martineau interviewed Jonty Blades later that afternoon. When he was informed that his son had given an eyewitness account of Luke Glover's murder, the little man shrugged and said that it no longer mattered, because the killer had himself been killed. He claimed that he had advised Gaylord to remain silent simply to protect Uncle, and for no other reason.

He was regretful when he was told that Gaylord was in trouble for removing the ax after the crime. His comment was typical. He said, "He shouldn't a-told yer that. But it's only what yer can expect from a lad."

"Did you tell anybody else besides Sam and Billy Glover that Uncle was Matthew Glover?" Martineau asked.

"No, not a soul."

"You received money, didn't you?"

"Just a quid or two. I didn't ask for it. I weren't tryin' ter blackmail nobody."

"You thought you were on a good thing, all the same. Did you tell anybody at all that Uncle had killed Luke Glover?"

"I did not. Do yer think I wanted ter get Uncle sent up fer life?"

Martineau nodded. Jonty's sworn word was not worth a last year's calendar, but he did seem to have been genuinely fond of Uncle, and it was unlikely that he had passed on Gaylord's story to anyone else. Certainly it was not likely that he had given the story to Billy, the son of the killer, or Sam, the son of the victim.

Jonty went into the cells on a charge of Misprision of Felony through his influence on his son. Martineau guessed that the Stipendiary Magistrate would raise his eyebrows at this unusual charge, but he had no doubt that it would be good enough to hold Jonty.

Sam Glover was interviewed that evening, and he stated that at twelve noon that day he had been sitting in a car with Ellie Blades, in a street not far from Holly Road, beside a church. The car, he said, had not been his Ferrari, but his 3.8 Jaguar. He mentioned certain matters which had been discussed. He had not noticed any passers-by. It was a quiet street, he said.

Martineau frowned when he heard Sam's alibi. He had expected something more solid. But when Ellie was seen she corroborated the story without hesitation, and she was able to remember some of the conversation. Martineau had to be satisfied with that.

Saturday and Sunday were filled in with routine activities, with many fruitless but necessary questions addressed to people who might have known something but did not. After a quiet weekend, there was a flare of activity on Monday morning.

The two teams of Robieson and Brabant, and Evans and Murray, took turns in keeping surreptitious observations on Gordon Barnes throughout the weekend. Barnes seemed to spend his time going to and from his favorite pub, the Northland Hotel, but in gait and appearance he was at all times sober. If he met any persons on business or pleasure, honest or otherwise, he met them in the hotel. If he made any telephone calls, he made them from the hotel, or from his lodging house. He did not use a public call box.

But at eleven o'clock in the forenoon of Monday, a cool but sunny day, Barnes seemed to be in some anxiety about using a public call box. And his behavior was so peculiar that Brabant, who was watching him, was also worried about what he ought to do with the man. The place was the concourse of the big and busy North Central Railway Station, and the public telephones were in a line of half a dozen, in an alcove set at right angles to the side wall of the concourse. For twenty minutes Barnes had watched the alcove, from a distance but from a position which enabled him to look right along the row of booths.

Before he did move toward the telephones, Barnes turned and methodically scrutinized the concourse and the people in sight. Brabant was watching from one of the main entrances, and he barely had time to step out of sight. When he ventured to look again, Barnes was approaching the alcove. The detective slipped across a section of open concourse and reached the spot which Barnes had vacated, at the further end of the bookstall. He put down a few pennies and picked up a newspaper, and opened it. Over the top of the paper he watched Barnes. It was an old trick, but he had been taught that old tricks were usually effective, except in dealing with professional crooks of great experience.

Barnes was at the telephones, but a small, stout man had bustled into the alcove just ahead of him. Evidently the first five booths were occupied, because the little man walked along and entered the last one. Barnes also went to the end of the line, and waited beside the last booth, and he also appeared to be watching its occupant intently.

It was then that Brabant became bothered by the feeling that he would soon have to make a difficult decision. The feeling grew when one and then another of the first five booths became vacant, while Barnes remained watching the man in the sixth. It became obvious to him that someone had left an important article or document in booth No. 6, for Barnes to collect. Barnes had been watching the booth as a general safety pre-

144

caution, but now, when he had decided to enter it, he had been thwarted by the little man whom he was now watching. Perhaps he was in fear that the man might accidentally find that which he intended to collect himself. Perhaps he suspected the man of trying to intercept the transference of the coveted object, whatever it was. He was watching the man's every move. "Oh hell," Brabant muttered. "What shall I do?"

He was alone. That morning his teammate Robieson had reported for duty at the last minute, having had no breakfast. Later, when Barnes had been followed to a shop in Derbyshire Road, Robieson had slipped into a nearby snack bar for coffee and a sandwich. But Barnes had stayed in the shop only a few seconds. He had got into his car and driven off. Brabant had had no alternative but to follow at once, leaving Robieson behind. He had assumed that his mate would be able to rejoin him later with no superior officer being any the wiser. He was driving one of the oldest of the C.I.D. cars, with no radio. He had been able to make one telephone contact with Div. 1, giving his position. Since then he had moved across the city. Now, when it looked as if he would need Robieson, he was completely out of touch with him.

The stout man emerged from No. 6 booth, and departed without a glance at Barnes. Barnes entered the booth. In a very short time he was out again, moving away. Brabant was in an agony of indecision. He had no time to telephone for instructions, because that would mean losing Barnes among people and traffic. In ordinary circumstances the man was not to be approached, but the circumstances were not ordinary. It was obvious that he had picked up something which might be evidence of complicity or guilty knowledge. This might be the only chance to catch him with the evidence in his pocket. If not intercepted immediately, he might be able to hand it over to someone else, unobserved.

Barnes was making for a main exit. He appeared to be nervous and alert, constantly looking around as he walked. As soon as he was out of sight, Brabant sprinted to another exit. Outside the station, Barnes was walking toward his car. As he walked round the front of it, to the driver's door, Brabant came round the back. The two men came face to face. As Barnes reached for the door handle, Brabant seized his arm. "Just a minute," he said. "You're under arrest."

By police standards Brabant was a small man, while Barnes was a big man by any standards. But the detective had been trained in unarmed combat, and he was confident. He overlooked the fact that there were many young and youngish men in the country who had been taught that sort of fighting in the armed forces. Barnes was not the cheerful fellow of his police photographs. He was tense and grim, and he reacted at lightning speed. He flung off the detaining hand and grabbed Brabant's lapels. He used his knee and his head at the same time. The detective was taken by surprise. He blocked the crippling knee, but he was butted in the face. Though dazed and shaken, he kept his face out of further trouble and sought an arm lock. The lock was broken before pressure could be applied, and he was sent reeling against the car. Then his prisoner was running, dodging and swerving across the busy station approach at top speed.

Brabant gave chase, in a fury because he might have done the wrong thing and then muffed it after all. It was the busiest time of the morning, in a busy part of town. He was shouting, "Stop that man!" and according to normal English behavior it was only a matter of time before some adventurous citizen would obey the appeal. No doubt the fugitive realized that. He made a skidding turn into the first alley he saw. He ran along the alley, took a turning at the end and found himself in a cul-de-sac blocked by a seven-foot wall. He ran straight at the wall, leaped, caught the top and pulled himself up and over. Brabant did the same thing four seconds later.

Then there was a chase through back yards, over walls, along alleys, across streets into other alleys, along a loading bay and through a warehouse packing room and out by another bay, until the younger man's superior agility and stamina had its effect, and he brought his man down in a quiet street of shabby offices.

In a rage, barely restraining himself from cuffing his exhausted prisoner, Brabant hauled the man back toward the railway station. As they walked along a main street, Station Road, he saw a police patrol car moving along in the traffic. He hailed it, and asked to be taken to Headquarters with his prisoner. There was no conversation on the way. From the beginning, Barnes had not uttered a word.

While Barnes waited under guard in the main C.I.D. office, Brabant told his story to Martineau. The chief inspector showed no sign of approval or disapproval. "Have you searched him?" he asked.

"No, sir, but I've made sure he hasn't slipped anything out of his pocket while I've had him in custody."

"All right. Bring him in here."

When Barnes was ushered into his office, Martineau grinned at him. "You're soon back," he said. "All right, where is it?"

"Where's what?"

"You know what. You picked it up at North Central Station."

Now that the time for action was past, Barnes was more like his old self. "Gorblimey," he said, in tolerant disgust. "What is all this? All I did was make a phone call."

"Why did you assault the officer?"

"He tackled me first. I thought he was bogus. He doesn't look big enough for a bobby."

"Mmmm. Empty your pockets. On the desk here."

Barnes complied, a little too willingly perhaps. Then he was searched. When that had been done, there was nothing on the desk which any man might not have been carrying. There certainly was nothing which could be called evidence.

Martineau's good humor vanished. His sarcasm was biting when he spoke to Brabant, "You've done well, haven't you? You'll have to scrub the assault charge and let this man go. All right, Barnes. Pick up your stuff and beat it."

Barnes moved to the desk with alacrity. He made two handfuls of his personal property and dropped them into the pockets of his coat. He went. White-faced, Brabant remained. He was wondering if Martineau would kick him out of the C.I.D., or give him another chance and the roughest dressing-down of all time.

Martineau did neither: there was no time. He went and looked into the main office and called, "Cassidy. Ducklin. Hearn."

The three men came. Martineau said, "Ducklin and Hearn, go after Gordon Barnes and stay on his tail. It doesn't matter if he spots you, just so as you see every move he makes. Sit next to him at a bar if you like. After two hours, not less than that, let him give you the slip, and come back here. Understand?"

The order was understood. Ducklin and Hearn hurried away.

Then Martineau said to Brabant, "Take Cassidy with you and go over Barnes's line of flight again. Climb over the walls again, and go through all the back yards. Look in every dustbin and every other likely place. When you've found what you're looking for, stay and watch it from some spot where you can't be seen. Cassidy will give me your position."

Three quarters of an hour later Cassidy spoke to Martineau on the telephone. "We found a fat envelope," he said. "There's Cellotape stuck to it, as if it's been attached to something. It looks like money to me. We found it among the rubbish in a dustbin without a lid. I'm guessing Barnes will be back for it."

"Where is it, exactly?"

"In the yard behind Merida Modistes. There's all sorts in

there. Wooden legs with silk stockings on. Shop-soiled falsies. Pin-up girls in their undies. The lot."

"Where is Brabant?"

"There's a fire escape. He's up on the first landing. He has a good view and good cover. He can drop straight down into the yard."

"Go back and stay with him. I'll arrange for your relief, if it becomes necessary."

"It won't be necessary, sir. Barnes will be back as soon as he gets rid of Ducklin and Hearn."

"See that you get him right," said Martineau. "He'll have to have the stuff in his possession."

Chapter Eighteen

At four o'clock in the afternoon Cassidy and Brabant brought in Gordon Barnes, having caught him with the fat envelope in his possession, and having seen him take the envelope from a dustbin.

Barnes was more angry than crestfallen. He was inclined to bluster. "You can't touch me," he said. "I found that envelope in a dustbin. I was going to hand it over to the police."

While he spoke, Martineau was opening the envelope. It was packed with five-pound notes. He put the notes and the envelope down on his desk, and looked at the man standing before him.

"Let me tell you the legal position," he said coolly. "You didn't *find* this money. The contents of dustbins are the property of the City Corporation. You *stole* this money from the Corporation."

"That's rubbish."

"Correct. And all rubbish is the property of the Corporation. It has a value. It gets sorted. Empty salmon tins and such like are pressed and sold for scrap. Rags are valuable. Paper is valuable. You must not steal from the Corporation."

"The stuff in dustbins is what people have thrown away. It doesn't belong to anybody."

"I've just told you who it belongs to. Now let's talk a bit of sense. If you claim that you were collecting your own property which had been inadvertently put in a bin, the Corporation might allow your claim. You have some backing. The police know you put it there."

"The police never saw me."

"No, but they know you passed that way earlier in the day, and they have a reasonable suspicion that you had this money at the time. Later, you did not have the money. Later still, you returned and went straight to the bin and picked out the money. It could be yours."

"All right, it's mine. So I didn't steal it."

"Ah ah. Steady. If you want support for your claim, you must furnish some evidence that you are truly the owner of the money: where you got it, who you got it from and so forth."

"I'll tell you nothing."

"In that case we can't help you, because there is a possibility that you're not the legal owner. We'll just have to hold you on the charge of larceny from the Corporation."

"You'll never get a conviction."

"You don't know that. And anyway it's a nice little charge to hold you with, while further inquiries are made. How much is there, five hundred? Five hundred pounds stolen from the Corporation! The Stipendiary will give us a remand in custody without batting an eye. And, furthermore, you'll never satisfy the Corporation that the money is rightfully yours if you won't tell where you got it. If our inquiries in that direction turn out to be a waste of time, I shall recommend that the whole five hundred be donated to the Dustmen's Widows and Orphans Benevolent Fund."

"It's a bloody swindle!"

"You're referring now to your reason for being in possession of the money?"

"The Corporation just can't take people's money like that."

"You're not thinking clearly. Until the contrary is proved, this is the Corporation's money. It is you who are seeking to take it from them. In order to do so, you'll have to prove that it's yours by saying where you got it."

"I'm saying nothing."

"Very well. You'll appear in court charged with stealing it. The circumstances will have to be given in police evidence. It'll be in the paper. It'll make interesting reading for somebody I know."

"Who's that?"

"I don't need to mention his name, but only you and I know to whom I'm referring. I heard a whisper a little while ago. Let us say I heard it on my transistor set."

Barnes turned pale. He looked around for a chair, and sat down. "Oh, hell," he said. "He'll think . . ."

"Yes, he'll think. Five hundred pounds is five percent of ten thousand. Your cut for fingering the job."

"He'll have me killed."

"He need never know. I'm busy with a murder job, but I'll always take time out to get my hands on that man. If you can put me on the trail of those transistors, I can backtrack until I eventually get him for receiving stolen property. He'll think I got my information, not from you, but from the people found in possession of the property."

"Look, Inspector, you've got it wrong. All I know about the transistor job is that I took a hiding from a bunch of thugs who tried to make me admit I was in it. I honestly don't know a thing about it. But I know what those fellows will think if they hear about this money. They'll think the same as you. Ooh-h-h! They'll murder me."

"If you're telling the truth, you certainly are in trouble. *If* you're telling the truth."

"I am. Believe me, I had nothing to do with those transistors. That money is something different altogether."

"Where did you get it?"

"I—I'm not prepared to say."

"You have no alternative, unless you want your head beaten in. They'll probably blind you before they kill you. And we'll never find your body."

"Oh, God, don't lay it on," the prisoner begged. He put his hands to his eyes. "Give me time to think."

"Very well," said Martineau, quite without sympathy. He lit a cigarette and waited.

"I don't know what to do." Barnes sighed, and again there was silence.

"I want you to know this," said Martineau eventually. "I can't hold you without charging you. Once you're charged, you'll have to appear in court, and the sum of five hundred pounds will be mentioned. You'll have to make up your mind in the next few hours. Either you give me the transistor job on a plate, or you appear in court charged with stealing five hundred pounds, or you give me some other acceptable story about the money."

"If I tell you the truth, that I borrowed the money, you won't accept it."

"I might. *Where* did you borrow it?"

Barnes shook his head, and again there was silence until Martineau said, "It occurs to me that we might have caught you in possession of blackmail money. It would be better to go down for blackmail than to have a gang of tearaways after your blood."

"You have no evidence of blackmail."

"That's true. We only have evidence of larceny."

Suddenly Barnes raised his head. It could be seen that a new thought was in his mind. And it seemed to make a new man of him.

"All right, go ahead with your damned silly larceny charge," he said. "I'm saying nothing."

That afternoon Devery and Cassidy drove to Anvil Yard for a second talk with Ben Chase. The engineer sighed when he saw them. He stopped his lathe and came over to them. "All right," he said. "What is it you want to know? I'm busy."

"I understand you had Jonty Blades to see you last Wednesday," Devery said. "Is that right?"

"Yes. He was trying to pump me about the Glover family, I don't know why. I didn't tell him anything."

"You think you didn't. How do you come to know the Glover family?"

"I'll tell you. I worked for Matthew Glover, making carburetors. Eventually I became his partner. We were doing well. Then Luke claimed the patent and ruined the business as far as we were concerned."

"So you didn't like Luke?"

"That's one way of saying it."

"You've known for some time, then, that the man called Uncle was Matthew Glover."

"Yes. Six or seven years. He saw my sign out in the street and came to see me. He said he didn't know me, but my name rang a bell. He seemed surprised at my rather effusive greeting, but as it happened I hadn't mentioned his name. I thought I'd hold back a bit, to see how things were. I said I'd mistaken him for somebody else for a minute or two. When I found out he didn't know his own name, I was glad I hadn't mentioned it."

"Why?"

" 'Poor and content is rich, and rich enough.' If he was happy as he was, I didn't want to put him into the tender care of Luke Glover. He would simply have started to exploit him again."

"I thought Luke wanted to make amends."

Chase's answer was to spit on the ground.

"And did you find that Matthew was happy?"

"As happy as a man could be. He didn't seem to have a care in the world. He lived rather raffishly; drank a lot, you know, but on his sober days he was immersed in making his little contraptions. He used to bring them to me to make for him. Jonty exploited him, but he also looked after him like a brother. I didn't interfere with Jonty."

"So you left it at that, and never told anybody?"

"That's true. I was tempted to tell Janet Glover, because she was a good soul. But I knew she'd tell Luke, so I kept quiet. I wouldn't have told Luke Glover the time if I'd had fifty gold watches."

"What about the wife, Matthew's wife?'

"She was dead."

"The son, then?"

"He had a good position at G.D.M. Luke was looking after him. He seemed happy enough, what little I saw of him. There was no point in telling him anything."

"What about the reward for information about Matthew? Wasn't the reward still standing?"

Chase spat again. "Luke offered the reward."

"Suppose one of Matthew's little inventions had turned out to be something good, would you have told him his name then?"

"I'd thought of that. I was going to cross that bridge when I came to it. I would have seen that everything was done right and proper. Any invention which was worth patenting would have been patented in his name, not mine. If you think I'd have robbed Matt Glover of a single penny piece you're grievously mistaken. Matt was good to me. We'd have made a fortune out of carburetors if we'd been left alone."

"How do you feel, now he's dead?"

"I hope the murderer rots in hell after he's been hanged."

"Strong feelings, Mr. Chase."

"Yes. It's no crime to have strong feelings, I hope."

"Have you any idea who might have done it?"

"None at all. I can't see a motive. He was just a poor fellow, living his own life and doing no harm to anybody."

After a few more brief questions, the two policemen departed. Devery commented as they drove away, "He seems to be pretty genuine. Now that he sees no point in being reticent about Uncle, he's told us everything he knew."

"Apparently, Sarge, apparently," Cassidy replied.

Chapter Nineteen

At ten thirty the following morning, Gordon Barnes appeared
before the Stipendiary Magistrate of the Granchester Central
District, charged with larceny. Barnes, without legal representa-
tion, reserved his defense and elected to go for trial at the Quarter
Sessions. In the same breath he asked to be allowed bail. Depositions were taken. When the magistrate became aware of the
amount of money involved he frowned. When he heard that
the money had been taken from a dustbin, the frown cleared
and he began to look interested. When he heard that Barnes
had claimed the money as his own he almost smiled. When he
heard that Barnes had refused to reveal the source of the money
he nodded grimly. He found that there was a case to answer,
and depositions were taken. Then the question of bail came up
again.

"Normally one would not regard theft from a dustbin as a
serious offense," the magistrate observed. "It is the amount of
money involved which makes it worthy of some thought. The
whole of the money is in police hands, I presume?"

The police solicitor agreed that the police were holding the
money.

"What are the prisoner's circumstances? Does he have roots
in the town?"

"He has a position as a salesman, and he lives in lodgings. So far as is known, he has no relatives in the town."

"H'm." The magistrate turned to Barnes. "What is to prevent you from running away if you are released?"

"Well, sir," Barnes replied boldly, "You said yourself that the money was more important than the offense. That money is mine. While the police have it, I won't run away from it."

"Mmmm. What about the police?"

Martineau had been whispering to the police solicitor. The solicitor said, "The police do not oppose bail, Your Worship."

Then the magistrate actually did smile. "With the money in custody, I think we can let the prisoner go."

Martineau slipped out of court while the terms of bail were being considered. He hurried round to the office of the inspector in charge of women police. When he entered the office the lady greeted him with a stare of mock hostility. She was an old friend. He grinned at her. "The time has come," he said.

"For what?"

"For the stalwart men in blue to seek the assistance of their gentler colleagues."

"Colleagues? Huh, we've been promoted. What sort of a hole do you want us to get you out of this time?"

"I need at least four smart girls in plain clothes—"

"You'll be lucky!"

"Silence. I need the girls. For two full day shifts. They'd better have a car. This is surreptitious observation. They've got to cling to the tail of a man who is expecting to be followed. My fellows wouldn't have a chance."

"Well, one team will do to be going on with, won't they?"

"Yes, and another to relieve them."

"Will they be expected to make contact?"

"Definitely not. They'll observe and report."

"Your men will take the night shift?"

"That's right, Sunshine."

"All right. You don't know how it's done. There'll be three

girls in each team. Two together and one to run the errands. Two and sometimes three girls together are seldom taken for policewomen. That is if they're noticed at all, which I hope they won't be."

"They might be. This fellow has an eye for the girls, I think."

"Who is he?"

"His name is Gordon Barnes, and he's just coming out on bail. He'll be collecting his personal property at the front office any minute now. You'll have to get your skates on."

The lady inspector reached for the telephone. "All right," she said. "Off you go, and hold the man back if you can. I'll be round there in a few minutes to take a look at him. When you see me, you'll know we're set."

With Barnes out on bail and under observation, the work of the murder investigation went on. Old and new witnesses were questioned. Jonty and Gaylord Blades were interviewed again, without changing their stories at all. Ben Chase was questioned by Martineau himself, without giving any additional information.

The transcriptions of the telephoned reports on Barnes, for the first few hours, were interesting without being exciting. His first act on being released was to make a telephone call from a public kiosk. Then he went to his lodgings and apparently packed his belongings. At any rate, he carried two battered suitcases and an assortment of coats out to his old Austin and drove away. He drove to the raffish neighborhood of Mossbank, with three policewomen in a car discreetly following. In Mossbank he made an inquiry of some men loafing on a street corner; then he drove around, apparently looking for fresh lodgings. He carried his cases into the first house he called at, and the policewomen noted the address. On emerging from his new home Barnes drove his car to the nearby town of Boyton, some eight miles from the center of Granchester. In Boyton he went to a second-hand car dealer whose show place was an open yard.

159

The dealer's manner was contemptuous when he examined the car, but Barnes went with him to his wooden office, and apparently a deal was made. Barnes departed from there on foot. The inference was clear. He was breaking his normal contacts and covering his tracks before Dixie Costello or any of his men had a chance to open the local evening newspaper.

When the preliminary shifting had been done, Barnes spent half an hour in a public house—not the Lacy Arms and nowhere near it—then he had lunch at a quiet but reasonably good restaurant. While he lingered over the meal, his observers took turns in having tea and cake in a snack bar.

After the meal, Barnes seemed to have time to spare. He spent the best part of an hour in a news theatre, then he strolled up and down Lacy Street, looking in shop windows. His manner was uninterested except when he looked in the windows of tailors and the better sort of men's outfitters. As the hands of the big clock in Somerset Square moved toward four, he went into a big Woolworth store, which was packed with people at that time of day. He made his way, a slow and devious progress, up and down the same aisle a number of times. Along that aisle were sold, among other things, electric bulbs and small electrical fittings, hand tools, gardening requisites and plants. It was the one aisle along which a number of masculine heads could be seen among the throng of women. During his time in Woolworth's, the observers had no means of knowing whether or not he spoke to anyone, or received a letter or small parcel. In all his actions Barnes was alert, constantly looking around him and behind. The young women who followed him had to be very circumspect to avoid notice. Their reports were unanimous in stating the opinion that they had not been noticed.

Martineau perused the transcriptions while he waited for other reports which he expected to receive an hour or two after the evening papers appeared on the streets. Dixie Costello would not waste much time, he was sure. In anticipation of some move by Costello, he had taken the precaution of temporarily staking out the Palmer Radio store, the Lacy Arms, the Northland Hotel and Barnes's recently vacated lodgings.

The report arrived. At ten minutes past five a man called Ned Higgs, with two more men, called at Palmer Radio. At half past five he called at Barnes's old lodgings. From there he went to the Lacy Arms, where he stayed for only a few minutes. That was enough for Martineau, and he called off his watchers. Ned Higgs was Dixie Costello's lieutenant, and it was to be presumed that he was now looking for Barnes in pubs, clubs and other likely places in the center of town. Dixie Costello was seeking Gordon Barnes. Quite literally he was seeking him with a vengeance.

Only minutes after these reports came the news that Barnes had purchased two bottles at a liquor shop. With these he had retired to his new lodgings in Mossbank. It was reasonable to assume that he was safe for the night.

Martineau studied the Woolworth report a second time. Barnes had not been seen to speak to anyone, so it was reasonable to assume that something had been passed to him. Another fat envelope? It was possible, since he had lost the first one. *If* he had received another parcel of money, then his game certainly was blackmail. The men who had stolen Costello's transistors would not give him a second share of the proceeds simply because he had lost the first one. It was reasonable to assume that he would not dream of asking. Probably he had been telling the truth when he denied any involvement in the transistor job.

Blackmail, normally, meant the extortion of money. The only people whom Martineau could see as victims of extortion were the four remaining members of the Glover family, Billy, Diana, Janet and Sam. And for one of them to be victimized did not mean that he or she must have committed a crime. Janet, for instance, could be paying blackmail to protect another member of the family. Janet was already wealthy. Sam *might* already be affluent, and he would certainly be wealthy after his father's will had been settled. Billy would not be entirely without money, and he had a chance of being as wealthy as Sam eventually. Diana would be more or less penniless until she received her paltry five thousand under the will.

At that stage of the investigation, Martineau doubted if he could get a court order to examine the bank account of any Glover. But he could bluff. He rang for Devery. "Bring the car round," he said.

The time was six o'clock, and for most people the day's work was over. It would probably be over for Sam and Billy Glover. They might be at the Granchester Club. Martineau and Devery went there. Sam's Ferrari was in the car park, with the top up because the sky was gray with a promise of rain. Billy could also have been in the club. The two detectives did not know what sort of car he was using.

They walked up the steps of the club. It may not have been the best club in the city, but it certainly had the wealthiest members and the most imposing premises. The uniformed porter looked them over carefully. He saluted, though he looked doubtful.

"Police," said Martineau. "I'd like to see Mr. William Glover."

"I haven't seen him go in," the porter said. His glance moved over the gathering of cars in the club forecourt. "I'm afraid he's not here yet."

"In that case I'll speak to Mr. Sam Glover."

"Yes, sir. Just one moment, sir."

The porter entered the club and spoke to the hall porter. He returned. "There is no one in the reading room. If you'll wait in there."

He showed the two men into a side room which contained two writing tables, a number of comfortable chairs and a big round table which was almost covered with periodicals. He closed the door as he went out, so that these intruders would not offend the gaze of passing members. When he had gone, Devery opened the door so that he could see who passed. He had earned his reputation as a smart policeman by never missing anything if he could help it.

Sam appeared ten minutes later. "Sorry," he said. "I was just finishing a game of snooker. The black wouldn't go down."

"Did you win?" Martineau asked.

Sam shook his head. "I lost on the black. I'm only a moderate player. Not in the same class as Billy."

"Billy is good?"

"Billy is good at everything. Didn't you know?"

Martineau looked at the open, guileless face and wondered if he were hearing sarcasm or slightly salacious humor.

"He's a scratch golfer, too," Sam said, and then, "What did you want to see me about?"

Martineau looked at the fingernails of his left hand, then he said, "As you may know, Mr. Glover, the police occasionally have to seek the power to examine private accounts. We in our force do this most reluctantly. We prefer to ask a straight question first. Have you recently drawn two large sums of money from your personal bank account?"

He looked up at the end of the question, and met Sam's gaze. He held it until Sam turned away, to walk to a chair and sit down. The young man's face was troubled as he sat in thought. Eventually he asked, "Am I absolutely compelled to tell you?"

"No. You're not compelled to say anything. But I assure you that if you don't I shall take the usual steps to find out. Also, by refusing to speak you may draw a certain amount of suspicion on yourself. That isn't a threat. Supicion would follow such a refusal as naturally as day follows night."

"Suspicion of what?"

"Let us just say 'suspicion,' and leave it at that."

Again Sam became lost in thought. Then he said, "I don't

163

like this. May I have a word on the phone with somebody before I answer?"

"I can't prevent you, but I'd rather you didn't."

Sam shook his head and sighed. "You're on about those five hundreds, I suppose," he said. "I drew them out to lend to Billy. He's in some sort of a hole he doesn't want to tell me about yet."

"Did you get any sort of written receipt?"

"No. I never thought of it. Billy and I don't bother with receipts in transactions between ourselves."

"Didn't he give any hint of his reason for needing the money?"

"No. I asked him, and he said he'd tell me sometime. If he'd been a betting man I wouldn't even have asked him."

"He isn't a betting man?"

"No. He'll probably tell you all about it and clear it up. The only thing I'm worried about is the breach of confidence. He'll think I did the dirty on him."

"In the circumstances you had no alternative. Where would he be at this moment?"

"I couldn't tell you. He's usually here at this time, but he seems to have changed his habits recently. He may have stayed on at the works for some reason, or he may have gone home. He does most of the firm's entertaining, you know, though I don't think he has anybody today."

"Ah well, it doesn't seem to be urgent," said Martineau, though in his opinion it was. He rose. "Thank you, Mr. Glover. We'll be getting along."

The parting was amiable, but without handshakes. Sam went back into the club, and Martineau went to ask for the use of the porter's telephone. He called G.D.M., and was told that Billy had departed a few minutes ago.

"He may be on his way here," he said to Devery. "We'll wait a little while."

They went to sit in the car. Billy arrived before Martineau

had had time to smoke a cigarette. He was walking away from a new cream-colored Rover coupé when the chief inspector hailed him.

"I've been waiting for you," he said. "I'd like you to come along to Headquarters with me."

Billy's frown of worry was natural enough. "All right. I'll come," he said. "What is it this time?"

"I want to ask you a few questions," Martineau replied. "And in case you want to talk on the way, I must caution you that anything you say will be taken down in writing and may be given in evidence."

Chapter Twenty

On the way to Headquarters it was some time before Billy spoke. Martineau's cautionary remark seemed to have shocked him, and apparently he was considering its implications. The chief inspector, who had learned to have some respect for the young man's mental ability, reflected that he was being given time to think. But it was unlikely that he would have any notion of the disclosure which his cousin had made. He would be taken by surprise.

But eventually he did speak. "What about that murder and manslaughter thing?" he asked. "Did you get an opinion?"

"Yes. Didn't you?"

"Yes. I was hoping yours might differ from mine."

"Whether it's a case of murder or manslaughter, the killer cannot benefit under the victim's will. The late notorious Dr. Crippen is the case in point, I believe. Nineteen hundred and eleven."

"More than half a century ago. Surely there's been something since then?"

"I'm told not. I suppose Anstruther will be doing his best to find something?"

"Yes, and I've got myself another lawyer, too. Anstruther was my uncle's man, and the firm's man, and maybe Sam's man."

After that there was silence, with Martineau thinking that it was always the same: a debatable will always brought distrust into a family.

In his own office Martineau wasted no time. He said, "I am informed that you recently borrowed two sums of five hundred pounds each, one today and one a few days ago. I need to know your purpose in borrowing the money."

Billy appeared to be astonished, but he answered without hesitation. "You're quite mistaken," he said. "I had no need to borrow any money. I didn't borrow any. I haven't borrowed any money in years, and never more than a fiver."

"Two sums of five hundred each," Martineau persisted.

"No. Your information is wrong. I have that much of my own if I need money. You can see the state of my account if you like. I'll give you written authority to examine my account and all my transactions."

"You borrowed this money. You could have had money in the bank and have been reluctant to withdraw any of it, for secrecy's sake."

"Secrecy? There's not much secrecy in borrowing, is there? It's a lot more secret to use your own money, whatever you want it for."

"Not when your account clearly shows that you've withdrawn it. In this case there's no written record. You did not give any receipt."

"You're damn right I didn't. I never borrowed it. What was I supposed to want it for?"

"You didn't give a reason. *I* think you needed it to pay blackmail."

"Who am I supposed to be paying?"

"We'll get around to that later."

"*Why* am I supposed to be paying?"

"Obviously, to stop someone from blathering about a certain matter."

"What certain matter?"

"Look here, I bring you here to answer questions, and I always end up answering 'em. *I'll* ask the questions in the order they should be asked. We'll take first things first. And the first thing is, did you borrow two sums of five hundred pounds?"

"No. Who says I did?"

"Your cousin, Sam Glover."

"Sam says that? He must be mad. Or else he's acting the goat."

"Well, he says it. And he isn't joking, as far as I can see."

"Am I supposed to have told him what I wanted it for?"

"No. He says you said you'd tell him later."

"I'll tell you something. Sam wouldn't lend a thousand quid to his own brother—if he had one—without knowing all about it. He'd want security, too. Sam can spend money, but he'll spend it on himself."

"Are you saying that he's abnormally selfish?"

Billy's gaze was level. "I'm not here to chatter about Sam," he said. "But if he says I borrowed a thousand or a hundred from him, he's a liar."

"Why would he say that, if it isn't true?"

"That's for you to figure out. How did he come to tell you this?"

"I put it to him that he'd been drawing a lot of money out of the bank."

"And he didn't want to tell you why, so he blamed it on me. He used to do that sort of thing at school. I thought he'd grown out of it."

"Obviously you're not going to admit he's telling the truth. Suppose we have him here and let him tell it in your presence?"

"I think that's a damned good idea," Billy retorted belligerently. "Then at least I'll know it isn't you trying to work some stunt."

"Go get him," said Martineau to Devery, and the sergeant went out.

"While we're waiting," Billy said, "suppose you tell me what's on your mind. You seem to think *somebody* is being blackmailed. Tell me why."

"Did you always ask a lot of questions when you were a child?" Martineau countered. "Here, have a cigarette, and we'll wait."

When Sam arrived with Devery, Billy looked so truculent that Martineau said, "You hold your peace. I'll ask the questions."

Sam's rather pale face was expressionless. He looked from one to the other of the seated men. "What now?" he asked.

"Do sit down," said Martineau, himself rising. Then he said, "Your cousin denies that he borrowed any money from anyone."

Looking at the chief inspector, Sam said, "Last Saturday morning I went to the bank and got him five hundred in used fivers. Yesterday afternoon I got him another five hundred, also in used fivers."

"You gave those sums of money to him?"

"I *lent* them to him."

Martineau glanced at Billy. That young man had got his temper under control. His eyes were certainly unfriendly, but his stronger emotions were hidden behind a frown of concentration.

"Did you ask what the money was for?" was the next question to Sam.

"Yes. He said he didn't want to tell me yet."

"Did it occur to you that Billy's need for money could have anything to do with the two recent sudden deaths of members of your family?"

"I won't answer that question. I told you what happened. If I had further thoughts, they are my own affair."

"All right. Were there any witnesses to the two transactions?"

"No."

"So it's your word against Billy's"

Sam shrugged. "I suppose it is. A thousand is a lot of money,

169

but I can stand it. If he defaults on the debt, he'll never get the chance of doing it again."

"A thousand is a lot of money, I agree. But the important thing is, which of you used it after it was withdrawn from the bank?"

"I don't know whether he used it or not. He certainly got it."

"Look, let me ask him a question or two," Billy interrupted.

"I refuse to be questioned by you, after this," Sam retorted.

"Very well. I'll put the questions up to the inspector, and he'll certainly ask you. He certainly will. This thing will go on for hours."

"Perhaps it will save time if you do answer," Martineau suggested mildly. He had no wish to aggravate trouble between cousins who were also business partners, but the trouble was there, and there might be less damage done if the rights and wrongs of it were ascertained immediately. It surely would be better for Martineau's investigation.

"Very well," Sam agreed reluctantly. He was slowly being stirred to anger. He glowered at Billy.

"You were awfully busy Saturday morning, weren't you?" Billy pursued. "You told me so when I went in to see you about that Mackray job. And we can prove it by your secretary if the inspector can get hold of her before you do."

"No need for that," Sam replied. "I was busy."

"And you were busy all day yesterday, weren't you?"

"Fairly busy."

"Then, if I went to you *twice*, not once, why didn't you simply give me a check each time, or at least *one* of the times, instead of trailing off to the bank yourself? That way, too, you'd have had a record of the transactions, to back up your word."

"Apparently that's what you wanted to avoid. You begged me to go myself and get you the money. I supposed you had your reasons. It was only afterward that I realized you were acting in a very funny way."

"What a lie! Never mind, we'll go on to something else. You can look innocent, but you know as well as I do what the inspector is getting at. That money was needed to pay somebody off. The person doing the paying was as guilty as hell about something. Guilty of murder, maybe. Somebody knows he did it, and is putting the squeeze on him. We know where you were when your father was killed. You were right there on the spot. Where were you when *my* father was killed?"

"Mr. Martineau knows where I was. Where were you?"

"The inspector knows where I was, too."

"Were you with Diana?"

"Mind your own business."

"I'm doing so. Inspector, if he says he was with my stepmother his alibi isn't worth a tinker's curse. I used to think he danced around her to keep in with my father. Now I know he's been carrying on with her for months. Since my father's death I've had the whole story from Styles, the housemaid."

Martineau said, "If you'll instruct Styles to tell her story, I'll send one of my officers to see her."

"I'll do that," Sam rejoined.

"You bloody rotter," Billy said.

"You're the rotter in this company. But you're not going to make a liar out of me and get away with it. I know very well Diana would put her name to anything to save your hide."

"If I'd known what was going on, I'd have made damn sure Styles *did* see me last Friday morning."

"Hah! Whatever you're up to, I'll bet Diana is in it with you."

"Blast you!" Billy sprang to his feet, red with fury. But Devery moved to hold him, and Martineau said, "Sit down. You're in the wrong place for brawling."

Billy sat down. Sam had risen to meet the threatened onslaught. The look on his face suggested that he would have welcomed it. He sat down slowly.

Martineau had not moved. Now, he addressed Billy as if nothing had happened. "You mentioned one of your cousin's visits to Grimwood. Did you know of those visits before the day of your uncle's disappearance?"

"I did not."

"But he did, Inspector," Sam interposed. "I told him. He used to rag me about it."

"*When* did you tell him?"

"Oh, ages ago. During the summer. One day when we happened to be going into the office together in the middle of the afternoon."

"You are a *bloody* liar," said Billy with contempt.

"Don't start that again," Martineau told him. "Do you happen to know a man called Gordon Barnes?"

"No, I don't. I believe Diana's name was Barnes before she married Uncle Luke."

"It was," the policeman admitted. He turned to Sam, "Do you know Barnes?"

"No. Is he Diana's ex-husband?"

"Yes. Are you both quite sure you've never communicated with him in any way? Any way at all."

Both the Glover cousins said that they were quite sure.

Martineau said, "Well, I think that's about it. And it's all very unsatisfactory. Has either of you anything to add to what has been said?"

Billy said, "No." Sam shook his head.

"Very well. I asked you that question with a special purpose. You don't seem to be very friendly at the moment, but you both have heavy business responsibilities and you'll have to continue working together. Since you've both said all you've got to say, there's no need for either of you to bring the matter up again and start quarreling. That is to say, if you can't be friends you can keep a sort of truce. Neither of you opens fire on the other with regard to the matter we have been discussing. If either of you finds he has something more to say, he can come and say it to me. Agreed?"

Billy said, "That's seems to be a sensible idea."

"It's the only way," said Sam.

"All right. The things you have said will be put into the form of statements, and later you will be asked to sign them. You may go, gentlemen."

Chapter Twenty-one

"Did you notice anything?" Martineau asked, when the Glover cousins and the silent, listening clerk had departed.

"I noticed that somebody was lying like hell," Devery replied. "I don't know which one it was. I wouldn't go on oath it was Billy, though the stuff we've got against him seems to be piling up."

Martineau had reached for the file of reports and statements on the Luke Glover case. "I'm thinking of that interview with Sam, after we'd found his father's body," he said, as he turned the typewritten sheets. "Ah, here it is. He states quite definitely that he'd told nobody about his meetings with Ellie at Grimwood. Now, he says he'd told Billy."

"And that means?"

"Either he was lying then because he didn't want to involve Billy, or he's lying now because he does want to involve him. He forgot what he'd said the first time. On that occasion, when he hadn't had time to think the thing over, it wouldn't seem to be important. I think I'd better see Diana and see if she can throw any light on the matter. And on other matters. While she's down here seeing me, you'd better go out there and see Styles."

Diana Glover walked into Martineau's office wearing a coat

of some rich black fur over a black dress. Pearls shone softly below her white throat. She was without a hat, and her hair was beautiful. As Martineau placed a chair for her he reflected once more that she was an extremely attractive woman. He also wondered, without being unduly concerned, whether the pearls would be her own property or part of her late husband's estate.

"I'm sorry to bother you at this time of day," he said politely. "Did you drive yourself down here?"

"Yes. I've been using the Rolls since you let me have it back. I might as well make the most of it. I expect I shall soon be running about in a minicar, if I can afford one."

That remark could have been interpreted as a whine, but it was uttered without bitterness. The policeman tried to look sympathetic. He said, "A girl like you won't be long without a husband, unless you don't want one."

"Nice of you to say so," she answered coolly. "But I'm sure you didn't bring me here to say nice things to me."

"I'm afraid that's true," he admitted. "I have one or two bones to pick with you. I'm still without a clue to the real reason for the post-mortem clause in your late husband's will."

"I've told you everything I know about it."

"Not quite everything, I think. You didn't tell me, for instance, that you and Billy Glover had been having something in the nature of a love affair."

"Somebody has been exaggerating. There's been nothing more than innocent fun."

"If that's all it was, your fun might have cost you plenty. Apparently Luke Glover didn't think it was at all funny."

"He could only have known what Styles told him. And she didn't tell the truth, I'm sure. She made something out of nothing and poisoned his mind. She hates me. I've realized that since Luke died."

"She had been in Luke's service a long time. Throughout most of his previous marriage, I believe. A certain resentment against

175

you is understandable. Anyway, it does look as if somebody told Luke a tale, and it could have been Styles. That explains why your legacy was cut, but it doesn't entirely explain the postmortem thing. That looks as if your husband thought you were so much in love with Billy or some other man, that you might try to make yourself into a widow."

"Really, that's ridiculous."

"He had some stomach trouble, and he thought he was being poisoned. That's how ridiculous he thought it was. He changed his will, but not at Billy's expense. I don't quite understand that. There might have been some other reason for him to think somebody wanted him out of the way. Were you having, er, innocent fun with another man besides Billy?"

"I certainly was not."

"I'll use an old-fashioned word. Did you have any flirtations or affairs with any other man before Billy?"

"No."

"Sam, for instance? He's a good-looking boy."

"No. Not Sam and not anybody."

"If you're telling the truth, it appears that Luke took a dim view of you and Billy, but he put the blame on you. At any rate his desire to do right by his brother Matthew, ultimately for Billy's benefit, was stronger than his resentment against Billy. If he had any such resentment. I'm still·inclined to think there's been another man in it somewhere."

"You can think what you like. It's over. Luke is dead, and you can't lay that at my door."

Martineau stared coolly at the girl's defiant face. "That depends how you look at it," he said easily, but with as much conviction as he could muster. "It was you who sent Luke to Grimwood last Tuesday afternoon."

The random shot hit the mark. Diana was dismayed. But she recovered quickly. "So Styles also listens at keyholes," she said scornfully. "She'll be out of a job soon. You ought to recruit her into the police force."

"It wasn't Styles who told me."

"Then who did?"

"The police don't normally divulge sources of information, so we won't go into that. What I'm really interested in is who told *you* about Sam's visits to Grimwood. Who did?"

"I'm like the police. I don't divulge sources of information."

Martineau grinned. "*Touché*. Was it Billy who told you?"

"No. And if you ask me who else it was I won't answer."

"Would you go on oath that it was not Billy?"

"Yes, I would."

"Would you go on oath that you haven't seen Gordon Barnes since he came to this town? And that there has been no contact apart from one brief telephone conversation."

Diana's gloves and handbag lay on the desk. She picked them up. She said, "I refuse to answer any more questions, and you can't make me. I've done nothing illegal."

"Not one of the seven deadly sins is illegal, Mrs. Glover."

She was on her feet. "When you start wearing your collar back-to-front you can tell me that again," she said. "I'm going."

Martineau also had risen to his feet, but she was at the door before he could walk round the desk.

"I know my way out," she said, and she departed, leaving the door open.

The chief inspector grinned ruefully as he listened to the brisk clicking of her heels on the hardwood tiles of the main office. The interview had not been entirely successful. He had learned something, but not everything. But it was a small achievement to have learned anything at all from such a woman. Nothing she said could be regarded as reliable. Nevertheless, she had left him strongly inclined to the belief that it was not Billy Glover who had told her about Sam Glover's little affair at Grimwood.

Chapter Twenty-two

Later that evening Martineau was studying the statements of Hannah Styles when he received a telephone call from the superintendent of the Granchester Remand Home.

"Something will have to be done about the Blades boy," the man complained. "He has bad dreams and wakes up screaming the place down. The doctor refuses to give him any more sedatives. He's decided sedatives aren't the right treatment. He says the lad has something on his mind and needs to tell somebody about it."

"He certainly has something on his mind. He witnessed a bloody murder."

"We know that. But this is something worrying him."

"Have you tried to get him to confide in you?"

"Yes. The doc has too. He won't say anything. He keeps asking for his father."

"Oh, he does? Not his mother?"

"No. Would you bring his father here? It might help."

"Er, we're awfully busy just now. Could you bring the boy here? He can see his father and stay the night here by his own agreement. Then his father will be on hand if he gets the horrors again."

"That might be just the thing," the superintendent said. "I'll see if he's agreeable to spend the night in a cell near his father; then I'll bring him over myself."

Martineau put down one telephone and picked up another. He dialed a number on the internal line. There was no reply. He went and looked out into the main office and saw Detective Constable Ainslie.

"Take a car and go to Sergeant Bird's house," he said. "Bring him here no matter what he's watching on the telly. If he's gone to bed let him come in his pajamas. If he's round the corner having a pint, don't give him time to drink it up."

"I gather it's urgent, sir," said Ainslie on his way out.

Martineau returned to his perusal of the Styles statement. Now that Mr. Sam had made the matter official by informing the police, she went into details of a love affair which she described as "shocking," but which would have seemed comparatively harmless had it not been for the implications brought up by the subsequent murder. Nevertheless, infatuation had undoubtedly been there, on one side at least. In Styles's opinion, Mr. Billy had been "led on" by Diana. The maid had been so convinced of it that she had plucked up courage to mention the matter to Mr. Luke. Mr. Luke had questioned her, then told her to hold her peace. He would attend to the matter in his own way, he had said. The approximate date of this assurance had been a few days before Luke's visit to his lawyer and his doctor.

The chief inspector's cogitations anent the statement were interrupted by Sergeant Bird, collarless and wearing carpet slippers and an old pullover. "What's up now?" the sergeant wanted to know. "Somebody planted a bomb?"

"No, but you're going to plant something," was the reply. "You're going to bug Jonty Blades's cell without him knowing about it."

"I believe the mike's there in the ventilator. It only wants connecting. Anybody could have done that. Even you could have done it, sir."

"I don't understand the things. And I want to be sure nothing goes wrong. Also, I want it perfect, amplified so we can hear Jonty's brain ticking over. I shall want to hear every whisper. It may mean the clearance of the Luke Glover job."

"H'm. I thought that one was cleared," Bird grumbled as he turned away. Martineau grinned. He knew that Bird would obtain the best possible results with the equipment he had.

A few minutes later Ainslie appeared. "Sir, there's Mr. Harker from the remand home with the Blades boy," he announced.

"Ask them to wait just a few minutes," Martineau replied.

He looked over the Styles statement again, and then Bird looked into the office and nodded and went away. Martineau sent for Ainslie.

"I'm keeping out of this," he said. "Get the cell keys and take Mr. Harker and the boy to Jonty Blades's cell. Tell Jonty the boy wanted to see him. Leave the two together and lock the door. You and Mr. Harker must come right out of the cell corridor and shut the door loud enough for Jonty to hear it."

"Very good, sir." Ainslie turned about like a soldier and went on his errand. He had been a detective officer for more than six months, but he still had the carriage of a smart uniform man.

Martineau waited, not idly but in contemplation of the action which might be taken subsequent to a certain revelation. The tape now running silently from spool to spool might provide information which would turn the case right over, or it might simply prove that Gaylord needed the comforting presence of someone he knew and trusted. But why had he continually asked for his father and not his mother?

Eventually Bird reappeared. He was carrying a large tape recorder under one arm and a small spool of tape in his hand. He put the recorder on the desk, attached it to a wall plug and set the tape in place. "There's another tape running," he said. "But I think this one will be what you want."

He went to the door and called into the main office, "I want absolute silence in there. Stop that typing, Ducklin." The rattle of the typewriter ceased at once. Bird closed the door and returned to the desk. He started the recorder.

For a time the machine emitted nothing but very faint and distant noises, then there was a vague metallic clinking followed by the unmistakable noise of a big key turning in a lock. The two listeners exchanged a glance and a grin. That lock needed oiling.

The sound of the lock was followed by a brief confusion of noises: footsteps on concrete, the creak of a cell cot, the jingle of keys, someone sobbing, a muffled exclamation.

Then Jonty's voice came clearly, and it was hoarse with strain. "What's up, lad? What they brought yer here for?"

Obviously it was Gaylord sobbing, and no doubt he was in his father's arms. Another voice answered, and it was presumably Harker's. "He kept asking for you, Mr. Blades. The police have allowed him to see you. He's going to spend the night in a cell, so that he'll be near you. I'm going to leave him with you for a while."

The sobbing could be heard as a background to the noises of departure, then came Jonty's voice: "Now then, lad. What's upset yer? Aren't they treatin' yer right?"

"It isn't that, Dad. I just can't get over what I've done."

"Sh-h-h-h!" Jonty's voice betrayed anxiety. "Not so loud, lad. They'll be tryin' to listen."

"I don't care. I can't stand it."

There was the sound of a slap. "Quiet, I said," came Jonty's voice, and then the command was followed by an urgent plea, in a voice only a little stronger than a whisper. "Yer all right, lad. I'm standin' by yer. All yer've got ter do is remember what yer've said all the time. Then they can't touch yer."

"Ah, but—"

"Yer dreamed it, lad. It were Uncle who did it. Don't yer remember? We went over it time an' time again."

"Well, it's not what I dream now. I dream—"

"Sh-h-h-h!"

"—about Uncle walkin' away, an' that man callin' after him, an' shovin' me outer the way. An' me—"

Again there was a slap; not a very hard one perhaps. "Make less noise, I tell yer!" Jonty exhorted fiercely. Then again there was a plea. "Look, lad. Yer don't want yer dad ter go ter the nick for years an' years, do yer?"

"No."

The strained voice dropped still more, but it could still be heard. "Yer don't want ter be hanged, do yer?"

"Hanged?"

"Yers. They hang folk for murder, yer know. They'll hang yer if yer don't keep yer trap shut. That's all yer have ter do. Uncle's dead. They can't touch him. He's safe."

"Well, who killed him? What for?"

"It were summat as had naught to do wi' you. Don't bother yer head about that. Let police bother."

"But I talk in me sleep. I know I do. The more I make up me mind not to think about it, the more I dream. I'm flayed a-goin' ter sleep."

"Yer'll get over it, I know yer will. Just yer stick to yer guns. It'll pass, an' then yer'll be all right. We'll all be all right, yer mam an' all. We won't get off scot-free, but it'll be naught serious."

The anxious persuasion went on, Jonty talking and his son apparently listening. When the tape ended Jonty was still talking, in a voice which grew easier and more confident all the time.

Bird stopped the recorder, and started to rewind the tape. Martineau said, "When you've done that, go and collect the second tape, and we'll see what's on it as far as it goes."

182

He went to the door, and saw that Ainslie was back in the C.I.D. "Go and bring out that boy now, and stay with him until I need him," he ordered. "You can talk to him, but not about the job. Nothing at all about the job."

To Ducklin he said, "Get a car and go pick up Mrs. Blades and bring her here. Tell her her son is here. The daughter Ellie can come too, if she wants."

He returned to his desk. Bird brought the second tape, and played it. It was a monologue, Jonty talking quite happily about good times in the past and good times in the future. It was interrupted only once by Gaylord, who wistfully mentioned that there had been some good times with Uncle.

"I'll make up fer Uncle," Jonty told the boy. "Yer'll see, when this is all over. Everything will be fine."

"It was about time we got the lad out of there," Martineau commented. "Happen we made a mistake. We should have let him see his mother."

"Oh, he'll cough when he hears the playback," Bird said confidently. "Shall I put on the first tape again?"

The machine was ready when Gaylord and his mother were ushered into the room. "Ellie couldn't come," Ducklin reported. "She had to stay with the youngest, Caroline."

"Right," said Martineau. "Stay outside and keep everybody quiet."

He offered a chair to Mrs. Blades. Gaylord went to stand beside her, very close to her. She sat with her arm around him.

"This lad's not lookin' so well," she accused. "He's not bein' tre't right."

"I assure you he is, Mrs. Blades," came Martineau's assurance. "I want you to listen to the recording we've just made, and then you'll know what's the matter with him."

Bird set the machine going. The woman's pale face went chalk white when she heard the first words of Gaylord. The boy himself stood stricken. They heard the recording in silence.

"Oh, dear. Oh, dear," the woman moaned when it was over. She hugged her son.

Martineau spoke carefully to her. "You're here to witness that this interview is conducted in all fairness to Gaylord. This tape recording cannot be used as evidence in a court of law. But it tells us the truth, doesn't it? We *know* the truth. Gaylord has been sleeping badly and waking up screaming. Isn't that so, Gaylord?"

"Yers, sir," the boy whispered.

"He is mentally ill, and he won't be better until he gets rid of his trouble by telling the truth."

"They wouldn't hang a child like this, would they?" the mother asked fearfully.

"Of course not. He's much too young. Furthermore, though we now know what he did, I am morally certain that he won't be charged with murder. A man was pushing him out of the way, it seems, and he was in a panic about what the man might do or say. And he happened to have a weapon in his hands. If he is found guilty of manslaughter he'll probably be detained at Her Majesty's Pleasure for a few years. The length of time will depend on his behavior. He will be educated and well fed. He'll be well treated if he's a good boy, as I believe he is. Now, Gaylord, you aren't compelled to speak, and what you say will be taken down and given in evidence. Would you like to tell us the exact truth of what happened last Tuesday afternoon, a week ago?"

The boy hesitated. He looked at his mother.

"Will he go to Borstal?" she asked.

Martineau shook his head. "He's too young to mix with Borstal boys. I assure you if you want him to grow up healthy and right in his mind, with a clear conscience, you would be wise to advise him to tell the whole truth."

"Happen yer'd better tell, Gaylord," the woman said.

Still the boy hesitated. "Dad said to say it were Uncle," he objected.

"But that isn't true."

"No. That's why I have bad dreams."

That remark decided the mother. "Tell the truth, and never mind yer dad," she said. "Tell the truth about poor Uncle."

The mention of Uncle in that sympathetic tone made Gaylord cry. Then drying his eyes he told his story. He and Uncle had arranged to cut wood at three o'clock that Tuesday afternoon. Just before three he had climbed over the cemetery wall and borrowed the ax from the Grimwood Inn. As far as he knew, no one had seen him take the ax, and it had not occurred to him to ask permission to take it.

Waiting in the cemetery with the ax, he had seen to his disappointment that Uncle was drunk, and of course he would go to sleep in front of the fire instead of stirring himself to cut wood. Then the Rolls-Royce had stopped in Grimwood Road, and the little man had got out and followed Uncle into the cemetery lane and stopped him there. He had called him "Matthew" and "Matt," but Uncle had looked at him drunkenly and turned away without speaking.

Gaylord had moved nearer, unobserved, to look and listen. He saw the little man take Uncle's arm again, and heard him say that he would have Uncle sent away and "made right," with the best doctors money could buy. But Uncle had pushed him, telling him to go away, and he had staggered back several yards. Uncle had then turned to go home, and, as far as Gaylord knew, he had done so without looking back.

The little man had started after Uncle again, but Gaylord had vaulted over the wall to stand in his way. He had been frightened that the man would indeed take Uncle away, and he wanted to stop him from following and speaking to him again. The little man, very agitated, had told him to get out of the way, and had tried to push him aside. Gaylord, also extremely agitated, had barred his path, and rather hysterically—so the listeners gathered—had told him that he was not going to be allowed to take anyone away. After a brief argument, during which Gaylord's agitation did not diminish, the little man turned away saying that he would settle the matter by bringing a policeman. It was then, apparently, that Gaylord lost his head. He caught the man by the shoulder and yelled that he could not fetch the police. The man replied that he certainly would fetch the police, and he turned away again. Scarcely realizing what he was doing, Gaylord raised the ax and struck. He said that the only idea in his mind at that time was that the man must not be allowed to go away and return with a policeman who would take Uncle away. The man uttered a sort of grunt as he fell, and thereafter he neither moved nor spoke.

At this point Gaylord broke down again, but after he had been comforted and encouraged by his mother, herself in great distress, he went on with his story. After striking the blow he looked this way and that, but in spite of all the noise which had been made, there seemed to be no witnesses. Uncle was the only person in sight. He had reached the back door of the lodge, and if he had heard the shouting at least he had paid no attention to it.

In a panic Gaylord threw down the ax and fled into the cemetery, but quite soon he returned to lift the dead man and drop him over the wall, having no doubt at all that he *was* dead. Then he picked up the bloody ax and carried it back to the inn, going straight across the cemetery and over the further wall.

That night, after the removal to Holly Lodge, Gaylord told his mother that he did not want to sleep with Uncle, giving an excuse and hiding his real reason, that he was afraid he would talk in his sleep. It was then elicited that his sleep-talking performances had often been a matter of comment in the family.

At bedtime Gaylord curled himself on the settee with a

blanket, but later his father came to him and asked him why he had been so silent and strange during the evening. Eventually he told his father what had happened. His father was silent for some time, and then he said that Gaylord must pretend to know nothing about the affair, and breathe no word of it to anyone. But, he said, the police would be coming eventually. Gaylord was to play dumb as long as he could, but if driven to it he was to say that Uncle had had the ax and that he had struck the little man down because he had seemed to be furious with him about something or other. Uncle had been drunk, he said. Uncle "wouldn't know any different."

Gaylord had been reluctant to blame Uncle, but neither had he wanted to shoulder the blame himself. At the first attempt by the police to question him he had remained silent, afraid to speak. But after Uncle's death it had seemed to be a good idea to do as his father had suggested. It was a good story, and Uncle was safe from the police. At that time it had seemed that all Gaylord's problems were solved.

The mother's sorrow deepened as the story went on, but at the end she said, "Well, yer can't blame a man fer tryin' to protect his own son. An' yer can't blame Gaylord for sayin' it were Uncle, after Uncle were dead. When all is said an' done, it were Uncle's brother what started it."

"I quite see the points you make, Mrs. Blades," Martineau replied. "Fortunately for us here, we aren't asked to apportion blame. You can still believe me when I say that I think Gaylord was wise to tell the truth."

"What'll happen?" the woman asked.

"Gaylord will be in court in the morning, and no doubt he'll be remanded again. But don't worry too much about that. He'll be well treated."

"What about his father?"

"Ah," said Martineau. "I'm afraid I'm going to have to speak to his father again."

Jonty Blades was visibly shaken when he heard the tape re-corder, but he did not panic. "Somebody told me a judge won't accept them things," he said. "Is that right?"

"Up to now, it's correct," Martineau admitted. "But it will come sometime. There's got to be a first time for everything."

Jonty's confidence was somewhat restored. "Yer won't be able to use it," he said.

"We won't need to. Gaylord has told us everything, in his mother's presence. Now we know who killed Luke Glover."

The prisoner looked sad. He sighed. "Well, I did me best," he said. "That business were none o' my startin'."

"Nobody could blame you, if you'd left it at that. But you didn't. You sought to make yourself snug for the future. That idea came after you had dreamed up the idea of blaming Uncle to cover Gaylord. As soon as you found that Uncle was Matthew Glover, you were set."

"All I did was try to help."

"To help yourself, you mean."

"Yer can't prove none o' that. All I got was a pound or two fer my services. I didn't threaten nobody."

"The few pounds you got were only a beginning. I don't suppose you would ever have asked for a great deal, but you expected to live in comfort for the rest of your life."

"Yer can't prove none o' that," Jonty persisted.

"You proved it, by your actions. But the game's up now. You've got all you're going to get in the way of remuneration. Now, you've got to consider your own position. The only way to persuade a judge and jury that you meant well is for you to tell the whole truth *now*."

Jonty was startled. "Judge and jury? What charge?"

"Conspiracy, for a start. And a very serious conspiracy. It led to Uncle's murder. You can take it from me, that fact will be pointed out to the jury."

The prisoner sat in thought. "I did naught wrong, only try to protect my own lad," he said at last.

"You can continue to hold that idea, but you must tell everything you know. Let me give you some inkling as to what will happen to you when a prosecutor gets hold of you. If you wanted only to protect your son, why did you stick your neck out at the register office? Then why did you visit Sam Glover so secretly? You knew even then that it might be necessary to lay the blame for Luke's murder on Uncle. Uncle was your friend, but you went to the son of the man who had been murdered."

"It were only after I couldn't get hold o' Billy."

"There is no evidence of that, except yours. We have made inquiries. Nobody at G.D.M. can remember anybody persistently trying to telephone Billy last Wednesday."

"I found his name in the phone book and tried there. I couldn't get no answer."

"See what a mess you'd get yourself into, in court? Billy's name isn't in the phone book. He lives with his aunt, and the phone is under her name. He has never bothered to have his own name listed."

Jonty was silent. Then he admitted, "That were a slip, but it were naught. I went to Sam an' ast him to put me in touch wi' Billy."

"He did that after he'd had a talk with you. I want to know everything you said to him, and everything he said to you."

"Yer know that already."

"I doubt it. Remember, the game's up. There's no longer any chance to profit. You might as well tell the truth and save yourself from getting deeper into the mire."

Again Jonty took time out for meditation. Eventually he said: "There were only one little thing, an' I can't see as it matters much. When I told Sam I'd found his uncle he ast a right lot o' questions, reckonin' not ter believe me, like. At finish up I had ter tell him it were his uncle what had killed his father. He were mad at first, an' then he seemed ter think it over an' come round a bit. He said he'd get Billy over, an' he phoned him. Then he said we'd tell Billy his father had been found, but we wouldn't let on he had aught ter do wi' Luke's murder. What were done were done, an' couldn't be mended, he said. Him an' Billy was friends, an' there were his aunt, Luke's sister, ter consider. It were no use makin' more grief than there were already. Which I thought were very decent of him, considerin'."

"Quite. And at that point he gave you some money?"

"Just a quid or two, what he had in his pocket. Oh, an' he did say if I was a good lad I wouldn't regret it."

"Nothing more than that?"

"No. Billy came then, an' I told him my tale, not mentionin' about Luke at all. We made arrangements fer him ter have a look at Uncle—his dad—unbeknown. Then Billy said he'd run me home in his car. So we went. That's all."

"So Billy never did learn from you that his father was supposed to be involved in Luke's murder?"

"Not unless he were a thought reader. I were very careful, an' by gum I had ter be. He's as sharp as a needle, is yon. In the car he ast a right lot o' questions, but I didn't make the same mistake I'd made wi' Sam. He weren't right pleased wi' me, but he didn't get ter know naught about Luke's murder."

"And the following day you showed him his father. Was he convinced then?"

"He didn't say. He seemed a bit sickened 'cause Uncle was in a state. He said we'd better leave it till he were sober. He gave me a fiver fer me trouble an' that were all. I went back ter Holly Lodge, an' that's when yer fellers turned up an' pulled me in."

"Mmmm. I hope you've told me the whole truth this time.

If there's more, it'll be brought out in court. And as far as you're concerned, that's the worst possible place for it to be brought out."

"I'm not bothered about that. There's no more ter come."

"Very well. You'll be taken down and charged."

Chapter Twenty-three

In the past, Martineau had often remarked that Dixie Costello had a better intelligence system than the police, but even he would have been surprised if he had known how efficient the system really was. It was not merely a matter of being able to use the eyes and ears of innkeepers, barmaids, club owners, café owners, bookmakers, bookie's runners and rogues of all kinds. There was also a rootlet of Dixie's grapevine in the C.I.D., one which Martineau had for years been trying to uncover. And, among lists of informants of various kinds, including professional men, there was a list of the registration numbers of all local police cars which did not carry police signs, and also all the numbers of cars privately owned by members of the force. These latter lists were intended to be used when it was necessary to know what the police were doing about certain matters.

In the matter of Gordon Barnes, it became necessary for Dixie to know. On being shown the newspaper account of Barnes's appearance in court, with the mention of five hundred pounds, he immediately thought of stolen transistors, as Martineau had done. "So Barnes was in it," he said to Ned Higgs. "And the cops caught him picking up his cut. He's out on bail. I want him. He'll tell me what he knows and what the coppers know. When you pick him up, be careful 'cause he might have a tail."

An hour later Higgs telephoned, "He's left his job and moved out of his diggings," he reported. "I'm looking for him around town, but I'm afraid he's skipped."

"All right. Keep on looking," Dixie said.

The boss mobster sat in thought for a little while; then he picked up the telephone again and dialed a number of which he kept no written record. The call was answered by a woman, who gave her own number.

"Oh, I do beg your pardon," Dixie said. "I dialed wrongly. I'm trying to get six three six four."

"All right," the woman said.

Dixie put the receiver back and lit a cigarette, and smoked while he waited. Within five minutes his call came, in a man's voice.

"This is you-know-who," a man said.

"Ah," said Dixie. "You're prompt."

"I just happened to call home. What is it?"

"Gordon Barnes, who was in front of the Stipe this morning. Have your lot tied a can to him?"

"They're keeping it awful squat, but that's my impression. They want to know where the money came from. But it isn't any of our lot tailing him."

"Who, then?"

"Maybe the zombies. They've been used before for that sort of lark."

"Thanks. Let me know if you get a line on Barnes. I'd like a word with him."

"Roger," the man said, and that was all.

Dixie got out his list of cars, sighed as he looked at it and set to work to type copies. There were occasions even in these days of affluence when he had to do something with his own hands. Before he had quite finished, Higgs telephoned again.

"Neither hide nor hair of him," he said.

"All right, leave it," Dixie replied. "I want you here right away."

Dixie finished his typing and got out a map of the city. He wrote down the names of ten districts, giving main roads as boundaries. Higgs arrived.

"Ten of the boys are going to have to get up in the morning," Dixie said. "Here is each man's area, and here is each man's list of cars he's got to look for. I want these lists back intact, and they're not to be shown around. See if you can fix up tonight to hire cars for those men who haven't got their own. I want them on their beats before eight o'clock. They phone me here whenever they see one of these cars."

"What's the idea?" Higgs queried.

Dixie told him.

"Am I going on the job?"

"No. I want you here, with Waddy and the Dog. And you'll need a car handy, with a good wheel man. Put some wrong numbers on it, just in case."

"I'll do that little thing," said Higgs, and then he departed.

At eight o'clock the following morning Dixie was sitting up in bed, reading the paper and drinking the coffee which his daily woman had made for him. At nine o'clock the calls began to come in. There were three between nine and half past, all from those of his men who were cruising near the center of the city. At twenty minutes to ten there was a call from Mossbank, from a male adherent who went by the name of Ruby Atkins.

"Car number four two oh seven NCC," Ruby said. "That's correct according to this list. But I don't get it. There's three bits of stuff in it. Young pieces."

"They're policewomen," said Dixie. "Watch they don't spot you. Where did you see the car?"

"It's in Plum Orchard Street, standing at the curb. Leastways it was there a couple of minutes ago."

"Get round behind it, a long way off, and keep your eye on

it. And keep your gleamers busy watching for that fellow Gordon Barnes. You know him, don't you?"

"I know him."

"Right. If you see him don't lose him, and never mind the zombies. I'm sending you some help."

Thus, before ten o'clock on Wednesday morning, Costello's men were put on the trail of Gordon Barnes. Dixie explained the situation to Higgs and his men. "Barnes will be around there somewhere. Those lady coppers will know exactly where. When he moves, they'll spot him, and so will you. You'll have to snatch him from under their noses, and then give them the slip. Take him to the old bonding warehouse, it's the nearest place. You should be able to get him there before the zombies can put the patrol cars on your track. When you've got him safe, send the car away and give me the wire. And don't handle him rough. There'll be time enough for that when it becomes necessary."

Higgs and his crew went to their falsely numbered car and rode to Mossbank. They located Atkins, and they located the police car and its occupants. They watched from a safe distance.

Ten minutes before noon, Gordon Barnes emerged from his new lodgings and walked to the news agent's shop at the end of Plum Orchard Street. He came out of the shop slapping his leg with a folded newspaper. He looked all around, and his glance lingered on the police car for an appreciable time. He did not look at the two mob cars standing close together at the curb. Possibly he thought that they were too far away to be occupied by people who were watching him.

Apparently satisfied that all was well, he crossed the street and entered the Plum Orchard Inn. When he was out of sight, the police car moved forward, going on straight past the inn and stopping in a position where its occupants could watch the inn through the rear window.

"Anybody know that pub?" Higgs asked from his car.

"I been in once or twice," Waddy replied.

"What's the layout?"

"Well, the back door's at the side, if yer know what I mean. In a little blind alley where the brewery men back their trucks in to be near the cellar door. That's why the zombies have moved, so's they can see the alley."

"If we backed our car in there, we could whip Barnes outa the boozer an' into the car, an' away. That right?"

"Yeh, it could be done that way."

"Right. Flag Ruby. We need him."

Ruby came. "A job for you," said Higgs. "Drive on an' draw up right behind those wenches in that car. Block their view an' stop 'em from backin'. Don't look back at us. We'll give you the word ter scarper with a couple of sharp toots on the horn. Then the job'll be over for you. You can go an' have a pint. Right, get movin'."

Ruby's car moved forward, and stopped behind the police car as directed. Close behind came the car with the false number plates. Sitting beside the driver, Higgs continued to give his rapid, confident instructions.

"Stop for a second at the front door an' let me an' the Dog get out," he said to the driver. "Then back into the alley as far as the side door. Waddy, you be standin' with the car door open. The Dog gets in first with Barnes, then you follow. I get in at this door. Right?"

"Right," Waddy and the driver answered together.

Higgs spoke to the Dog: "Wolfe, slip on that spiked knuckle of yours. You just let him see it, see? Scare the livin' daylights out of him. But for Christ's sake don't hit him with it. I'll do all the talkin' there is. Right?"

"Right," growled the Dog. He was a man so big and strong that it was not really necessary for him to carry a weapon. But he took his dreadful instrument from his pocket and slipped it over the knuckles of his right hand. It was a homemade affair, composed of two layers of leather with four dozen one-inch nails protruding through the outer layer. When he had adjusted the thing to his satisfaction, he pulled down the sleeve of his coat to conceal it.

The operation was carried out without a hitch. Higgs and the Dog entered the inn. Barnes was sitting on a tall stool at the bar. He had a glass of gin in front of him and he was just opening his paper. The only other person in sight was a small plump man who was obviously the landlord. Barnes looked up as the two men entered. He recognized them, and slid from his stool and looked around for a way out. Then they were there with him. He stared speechlessly at the Dog, who grinned ferociously and showed him the spiked knuckleduster. Higgs said, "Somebody wants to talk to you. That way out."

The Dog led the way, and Barnes followed meekly. Before he followed also, Higgs turned to look at the landlord. He held up a clenched right fist and put the forefinger of his left hand to his lips. The landlord nodded. He wanted no trouble with men like Higgs and the Dog.

Outside, Waddy was holding open the door of the car. The Dog climbed in, Barnes followed him, Waddy went last and squeezed his plump behind into the space available. The slam of the car door was almost echoed by the sound of Higgs closing the other near side door of the car. The vehicle nosed out of the alley. The driver gave Ruby Atkins the signal that he was free to depart.

The occupants of the police car had quickly realized that some mischief was afoot. When the view was blocked by Ruby's car, the policewoman at the wheel drove forward and started to turn. When the car had been turned until it was facing the inn, Ruby got his signal. His car shot forward and away.

"We've had him, girls," one of the policewomen said. "But I've got his number and description, for what it's worth."

"It's the other car we want," said the driver as she drove out into the cross street. "There he goes, half a mile away. We've had him too."

"We don't know anything yet, Vi," the third girl said. "We can't catch that lot. Let me go into the pub and see if we've guessed right. If we have, we'll have to tell Headquarters."

The old disused bonding warehouse in Mossbank had been acquired by Dixie Costello, through a nominee, with the idea that it could be used for various purposes: storage, a meeting place, an interrogation room, even a torture chamber. It was surrounded by streets of empty, condemned houses. A man could yell his head off there, and only his inquisitors would hear him.

Dixie arrived on foot, having left his car at a shabby little club a quarter of a mile away. He owned the club, and with due respect to the antislavery laws it could also be said that he owned the management and staff, right down to the red-headed cigarette girl. So that was all right. Everything was under control.

When he arrived at the warehouse he noted that the kidnap car had been driven away, according to orders. As he knocked three times loudly and three times gently on the back door, he wondered briefly how long it would take the coppers to find a body covered with a flagstone and rubble in one of the condemned houses. He hoped it would not come to that, but he had known weak characters to flake out and croak before when questioned by Higgs and the Dog.

Waddy let him in. "All right?" he asked.

"Beautiful, Dix," Waddy said. "We done a good job. We was outa sight before they could shake the mascara off their eyelashes."

"Good. I'm pleased," said Dixie, who always gave praise where it was due, so long as it did not cost too much. He walked into the main chamber of the warehouse. All the occupants were standing because there was nothing to sit on but a cold stone floor.

"Hello, there," he said to Barnes. "I see now we didn't talk to you proper the last time."

"Ah yes, you did," Barnes replied, though his voice shook with nervousness. "I know what you're thinking. It's the obvious thing. Martineau thought the same."

"He did?" Dixie was perturbed. "I wonder how he got on to that. What did he say?"

"He was cagy about it. He didn't say anything outright, but he said he'd heard something on his transistor set. He was referring to the five ones they lifted off me."

"Yeh. He knew why you got it. And so do I."

"No, you're wrong. This is another job altogether. One of my own. I'm leveling with you because I know it's the only way I can keep my face the way it is. These men of yours have taken just short of five hundred quid off me. They divvied it up. They said they'd slice my throat if I told you."

The Dog stepped forward. "You bloody pansy, you," he threatened thickly. "I'll cut your nose off."

"Down, Doggy, down," said Dixie. "You mind I don't have *you* beautified. Robbing me like that. Come on, shell out. Let's see if he's telling the truth."

Reluctantly the three mobsters produced wads of five-pound notes. Higgs had one hundred and ninety-five pounds. Waddy had a hundred and fifty and so had the Dog.

Dixie held the money in his hand. "Do you think I keep you lot in luxury so's you can pick up lolly on the side?" he demanded sternly. "If this money don't belong to this fellow here, it belongs to me. And don't you forget it. Now, Barnes, how did you come by this? I thought the bogeys had your five ones."

"They did. That's another lot I got. I tell you it's a different job."

"It looks as if it must be," Dixie admitted thoughtfully. "And it sounds like a damned good one. You'd better tell me. I like to be in on these things."

"The money in your hand proves it isn't the transistor job. I realize you're entitled to something for your trouble. Can't you take what you've got and let me go?"

Dixie whistled. "My word, you certainly are on a good thing, giving up five ones like that. I certainly must be in on this."

"All right," said Barnes wearily. "I know I have to tell you. But I want a reasonable share. I'll let you kick me to bits before I'll lose the lot."

"A reasonable share I'm always willing to concede," said Dixie generously. "Let's say ten percent. For you I mean. I've got to pay these boys, you know."

"Twenty," said Barnes. "Flog me and I won't take less. It's my idea, you know."

Dixie studied him. He knew the type. Here was a man with enough common sense to do a deal when he was cornered. He also looked as if he could be fatally obdurate if treated too badly.

"All right, twenty percent," the boss mobster agreed. "Now, give me the good news. You boys step outside while I listen."

"What about the money you've got there?"

Dixie smiled. "You get twenty percent, if the job's a good 'un."

Chapter Twenty-four

A few minutes before noon on Wednesday, about the time when Gordon Barnes was buying his morning paper, Detective Constable Brabant knocked on the door of Martineau's office. He entered and said, "A little something, sir. I think we've broken an alibi."

"Which one?"

"Sam Glover's."

"How?"

"The Blades girl is out of work. It occurred to me that she might be signing on at the Labour Exchange. Well, she is."

"And?"

"Friday is pay day at the Labour Exchange. I wondered if she drew her dole last Friday. She did."

"Ah. What time?"

"Twelve o'clock within minutes. There's a clerk called Humphries who knows her quite well. She was the last of his morning's lot. She always is. Twelve o'clock is her regular time. He remembers thinking that if Eleanor Blades appeared at her usual time there would be nothing more until after lunch. He's quite positive. I got his statement."

"So Sam Glover was lying. If he's our murderer, I still can't see his motive. You've done very well, Brabant. Very well indeed. Now let me think about this."

While Martineau was thinking about the new development, his thoughts were interrupted by the telephone. An agitated policewoman informed him that she was out of touch with Barnes and that he appeared to have had assistance in getting away. Martineau listened to the story, and then he said, "You stay within sight of his lodgings. Let me know when he comes back. And take notice of what shape he's in. It's my opinion that he's been picked up by a mob, and a very rough mob at that. I'm glad you didn't have the chance to interfere."

Martineau was reasonably certain that Barnes was in the hands of Dixie Costello. And to save his own neck, Barnes would have to tell the truth about the two sums of five hundred pounds. Because of the second batch of notes, presumably now in Barnes's possession, Costello would believe the story. Now Barnes would have a partner in extortion, one who would take the lion's share. Sam Glover, or alternatively Billy Glover, was at the mercy of a blackmailer who would never cease in his demands. He would not ruin his victim. He was too wise for that. He would merely keep him hard pressed for money.

There was no point in starting a hunt for Costello and his men, or even in troubling to trace the driver of the car which had obstructed the policewomen. There would be no complaint of kidnaping, no complaint of any kind. Barnes would know when he was beaten. Against his will perhaps, he would have become Costello's creature.

Martineau reflected that quite soon Sam Glover, now the chief suspect, would be receiving a demand for a really large amount of money. Probably the demand would be made by telephone. The police were not allowed to tap telephones. Sometimes that was a great pity.

Thinking about telephones, Martineau wondered how many Sam Glover had. He sent for Devery.

"I've decided to put all my eggs in one basket," he said. "I'm going to concentrate on Cousin Sam. Take Cassidy and scout around the vicinity of his flat, while I get a warrant to search. See if the place is staked out by any of Costello's boys. Mind you're not spotted. You've got plenty of time."

"Costello?"

"Yes. He's in it now, or he soon will be. Off you go, and stay around till I arrive."

Devery departed, and Martineau had words with the warrant officer on the internal line. Then while he waited, he brooded on the mystery of how Costello had so quickly located Barnes. It did not occur to him that the mobster might have a list of the numbers of police cars, but he did guess that there had been a leak of the information that policewomen were being used to watch Barnes. "If I could only find that damned traitor," he muttered savagely. "If I could only get a clue to him."

The search warrant arrived. Martineau took Brabant with him to Sam's flat. First, he located Devery.

"All clear, Guv'nor," the sergeant said. "But there's a maid or a cleaning woman in there. I saw her at a window for a second or two."

"She's a cleaning woman," said Martineau. "Sometime this afternoon she'll finish for the day and go home." He looked around. Three hundred yards along the street there was a high-class private club which was impeccably conducted. He knew the proprietor well. He nodded in that direction. "Brabant and I are going there for a tankard of ale and something to eat," he said. "Let me know when the cleaning woman goes."

They had eaten a meal and were lingering over coffee when Devery appeared. "She's gone," the sergeant said. "And still no sign of Dixie's mob."

They returned to Sam's flat. On Martineau's instructions, Brabant stopped the car out of sight of the flat, round a corner.

"Bring those keys," Martineau said as he alighted. "Here, you take them, Devery."

Devery was something of an expert with the C.I.D.'s skeleton keys. Within three minutes Martineau, Devery and Brabant were inside the flat. Cassidy was stationed outside, to watch for enemy reconnaissance.

Martineau went straight into the largest of the two bedrooms. He nodded in a satisfied way when he saw a telephone. "I hoped he'd have an extension in here." He looked around. "Now then, where can our man hide?"

The bed was low and luxurious. A child could not have crawled under it. There was a long built-in wardrobe, full of clothes on hangers. "That would do at a pinch," Martineau commented, but even as he spoke he was gazing at a big winged chair which stood in a corner of the room.

"Brabant, let me see you get down behind that chair," he said. "You've got to do it without noise."

Brabant obeyed. He disappeared. Martineau walked across the room, from wall to wall and from door to window. He walked around the bed. He went to the chair and looked over the back, meeting the upturned gaze of the man behind it.

"That's the only way for anybody to find you," he said. "You're going to stay here, and you'll get behind that chair when you hear Sam come home. If he looks for somebody hiding in the place, he'll find you. If he doesn't, he won't. Now let me see you come out of there and go to the phone, and pick it up and put it down again, all without making a noise."

Brabant rose silently and carried out the order.

"That's fine," Martineau said. "I'll get Sergeant Bird to bring you a little battery tape recorder. He'll set it for you and show you what to do. You'll make a recording of any phone calls, but you'll also listen. It'll be you and not the tape recorder who is the witness. Take this warrant and keep it in your pocket. It'll cover you if you happen to get caught."

"Suppose Sam doesn't go out tonight, how do I get away?" Brabant wanted to know.

"If you're not back at the office by eleven o'clock, I'll arrange some sort of diversion to get you out. Right, that's settled. But I suppose I'd better have a glance round this place before I go away. Sergeant, have a look in some of these drawers, but don't disturb anything."

While Devery searched the bedroom, Brabant was given the task of searching the living room. Martineau looked in the kitchen, then crossed to the bathroom. He found that it was well-appointed but strictly functional, definitely a man's bathroom. There was no odor of bath cubes or perfumed soap, and the only thing which Martineau might have considered womanish was the collection of half-empty bottles, of all shapes and sizes, which filled the bathroom cupboard.

He began to read the labels on the bottles: Silvikrin, Vosene, K.D.X., Selsun, Loxene, and half a dozen more hair tonics and medicated shampoo preparations. Why so many? He remembered Sam Glover's thick dark hair. Sam had one of those heads which would never go bald, Martineau felt sure. He studied the bottles. Sam suffered from dandruff.

"Sergeant," he called. And when Devery came: "Do we still have that hat from the murder car?"

"Yes, Guv'nor. At least, the laboratory has it."

"Look here. Look at all these dandruff preparations. Do you remember that young pathologist at the general hospital telling us about some experiments for the positive identification of dandruff? I wonder if they were successful."

"We could find out."

"Happen we could. Material evidence. Just the job. Have you an evidence envelope? Good. I'd like to take Sam's hairbrushes with me, but it might put him wise. We'll give them a right good combing, and then we'll get out of here. I've a feeling we're going to wrap up this job sooner than I expected."

Still concentrating on the affairs of Sam Glover, Martineau sent out men to look for new sources of information, and he personally visited certain old ones. At the Grimwood Inn he learned that Sam Glover and Ellie Blades had met there, on the afternoon of last Thursday, about the same time that the police found the rest of the Blades family at Holly Lodge. They had also met on the following day, Friday, at about the same time. The chief inspector reflected that this was a case which would already have been cleared if he had had a squad of invisible men to follow a few people around.

Ellie was brought in for questioning, and when she was confronted by the statement of the clerk at the Labour Exchange, she tearfully admitted that she had wrongly given Sam an alibi for Friday noon.

"He had nothing to do with it," she maintained. "It was just that he didn't want to be questioned. He was doing something for his cousin, Billy. He was trying to help Billy."

Martineau nodded, refraining from comment. "I suppose you fixed up the alibi on Friday afternoon?" he asked, casually enough to give the impression that he was not greatly interested in the time.

"Yes," she admitted. "He told me what to say."

"That would be between two and three, before the inn closed for the afternoon?"

She looked doubtful, sensing a trap. She took a little time to consider the matter and failed to see the trap. And no doubt that was because she believed that Sam was an innocent man.

"Yes," she said. "I met him about quarter past two and left him just after three. He took me in his car to a bus stop in Derbyshire Road."

"At any time during the meeting, did he actually mention Uncle's murder to you?"

"No. I told him. He was shocked, and when he'd thought about it a while he said I'd better be his alibi, because he didn't want to be involved."

Impassively, Martineau nodded again. Either the girl had eventually seen the trap and neatly evaded it, or else she was now telling the truth. It would have been a point of tremendous importance if Martineau could have proved that Sam was faking an alibi for murder at a time when he was not supposed to have known about the murder. Now, that point was covered. Ellie could have got the story from her mother when she returned from the Labour Exchange, and it would be a natural thing for her to tell Sam when she met him.

Still, would an innocent man fake an alibi? Martineau thought not. He began to stalk his quarry from another angle.

"You've seen a true statement," he said. "Now I'll show you another statement, signed by you, which isn't true. I'm referring to your first statement, given on Thursday afternoon. In it you said that you had not seen Sam Glover since Tuesday, and actually you had been with him only an hour or two before, that is to say on that same Thursday afternoon. I have the word of Mr. and Mrs. Wensley from the inn on that."

The girl looked down at her hands, twitching with interlaced fingers on her lap. "Yes, I lied about that," she admitted. "We should never have gone there. We should have gone somewhere else."

"Ah, but at that time it didn't matter to either of you. Now, it does matter. Tell me, what did you talk about on that occasion?"

Fingers twisted fingers painfully. The girl's face also showed the agony of indecision. "Does it matter?" she asked.

"Not to you directly. It matters to me."

"Well, there'd been Sam's father murdered, and he asked me if I'd seen or heard anything. I said I didn't know anything about it."

"And was that true? You can't get Gaylord into trouble now, you know. He's confessed that he killed Luke Glover."

"It—it was true."

"Now I think you're being dishonest again. Didn't Sam tell *you* anything?"

"No."

207

"Didn't he tell you he'd seen your father the night before? I know your father went to him."

"Yes, he did tell me that."

"And did he tell you that the man you called Uncle was his own uncle, Matthew Glover?"

"Y-yes."

"And what else did he tell you about Uncle?"

"Nothing."

"Now, now. You were terribly worried, weren't you? You were terribly worried because someone you knew had killed Sam's father. You felt that you ought to tell him, but you couldn't, could you?"

"I tell you I didn't know."

"I don't think that is quite true. Were you very fond of Uncle?"

"I suppose I was. He was like a member of the family. And he was jolly when he was sober. He was good and kind, too."

"And you were awfully worried, weren't you? And Sam wondered why. So he told you what your father had told him, that Uncle had killed Luke Glover. Did he, or did he not?"

"Yes, he told me that. He said he didn't know what to do about it. He said he had other members of the family to think about. They'd be terribly distressed, he said."

"Naturally. But you were terribly distressed too, weren't you?"

"Yes."

"His family was going to be torn apart because they believed that Uncle had killed Luke Glover, his own brother. Did *you* believe that?"

The girl was silent.

"You can tell me," said Martineau. "The truth can't hurt Gaylord now."

"I told Sam," she said. "I told him I could stop the trouble inside his family if he'd swear not to tell the police. He said he wouldn't tell the police. So I said I was certain Uncle hadn't hurt anybody. I said I could prove it. I made him believe me."

"He wouldn't believe you unless you told him how you knew. Did you tell him?"

"Yes," she admitted. "I told him Gaylord had done it."

"How did you know that?"

"That Tuesday afternoon, before anything had happened, when everybody was happy, I saw Gaylord climb over the cemetery wall and borrow the ax. I thought nothing of it at the time. It happened while Uncle was in the taproom. He never had the ax at all."

"How did you come to see Gaylord take the ax?"

"Sam had said something a bit cheeky, and I was pretending to be mad. Only pretending. I got up and went to the back window and stood looking out into the back yard."

"Would you say that was conclusive, because Gaylord happened to have the ax in the first place?"

"It was to me. How could Uncle have got the ax? Gaylord liked the ax, and he always wanted to use it first. Besides, Uncle would never hit anybody with an ax. Gaylord would, if he was frightened."

"Thank you," said Martineau.

A few minutes later, a policewoman telephoned with the news that Gordon Barnes had returned to his lodgings, and that he was apparently unharmed.

Half an hour after that, the same girl informed Martineau that Barnes was now in his old haunt, the Northland Hotel. He was no longer a fugitive apparently. Obviously, he had come to an agreement with Dixie Costello. He was out of the picture until evidence of blackmail could be found. Observations on him could continue with that object.

"Many thanks for your help," Martineau said to the girl. "Keep up the surveillance, but take care to keep out of trouble. He'll probably know now that he's had policewomen on his trail."

Chapter Twenty-five

At half past eight Brabant returned to the C.I.D. and reported to Martineau.

"Well?" the chief inspector demanded. "Did our client get a phone call?"

"Yes sir," the detective replied, trying hard to hide the elation following a successful mission. "Two calls, actually."

"What time was the important one?"

"Bang on seven. The phone rang in the living room. I nipped out from behind the chair and listened in on the extension, according to the instructions of my superior officer."

"That's right. Don't forget to say that bit, in case the defense suggests you're a sneaking spy. Did you get it all?"

"Practically all, I think. I must have picked up the receiver nearly as soon as Sam. I could hear all right, though I haven't tried to play the recording yet."

"It's what you heard that matters. But run the tape now. We'll see what you got. Ah, I see you haven't run it back yet. We'll let Sergeant Bird do it, just to be safe. I'll get him."

They waited until Bird arrived and ran the tape back to the replay position. A voice could be heard as soon as the playback started.

". . . that the Ace?"

Martineau could not identify the voice, nor did he recognize the voice which answered.

"Ace of what?"

"Ace of Diamonds."

"Er, yes."

"I'm speaking on behalf of the Ace of Spades. It's about that life insurance you have with him, and he's here if you want to talk to him. Since he joined my company the premium has gone up. But don't worry about that. It'll never get too heavy for you to pay. You can afford ten thousand a year, regular. No more, no less. My firm will be happy and you'll be safe. The first annual payment will be tomorrow."

"Ten thousand! You're crazy."

"Nobody is less crazy than I, my friend."

"I can't raise all that money."

"I know you can. I've been studying your case."

"Ten thousand every year?"

"You don't understand. You're not dealing with a pipsqueak concern any more. This sort of insurance is big business. We provide a service for our clients. You'll get the residue of your father's fortune, and that will be practically all of it. Your cousin will get nothing. So, you see, you'll be prosperous enough to pay the premiums."

"I don't understand."

"You're not as bright as I thought you were. When your father died, your cousin's father inherited about half of the estate. But your cousin killed his father, so he can't inherit, so it goes to you."

"Ah. Can you prove that?"

"It'll be proved. The necessary witnesses will be found. Good witnesses, too."

"What about my cousin's alibi?"

"He won't have one. His witness is going to change her testimony. She'll be persuaded."

"Are you sure you can do all this?"

"I'm sure. One thing I'd like to know. What's the position if I induce Spade Ace here to confess to the coppers that he put the black on your cousin? They know he got some money from somewhere. Would it work out?"

"Yes, it would. I have already told them my cousin borrowed two sums of five hundred from me."

"Fine. We might have to make it worthwhile for Spade Ace to do a little stretch. That'll be a small extra expense for you. He'll be a good witness against your cousin."

"You're beginning to convince me you can do it."

"But of course. Don't worry about a thing. All you have to do is pay the premiums. As your insurance broker, your prosperity will be mine. I want you to go back to work without a care in the world, and make a lot of money. And don't bother about the police finding out you've had to raise the money. Their interest in you will finish when Spade Ace owns up. They'll concentrate on your cousin, not you."

"Perhaps you're right. Anyway, I'll be careful."

"That's my boy. Now, here's what you do. Take the money as the bank gives it to you, old and new, ones and fivers. It'd look a bit suspicious if you insisted on every note being a used one. Buy a new suitcase at Marks and Spencer's, where they sell hundreds. Put the money in it and get into that Ferrari of yours. Set off about eight o'clock at night, when it's nice and dark, and drive out to Clingstone and get on the motorway. On the twenty miles between Clingstone and Belshaw you'll be able to do a hundred and fifty if you like. Anyway, go fast enough to shake any copper car which might be on your tail. Turn off the motorway at Belshaw and head back to town. You'll come in on the right side of town to get to Grimwood without being noticed."

"Grimwood?"

"Yes. Spade Ace suggested Grimwood because you know the

place well, and because it's so quiet it might as well be dead. Drive past the cemetery at nine thirty. Keep a lookout to make sure there's nobody in sight. When you pass the main gate, slow down enough to chuck out the suitcase, then drive on. That's all."

"Very well. Are you sure nobody is listening to this conversation?"

"Only Spade Ace, unless you've got somebody there with you. Only M.I.5 taps telephones. The ordinary bogies aren't allowed to do it. It's immoral, or something. Now, is all clear?"

"Yes. Quite clear."

"All right then. Let us hope this is the beginning of a long and profitable association. You can take my word for it, the premiums will not be increased. But if you've any idea of stopping your payments when things have blown over, you'll find you're making a mistake. You'll pay every year, regular. This is the Ace of Clubs signing off. Cheerio."

The tape ran soundlessly. At a nod from Brabant, Bird reached out to stop it. Martineau said, "That's better than I hoped for. The Ace of Clubs talks like Dixie Costello, but doesn't sound like him. I wouldn't have recognized Sam's voice, either."

Said Bird, "These little battery recorders don't always give the true timber of a voice. But the words were clear enough."

"Yes," the chief inspector agreed. "And Brabant heard them, that's the thing." Then he scowled. "Costello knows an awful lot. He's been getting information from this office again. Neither of you two must say a word about this to anybody at all. Understand?"

"Yes, sir," Brabant replied. "Would you like to hear the other call?"

"Yes. Put it on."

Bird restarted the tape. Sam Glover's voice was heard. ". . . Yes. Is that Ellie?"

"Yes. Listen. The police came for me again. They found out

I was at the Labour Exchange last Friday when I was supposed to be with you. A man there knows me, and he knows what time I was there."

"Oh hell. That's torn it. Did you admit to being there?"

"Yes. I had to. But I told Mr. Martineau I'd only given you an alibi because you didn't want to be involved. I told him you had nothing to do with Uncle."

"Ah. What else did you tell him?"

"Nothing else, really. He wanted to know about our last two meetings at the inn. He'd found out about that, too. So I had to tell him about seeing Gaylord take the ax."

"Did you tell him you told me? Does he know that I knew all the time that Uncle hadn't killed my father?"

"Yes. Did I do wrong?"

"I think you just about ruined everything. Look, I'd better see you, and I'll find out what else you told him. We won't go to the inn. You know that other little pub at the corner of Grimwood Road, just where you turn into Derbyshire Road? I'll meet you there in half an hour. What? Oh, bye bye."

Again Bird stopped the tape. Martineau was smiling grimly. "So the cat's among the pigeons," he said. "I fancy Sam will think he's not quite good enough to get around that one. I'm guessing he won't think Costello is good enough, either."

He looked at Brabant. "I suppose that's the lot? When Sam went to meet Ellie you cleared out of the place?"

"Yes, sir. I thought I'd better clear out with what I'd got. And according to your instructions, sir."

"Quite. I could pick up Sam right away, but I think we'll let this blackmail job roll. I might even get my hands on Dixie Costello. That would be worth a lot."

The following morning Martineau put his case to Clay, and received a promise of full support in what he intended to do. After that he heard the first report on Sam Glover's movements that day, from Devery and Cassidy. Sam had merely gone to G.D.M., as he would have done on any other working day.

Then the chief inspector remembered that Gordon Barnes was still under surveillance by policewomen. Now that Costello was taking a hand in the game, he felt that the work had become too dangerous for women. He hastily issued the order to call them off, but the message did not reach them in time to prevent their witnessing an interview in a city café between Barnes and a handsome blonde woman about thirty years old. Policewoman Violet Briggs reported that she and Policewoman McEvan had ventured to take a table at the far side of the biggest room of the café, and they had watched the interview. It had been a quiet talk, with no signs of heat. Barnes had appeared to reason with the woman, or as P.W. Briggs put it, he had seemed to present an unanswerable case to her, which she had appeared to accept with an expressionless face. Which showed that P.W. Briggs was intelligent, but not intelligent enough to remember that a police officer should report nothing but facts, without the use of imaginative words or phrases.

"That would be Diana receiving her instructions," he commented. He reflected that if it had not been for Ellie Blades's recent statement, coupled with the overhearing of Costello's plans, the boss mobster might have succeeded in building up a case against Billy Glover which would have convicted him in spite of police disbelief in it. Martineau never made the mistake of underestimating Costello. With regard to the statement, he was comforted by the knowledge that Sam Glover could not inform either Costello or Barnes of the new danger to himself. Those two were out of his reach until half past nine that night, unless he had made a shrewd guess at the identity of the man who had called himself the Ace of Clubs. This was possible, but not likely. Until now, the orbits of Glover and Costello had been far, far apart.

During the forenoon Sam was not reported to have left the

office to visit a bank. Martineau assumed that he had telephoned. City banks are accustomed to paying out sums of money far in excess of ten thousand pounds, but these are factory pay rolls and suchlike regular withdrawals. An *unexpected* demand for ten thousand, late in the day, could easily find a bank manager without so much cash on the premises. Sam would know enough about such matters to have given his banker reasonable notice of the withdrawal, and he would certainly have done so if he intended to raise some of the money by an overdraft.

While he waited for news, Martineau thought darkly about the traitor in the department. The younger men of his squad, Hearn, Ainslie, Brabant, Robieson, could not really be suspected. The leakage of information had existed for years, he was sure. He considered his older subordinates, Devery, Bird, Cassidy, Cook, Ducklin, Fisher, Evans, Murray, Wallace. One of those? He hated to think so. One of the clerks? Possibly. Detective Inspector Pearson or one of his squad? Not Pearson, but possibly one of his men. Or it could even be one of the sergeants or clerks in the front office. They usually knew what was going on.

But today they could not know, unless Brabant or Bird had talked out of turn. The tape which the young man had made was safe in Martineau's pocket, and had been there all night. So they could not know of the telephone conversation overheard by Brabant, or that Brabant had overheard a conversation. Therefore, they could not know of the trap which would be set at Grimwood. Only Devery and Cassidy could know or assume that a tape had been made, or that Brabant had overheard something. Martineau trusted each of those as much as he trusted any man, so he began to be reasonably satisfied that the secret would be kept. He studied a large-scale map of the district around Grimwood, and decided on his tactics without putting a single note on paper.

At three o'clock, Devery made a further report on Sam. He

had lunched at his club. At two o'clock he had gone from the club to the Northern Counties Bank. He had entered the bank carrying an apparently empty briefcase. When he had emerged ten minutes later, the briefcase had been bulging. He had locked it in the trunk of the Ferrari and moved along the street to the London and Granchester Bank. Again he had entered with an empty briefcase and emerged—in five minutes this time—with a full one. Then he had gone to G.D.M. and entered, taking both briefcases with him.

Martineau pondered. Ten thousand pounds in two briefcases? He remembered the loot of the Northern Steel pay roll job. Twenty-nine thousand pounds in a big leather traveling bag. He supposed that Sam could now be in possession of the whole ten thousand, especially if some of the notes were fivers.

Then he considered the times involved. Five minutes was pretty quick, if it covered the whole transaction of receiving some thousands of pounds over a bank counter. Five thousand pounds in ones was fifty bundles of a hundred, or a hundred bundles of fifty. Fellows didn't handle bundles of notes like bunches of bananas. Or did they? Perhaps they did, but a small doubt had been planted in Martineau's mind. This time he did make a brief note: the name of a man he had to see.

At four o'clock the team of Devery and Cassidy was relieved by Ducklin and Hearn, in a side street within sight of G.D.M. The new observers had no sooner settled at their posts, looking through the railings and across the huge forecourt of the factory, than they saw Sam on the office steps. A minute later the Ferrari came through the gates and went away at high speed. The following police car was left far behind, but its occupants were not greatly concerned. It had happened before. In the heavy traffic of the city center, they would spot the Ferrari again. If they did not, they would go to Sam's club and his flat and find the car at one of those places.

When they arrived at the flat, Ducklin sent Hearn on reconnaissance, and he found the Ferrari in the garage behind the flat. But, he reported, Sam's Jaguar had been taken out.

"I expect Sam's in the flat," he said. "Somebody else will be using the Jag."

Ducklin was a much more experienced man, and he was cautious by nature. "Who, do you suppose?" he demanded dryly. "D'you think the cleaning woman has gone home in it? I'm going to acquaint the Guv'nor with the facts."

Martineau did not seem to be perturbed by the news. "All right, stay on the job," he said. "I'll put out the word on the Jaguar, just in case."

The word went out. The chief inspector thought that perhaps Sam was using a less noticeable car to go to Marks and Spencer's, to buy a plain suitcase.

But precious time went by, and an hour later the Jaguar was found in a public parking place near Somerset Square. The parking attendant said that the occupant of the car had walked away in the direction of the London and Midland Station. He had been carrying a briefcase and a suitcase. The time, the attendant said, had been about a quarter to five. From his description, the man could have been Sam Glover.

Chapter Twenty-six

"There's a nonstop train to London at five o'clock," said Martineau. "I wonder if Sam has skipped."

"He could have," Devery replied. "He knows we're getting the evidence bit by bit. And he's being blackmailed. He'd feel like a man sixty feet up on a shaky ladder."

The older man reflected that his sergeant did not yet know of Dixie Costello's plans for Sam's future. Nevertheless, it was quite possible that the young man had fled. The breakdown of his own alibi, the knowledge that his deceptions had been fathomed and his motives revealed, the prospect of a lifetime in a blackmailer's hands and the doubt that the blackmailer would succeed in getting his cousin convicted of murder, could have made Sam decide to cut his losses and head for the horizon.

"Anyway, we'll have to do something about it," he said. "Whether he's at home or away, put it out to All Districts. Samuel Cartwright Glover wanted on warrant for murder. May try to leave the country. Believed carrying a large sum of money. Request the special vigilance of all airport police and dock police. I'll get the warrant."

He dialed a number on the internal line, and while he waited he had time to call after Devery, "Send Brabant in here."

Brabant came, and waited while Martineau spoke to the warrant officer. When the brief talk was ended, the chief inspector said, "We think Sam Glover might have cleared out. We've got to act as if he has. How much money have you got?"

"In my pocket, sir? Seven pounds and some change."

"Right. Take a car and go to Marks and Spencer's. Buy yourself a nice suitcase. Bring it back here and see if you can fill it with scrap paper without attracting too much notice. If anybody asks you what you're doing with a suitcase, say you're changing your lodgings and you need an extra case."

"Yes, sir," said Brabant, turning away.

"Just a moment. How good a driver are you?"

"Pretty fair, sir. I passed the Advanced."

"Think you could drive a Ferrari?"

"Yes, sir. I might need a few minutes to get used to it."

"You'll have time to get used to it. If Sam Glover doesn't show up before eight o'clock you're going to commit an offense: taking away a motorcar without the owner's permission. There might be some trouble about it later, but I'll take the knock. Do you get it?"

"Yes, sir. Out to Clingstone along the motorway, turn off at Belshaw, back to Grimwood, dump the suitcase at the cemetery gate at nine thirty and return the Ferrari to the garage. And not a word to a soul."

"Good man. Now go and get that suitcase. When you've filled it with paper, take it to Sergeant Bird. Tell him you want it treated with eosin or something of the sort."

Brabant departed. Martineau found Sam Glover's home telephone number and called his flat. The call was not answered. A man in Sam's harassed situation was not likely to let a call go unanswered. He was not at home.

It was not yet six o'clock. Martineau called the British European Airways office in Bishopsgate. He introduced himself and stated his urgent need. It was a matter of life and death, he said. He wanted a seat on the next plane from Granchester to London.

221

"Eight o'clock," the clerk said. "There will be a seat. Martineau, did you say?"

"The passenger's name will be Devery, Detective Sergeant Devery. Can he pick up his ticket at the airport?"

"That can be arranged, Inspector," the clerk said.

Martineau sent for Devery. "Go home and pack some pajamas and a shirt, and come back here to stand by," he said. "If Sam Glover is still missing at seven o'clock, you're flying to London Airport on the eight o'clock plane. Your seat is booked."

"I won't be in time to meet Sam at Euston," the sergeant said.

That was true. The five o'clock train would arrive in London a few minutes after eight o'clock. There had been no London plane since half past four, so no Granchester policeman could have been in time to meet Sam when he left the train at Euston Station. But Metropolitan police officers would meet the train. If they picked up Sam, Devery would arrive an hour or two later to identify him.

Martineau said, "If the Metro don't spot him, I think he'll make for one of the Channel ports. You'll have to do the best you can."

At seven o'clock, a phone call to Sam's flat again went unanswered. He had not been seen near his flat, and he had not returned to his Jaguar, which was still in the car park under surveillance. It was becoming increasingly clear that he had fled.

"You'd better go and get on that plane," Martineau said to Devery. When the sergeant had gone, the chief inspector sat and considered the things to be done and the precautions to be taken. A great weakness in his plans had been apparent to him since six o'clock. He had applied for a warrant for Sam's arrest, and he had put out an Express Message which would go to all policemen in all police forces. Unless the traitor in the department was at home, off duty, he would naturally know about the Express Message. If he also knew that Dixie Costello was interested in Sam's affairs, he would pass on the information, and Dixie would realize that the case had taken a new turn and act accordingly. There was a chance that the traitor would not connect Sam and Dixie at all. It was a chance which had had to be taken. The scheme to nail Dixie for blackmail and conspiracy was a project dear to him, but even so he had not dared to delay an announcement concerning a fleeing murderer.

Having accepted the hazard, Martineau went forward with his plans. There were certain people whom he had hesitated to approach in case they might somehow manage to warn Sam. The danger of that seemed to be over. He telephoned the Granchester Club and asked if Mr. William Glover was still there. Apparently Mr. Glover was there, engaged in a game of snooker. He asked if Mr. Glover could come to the telephone for just one minute.

Billy came. "Yes, Inspector?" he asked, and there was anxiety in his voice.

"Have you seen Sam since four o'clock?"

"No. Nobody seems to have seen him. He doesn't seem to have been in the club."

"All right. Listen carefully. The job is practically cleared, but tonight there still might be an attempt to put you in the middle."

"In the middle?"

"To frame you. You must have a cast-iron alibi between nine and ten. I advise you to pick up a good book and come here and sit in the C.I.D. for an hour under a policeman's eye. That's the best alibi you could have."

"Very well, I'll do that. Does this mean I'm out of it?"

"It seems that you are. But right now I'm the only person you can trust, if you can bring yourself to trust a copper. I want your word of honor you won't mention this to a soul. Not *anybody*."

"All right. I give you my word."

"Just come and sit here like a good boy. You've got more enemies than you know, so watch your step, now. Good-bye."

After that talk, Martineau told the duty clerk that he wanted to speak to Ducklin or Hearn when the hourly, on-the-half-hour contact with Headquarters was made. He intended to call those two in to H.Q. on the pretext that he needed them, so that they would not be near Sam's flat when Brabant took out the Ferrari. He wanted no witnesses to that illegal act. If all went well, the Ferrari would be out and back again before it was missed. At any rate, nobody would know who had taken it.

He intended to go with Brabant to make sure that he got away in the Ferrari. Also, by abetting the action of taking the car, he would show that he really did intend to take the responsibility. Before he went, he made one more phone call. He spoke to Diana Glover and arranged for her to meet him in his office at half past eight.

Chapter Twenty-seven

Martineau drove the C.I.D. car to Sam Glover's flat. Sergeant Bird sat beside him, holding a small Gladstone bag. Brabant was in the back seat, and the Marks and Spencer suitcase was on the floor beside him.

"A Ferrari is a rare sort of car in this country," Martineau commented. "I shouldn't think any of our keys will fit the ignition. Do you think you'll be able to start it, Sergeant?"

Bird was terse, as always when there was work to be done. He said, "We can hope the top is down. If it is, we'll be able to open the hood. We can start it then."

"You're familiar with the model?"

"I am not, sir. But as far as I've been able to learn, the two-seater Ferrari is the Scagliotti Spyder, and the hood can be opened from the driver's seat. For the rest, all coil ignition is alike in principle. There'll be a circuit which can be closed."

Martineau grinned in the darkness of the car. He made no further remark. He drove past the flat and saw that its windows showed no light. He took the car round the block. Neither he nor his companions could discern any lurking figure. There was one parked car and it was unoccupied. But it was an Aston Martin, a thoroughbred whose performance would compare with a Ferrari's. "I wonder what that DB4 is doing there," Bird muttered.

Martineau went halfway round the block again. He had noticed another entrance to the yard behind Sam's place. He stopped the car and the three men went into the yard by that entrance.

The Ferrari was still standing alone in the open garage. "The top's down," said Martineau with satisfaction. "Brabant, put your case in the corner there, and go and dog out for us. And keep an eye on that Aston Martin."

Bird was at the car, opening his Gladstone bag. He extracted a flashlight and began to look under the dashboard. He found what he sought, and moved to open the hood. He stood looking down at the engine. "Beautiful," he muttered.

With knife, pliers and a length of wire he set to work. Martineau stood looking up at the surrounding windows, to see if the neighbors were curious. Presently, at Bird's request, he sat in the car. "Try her now," the sergeant said.

The starter whirred momentarily and the engine caught. Its roar, as Martineau pressed a little more heavily on the accelerator, brought Brabant from his post. "Nobody has been near the Aston Martin," he reported.

Leaving the engine gurgling happily, the chief inspector climbed out of the driver's seat. "Get in," he said, when the hood was closed. "We'd better have that top up."

When that was done, and Brabant was at the wheel, the suitcase was propped against the seat beside him. He drove carefully out of the yard. His two companions followed him to the entrance, and stood scrutinizing the infrequent passers-by for several minutes after the sound of the car had died away. The Aston Martin was still standing at the curb.

"He'll be all right," said Martineau. "Let's go."

Diana Glover was a few minutes early for her appointment, but Martineau did not keep her waiting. He noted that she was wearing the fur coat and the pearls again. His greeting was civil, but her manner was cold and distant. He remembered that his last interview with her had ended on an unfriendly note. Apparently she was ready to start again from there.

When she was seated he said, "If we can settle one or two small matters, this should be the last time I need to trouble you."

She did not reply, nor did her expression change.

He went on: "I'm curious about a very recent meeting between you and Gordon Barnes in a café. At least I believe it was you, and of course you could be identified."

"Have you been spying on me?" she demanded.

"No, I've been spying on Barnes. And a very worthwhile operation it's been. He was seen to meet you. I want to know what he asked of you."

"I don't know what you mean."

"I'll be more explicit. Did he suggest that you should change your testimony with regard to a certain matter which seemed vital to Billy Glover?"

"No, but I was going to speak to you about that. You see—"

"Don't say it. I don't want to know what you intended to do, because it doesn't matter. Billy doesn't need an alibi. What I do want to know is whether you were threatened or otherwise coerced in this matter. You needn't be afraid to tell me. Nobody will hurt you now. There will be one or two arrests tonight, and after that a certain criminal scheme will be dropped. Were you threatened?"

"In a way. Gordon said he was afraid of a certain person, and he said he couldn't stop this person from having me disfigured if I stuck to my evidence about Billy's alibi. He sort of pleaded with me to save myself from this man."

"Did he name the man?"

"No. He said he was a gangster. I didn't say what I'd do one way or the other, because I was given time to think it over."

"I see. Were you seeing Barnes before your husband's death?"

She was silent. The policeman guessed at her thoughts. Would the police find out anyway?

"I saw him once or twice, always in a public place," she said.

"May I ask why you bothered?"

"I was bored. It made a change."

"Was it Barnes who told you about Sam's visits to Grimwood?"

"Yes. He knew there was a girl, but he didn't know who she was or where she lived."

"Was he nosing along Sam's trail at your instigation?"

"No." The answer was prompt. There had been talk of a criminal scheme.

"What was your real purpose in telling your husband about Sam?"

"It was my duty. The thing wanted stopping. Sam is engaged to a nice girl."

Martineau made no comment. It seemed obvious to him that Diana's aim had been to stir up trouble for Sam. Well, she certainly had succeeded.

He wondered what Diana would say if he told her that her stepson was wanted on warrant for murder. She would ponder the news in relation to herself. The murder of Matthew Glover had been a murder for gain. But even if Sam were sentenced to death he would have time to make a will. And the most certain prediction that anyone could make about Sam's will was that Diana would not be mentioned in it.

Martineau decided that it would be soon enough for Diana to learn about Sam's predicament when she read the morning paper. He rose. "That will be all, Mrs. Glover," he said.

Standing by his desk, she hesitated. "Did you say Billy would be all right?" she asked rather breathlessly.

"He seems to be quite in the clear."

"Will you tell him about—about what we've been talking about?"

The policeman looked at her. Anger rose slowly from some place deep inside him. What did these people have instead of a code of decent behavior? They appeared to value manhood in terms of money, and character by position and background. There was one set of rules for them, and another set for those they regarded as inferior.

"Will I run to Billy with an earful of tittle-tattle?" he asked dryly. "Is that what you mean?"

Her glance dropped, and she had the grace to color slightly.

"I don't handle divorce business or infidelity cases, either," he added coldly. "I believe you said you could find your own way out. Good night."

With that interview over, Martineau turned his attention to the arrangements at Grimwood. He looked at his watch. It was not yet nine o'clock, but his men would already be at their posts, ready to move into place. Behind the hoardings of the railway sidings there would be three men with field radio sets strapped to their backs. One would be opposite the Grimwood Inn, another would be opposite the cemetery gates and the third would be watching for the Ferrari's approach to the cemetery from the other side. There were teams ready to move in and block both ends of Grimwood Road, and more teams on the road which ran behind the cemetery, in case the person or persons detailed to receive the Marks and Spencer suitcase should decide to approach and depart through the cemetery itself. None of these men would move into place until the actual hour of nine thirty, but they would not be later than that time. Martineau was taking a chance that they might reveal themselves too soon, but he wanted to be certain that they would not be too late.

At twenty minutes past nine he was at his own post, near to

the Ferrari's line of approach and inside the area of control. It was a calm, clear night and dry underfoot. There was no traffic in Grimwood Road, and only one pedestrian in sight. This was an elderly woman carrying a large jug. She entered a street-corner pub: she was not in the scheme of things. Apparently there would be no disinterested witnesses to Operation Suitcase.

At twenty-eight minutes past nine Martineau heard the throaty voice of the Ferrari. It shot past the side street where he waited. He listened, and heard the driver slow down, change gear and pick up speed again. Brabant had passed the cemetery gates, and presumably he had jettisoned the suitcase. The walkie-talkie man opposite the gates would now be informing the check-point men that the trap was baited. The check-point men would be moving into place.

A few seconds later it became evident that other men must have been listening to the telltale changes in the Ferrari's engine note. Martineau heard two cars, and he knew that they would not be police cars. His own car was concealed round a corner, and he hastily dodged into hiding round the same corner. Peeping, he saw the cars go by. There seemed to be three men in each car. Well, there they were, inside the control area. They could have been waiting in that area for some time.

Two cars. One of them would be a decoy car, or at any rate its mission would be to obstruct or confuse pursuers. Martineau reflected that he was probably the only policeman on the operation who knew that the blackmailers were using two cars. He had a radio in his own car, but no time to use it: events would be happening too quickly.

He got into his car and drove toward the cemetery. He saw a car standing at the entrance to the little lane where Luke Glover had been murdered. He looked along the road to the Grimwood Inn, and saw red lights and the shapes of stationary vehicles. He could hear voices raised in protest. The decoy car had been caught, and its crew were playing their parts.

He alighted from his car and crossed the road, and walked beside the wall of the railway sidings. "I'm here, sir," somebody called. He moved toward the source of the sound. It was Cook, one of his own men, peering at him between the wall and the hoarding above it.

"What happened?" he asked.

"The sports car passed and the bag was dropped. Then two cars followed. The first car stopped and a fellow got out and grabbed the bag. The second car overtook and passed on, and got stopped further on. So the first car—that one there—reversed to that lane. Three fellows got out, without the bag, and pelted off into the cemetery."

"So we should have 'em bottled in," Martineau said. "All right, stay where you are and watch this frontage, in case they get chased back this way."

He walked to the car. One of the back doors was hanging open. The Marks and Spencer suitcase was on the back seat. It had been opened, and its worthless contents were disarranged and scattered. He closed the door of the car and went along the lane to the side gate of the cemetery.

In that ancient graveyard nothing moved. Even the trees were still. He guessed that the three fugitives would have gone straight through it and over the rear wall, with the idea of escaping in that direction. He did not follow, but took out his flashlight and entered Cemetery Lodge. He searched the place and found it unoccupied. He was in an upstairs room which had two broken windows when he heard a distant shout. Apparently some police-man had spied the fugitives. It was possible that the warning shout had caused them to turn back and seek another way out of the trap. Martineau stayed where he was at one of the broken windows. He gazed out across the graveyard and listened.

He suffered the fate of all watchers in darkness. The night played tricks with his eyes. Bushes moved and gravestones changed position. When he saw figures near the wall adjacent to the Grimwood Inn, he was not sure that he had really seen anything. But he left the lodge and went in that direction.

There was nobody under the trees by the wall, but there was a tree stump which would serve as a high step. He stood on the stump and looked down into the back yard of the Grim-wood Inn. The inn was inside the cordon. It would have to be searched if the fugitives were not found. As a last resort, would they take refuge there and hope to be overlooked?

He climbed over the wall and entered the inn by the back door. In the bar room, the landlady was behind the bar. She was filling a tray of drinks for the landlord to take into one of the rooms. The woman stopped her pumping when Martineau entered. She stared at him, and her expression was hard to define. The landlord turned to see who had entered. There was no doubt about his feelings. He was relieved to see a policeman, but he was also nervous about what might happen.

"Has anybody come in here in the last few minutes?" the detective asked.

"No, Mr. Martineau, nobody," the landlord answered loudly. Then he closed one eye momentarily, and his glance slid toward the open doorway of the taproom.

Martineau nodded. Understanding the man's predicament, he looked in the best room and the snug before he went to the taproom. Standing in the doorway of that room, he surveyed the customers. There were half a dozen men sitting round the fire talking quietly, and they were all strangers to him. At a table to one side, two men were deeply immersed in a game of dominoes. Of those two, the one facing the doorway had his hat well down over his eyes. He was Ned Higgs, Dixie Costello's lieutenant.

There was one other man in the room. He was sitting in the furthest corner, hunched in his seat, and holding a newspaper higher than a reader normally does. His face was hidden by the paper.

Without turning his head, Martineau called, "Landlord!"

The man came. Still watching the newspaper reader and the domino players, the chief inspector addressed him. "George Wensley," he said clearly. "I call for your assistance in the name of the law. Go outside to that road block and bring two or three policemen in here."

The landlord said, "Yes, sir," and departed. The men by the fire turned to look at the policeman. The two tough characters playing dominoes did not raise their eyes from the table. They appeared to have heard nothing.

The man in the corner did not have a mobster's nerves. Unable to stand the suspense, he lowered the newspaper to see what was happening. He was Gordon Barnes. Martineau saw the cornered man's look of alarm pass from his face, to be replaced by weary resignation. He was ripe for the inquisition.

Chapter Twenty-eight

Detective Chief Superintendent Clay came down to Head-quarters that night, to put his mind at rest by finding out exactly what had been happening. He did this because Sam Glover looked like the most socially eligible murderer he had encountered in thirty years of police work. The way the newspapers would play it, it would look as if another war had started. Clay wanted to be sure that no mistake had been made.

"We're doing reasonably well so far," Martineau told him modestly. "I think we'll get one or two convictions."

"How did the blackmail job go?"

"We wheeled in Barnes, Higgs and Waddy. There were three more characters in a decoy car, but it was their own car and we had to let them go. Barnes has eosin on his hands. He was the only one who handled the suitcase. The others were too fly. Barnes is so scared of them that he won't implicate them, and he's taking the rap. He's given a statement. He admits he was blackmailing Sam Glover, and he'll be a witness at Sam's trial."

"With what evidence?"

"On Friday morning he was on his way out to Broadhulme with the intention of seeing Diana and getting her to lend him some money. On the way he was overtaken by Billy Glover. He saw Billy leave his car outside The Beeches and he thought that was a bit odd. He dumped his own car somewhere and

234

hopped over a garden wall among some shrubs and watched from there. He saw Sam drive past in a Jaguar. Sam must have parked the Jag somewhere out of sight, because he was back in a minute or two on foot. He went to Billy's car and unlocked it with a key. He leaned into the car and stood up with something in his hand. He went to the back of the car and he was busy there for about half a minute. Then he got into the car and reached into the back. He took a hat from there and put it on his head. He drove off toward town, and Barnes noticed that the rear number plate of the car was covered by a duster or something of the sort, lightish brown in color. The time was about eleven thirty."

"And he saw Sam come back?"

"At twelve twenty-five, sir. He took the duster off the back of the car, threw it in the car with the hat, locked it up and cleared off. Barnes saw him go by in the Jaguar. Later on Barnes heard about Uncle's murder. He put two and two together and thought he was set for life."

"Where did Sam get keys for the car?"

"Billy kept his spare car keys in an unlocked drawer in his office. We have evidence that Sam knew they were there."

"Can you prove that Sam knew Matthew Glover by sight?"

"We can prove he knew Uncle by sight, and he'd been told that Uncle was Matthew Glover."

"As a witness, Barnes will be attacked. He might be discredited. You'll want more evidence."

"I've got more. Nowadays the lab can type dandruff, like blood. Sam's dandruff was found in Billy's hat, the one taken from the car. Unless Billy suffers from the same sort of dandruff, which is unlikely, we've got evidence."

"H'm. What else?"

"A real find. Sergeant Bird came up with it. Sam was wearing gloves when he handled Billy's car. But the duster was stuck to the back of the car with Cellotape. The Cellotape was still stuck to the duster when we found it. Nobody thought much about that till it occurred to Bird that Sam might have some trouble trying to handle Cellotape with gloves on. So he looked and found a nice thumb print on one piece, and a bad one on the other. The print compares with prints found in Sam's office and in his flat. It's his, all right."

"That's better. You *have* been busy. Now show me motive and opportunity."

"Motive. That had me beaten for a while. On Tuesday the twenty-sixth of September Sam didn't have a care in the world. He was dallying with Ellie Blades in a whimsical sort of a way, and it's my belief he'd grown quite fond of her. His father's murder may have bothered him, but it wasn't until he heard the new will that he was really hurt. The new will more or less gave Glover Carburetors to Billy, and left him with G.D.M. Now, just half an hour ago I learned a trade secret from Billy, which will of course be verified. G.D.M. has made a fortune, but times have changed in the washer business, and next year they expect to lose money. The future is not bright. On the other hand G. Carb. has also made a fortune, with a lot less sweat, toil and tears. And the G. Carb engineers have developed a new fuel injection system which is an improvement on any system Billy has ever heard of, both for power and economy. Luke Glover didn't have much faith in it, just as he didn't have any faith in the first carburetor till it started to make a lot of money. But both Billy and Sam were enthusiastic about it. And, remember, Sam is a motor enthusiast. When Sam heard the terms of the new will, he realized that his father was putting the new fuel injection system into Billy's hands.

"Perhaps that motive alone is not terribly strong considering that Sam would still have G.D.M., but Billy tells me that he can find plenty of witnesses to show that Sam has been pathologically jealous of him from their schooldays. Billy has always been able to beat Sam at everything, and I believe he is even a better car driver. When they were kids Sam cheated all ways to try and win. Recently they've been friends on the surface, but Sam hasn't taken Billy on for years at anything, even on handicap, because he can't bear to be beaten by him."

"That should help. But I'd like more."

"More came through disappointment after a great relief. Jonty Blades came on the scene to tell Sam his made-up story of Luke's murder. At that time Sam would have no reason to doubt the story, especially since he may have wanted to believe it. It would please him to know that Billy's father was a murderous sot. Now I must admit I'm making guesses, but I think they're good ones. I believe Sam took a subtle pleasure in with-holding Jonty's story from Billy, assuming that the police would eventually nail Billy's father for the murder in any case. He simply allowed Jonty to show Billy a sordid old drunk who didn't know what day it was. So far so good, and then the will was read. This great blow must have been followed some time later by the realization that when Uncle was convicted of murder, he would disinherit himself and Billy as well, and that he, Sam, as residual heir would get practically the whole of Luke's estate. So Sam would be on top of the world again for a few hours until he learned from Ellie that it was not Uncle but Gaylord who had killed his father. Imagine how he felt. Billy was going to win after all. Billy was going to get the new fuel injection system. The disappointment must have been enough to drive him slightly crazy, and maybe it did. Well, he assumed that he could control Ellie. If Uncle was put out of the way, he wouldn't be able to deny Gaylord's convincing story. What followed then would seem to be logical. And easy. Being jealous of Billy, he knew more about his movements than he was aware of. He knew about the visits to Diana. He didn't know how to walk along a street and steal a car, but he

237

knew how he could steal Billy's. And of course he could lay the blame on Billy. The whole thing would seem beautifully simple."

"Simple to him, crazy to you and me. But anyway there's an element of madness in nearly all murders. All right, that's motive. What else?"

"Well, Barnes started to blackmail him. When I asked him about withdrawals from the bank he thought he'd better admit them and say he'd lent the money to Billy. Then he got Dixie Costello on his trail. That was bad, but bearable as long as Costello was going to make sure that Billy took the blame for his father's murder. That would have been another case of automatic disinheritance, you see. Then we busted his own alibi for Friday. He found that out, and he learned that we knew he'd known all the time that Uncle hadn't killed his father. *He* thought we'd perceive motive there, all right. He lost his nerve and cleared out."

"Is there anything more?"

"Brabant's evidence of a telephone conversation. Also, we'll put Sam up for identification, to see if any of the witnesses of Uncle's murder can pick him out."

"I think you've got him right. It's a pity you didn't get Costello or any of his mob for the blackmail job."

Martineau sighed. "I'm sure that villain has a line into the C.I.D., and has had for years. I'd dearly love to find that traitor. As soon as I have an hour to spare I'll go to work on Higgs and Waddy. I can only do my best." Again he sighed. "Sometimes I wonder if I ever will lay hands on Costello. It always seems that the most I can do is ruin his day."

"I wouldn't worry too much about it," Clay said. "You've got enough to do as it is. When Sam is brought back here, you'll *really* start to be busy."

Detective Sergeant Devery was met at the airport reservations office by the airport police duty officer. The two men knew each other. They shook hands.

"You're late," the duty officer said, as Devery pocketed his ticket. "Only I can get you on the plane at this time. We're waiving quite a number of regulations in this life and death matter of yours. Come, this way."

Devery thanked him as he led the way to the plane. He grinned. "I suppose it's got something to do with this Sam Glover, wanted for murder," he said. "Where do you hope to find him?"

"We think he took the five o'clock London train. If the Scotland Yard lot pick him up as he leaves the train, I may have to identify him. If they haven't got him, I shall proceed with caution in whatever direction I think he's gone."

"What about London Airport? Or Gatwick?"

"We don't think he's had time to get on a flight."

"He may have got a cancellation," was the cheerful retort. "After all, you did."

At the plane a crew officer and a girl ticket checker waited at the foot of the steps, and a white-coated steward looked down from the plane itself.

"Is this the gentleman?" the crew member asked briskly, when Devery proffered his ticket to the girl. "Come on, up you go, sir. You're late."

Devery bade good-bye to the duty officer, and went up the steps. In the plane, the steward led the way to a forward seat. The crew member brought up the rear, rather testily urging Devery to get along and take his seat.

But the sergeant was not to be hurried. He looked to left and right as he moved up the aisle, scrutinizing his fellow passengers. He stopped when he saw a youngish man in a new hat and a new raincoat, wearing dark glasses and looking at a magazine.

"Really, Mr. Glover!" he reproved. "Dark glasses at night! The most fatal way of drawing attention to yourself. I didn't

239

expect to find you on this plane. A rare piece of luck for me. I'm afraid there's a warrant for your arrest. Come along, you'll have to get off. Steward! This gentleman's luggage will have to be put off the plane."

"Oh, hell," said the officer. "Now we *are* going to be late."

In the taxi which took Devery and Sam Glover from the airport to police headquarters, there was silence for some time. The sergeant was waiting for his prisoner to protest, demand an explanation, claim that a mistake had been made. But Sam had nothing to say.

Eventually it was the policeman who spoke. "Want to talk? It'll pass the time," he invited. "I don't mean talk about murder, this isn't the place for it. But there are other things."

Sam's lips moved briefly. His tone was sulky and contemptuous. "Such as?"

"Well, we never saw you go to the BEA office. I suppose you phoned them sometime today and arranged to pick up your ticket at the airport. Is that right?"

"Of course. I can tell you that much."

"And this, for instance." Devery took a passport from his pocket. "Made out in the name of John Henderson, engineering consultant, care of the Granchester Club, Granchester. It bears your description and your photograph. How come?"

"I don't see why I should tell you."

"Perhaps not," said Devery unconcernedly. "But there is a passport offense already, and I'm the man who will have to report it. An explanation will be required. It'll save time if you give it now. Here, have a cigarette."

"I'll smoke my own, thank you," said Sam. But he accepted a light.

"I think you must have been very clever about this passport," the sergeant pursued. "I don't quite see how you did it."

Sam was still contemptuous. "It was simple enough."

240

"Who is John Henderson?"

Sam sighed, and condescended to explain. "He's a draughts-man at G.D.M. Once—months ago—I was passing through the drawing office during the tea break. The talk must have been about passports or travel. I heard Henderson boast that he didn't have a passport. He'd never been overseas and he didn't intend to go. Old England was good enough for him. It occurred to me then that a spare passport might be useful someday. I had some new passport pictures taken, and I got an application form and got it filled in. I wasn't breaking my neck over the thing, but I did look for a chance of getting hold of some document of Henderson's, in case it was needed for identification. I got it during a cricket match at the works sports club. He was out there fielding. I'd noticed where he hung his clothes, and I bor-rowed his driving license and his club card. I went off and sub-mitted the application, then returned the things to Henderson's wallet. He was still fielding."

"Didn't the clerk at the passport office compare the signature on the driving license with your signature?"

"It was a girl. I exerted myself to be nice to her. She barely glanced at the club card and didn't open the license. Anyway, Henderson hadn't signed it."

"It sounds simple, but I can see snags. Who was your referee on the application?"

Sam allowed himself a sour grin. "My father. He was a J.P., you know. I put the form in front of him with some other stuff to be signed. He said, 'H'm, passport,' and did the necessary."

"But he should also have endorsed one of the passport photos."

"Yes, but he didn't know that. He never went abroad, either. I traced his signature on the back of the photograph."

"Didn't the girl query your address, the Granchester Club?"

"No. I told her I was unmarried. I said I'd just started as a consultant, and I expected to travel around a lot. I said I could always be reached through my club."

241

"When you'd made the application, the passport would be sent to the club under the name of Henderson."

"The hall porter sorts the mail at the club. I told him I was expecting a letter under that name. He gave me the letter, and I gave him a good tip. He knows how to mind his own business."

"A very nice little operation. It's better to have a good false passport than no passport at all."

Devery gently kicked the suitcase which was on the floor of the cab. "What about this? It's an awful lot of money. How did you raise it so quickly?"

"I got it from two separate banks with a tale about buying a private airplane for cash. Perhaps they didn't believe me but it was none of their business what I was doing. The security was there, and that's all they needed. I knew they wouldn't say anything to the police."

There was silence for a while, and Devery fell to musing on this clever young man's mistakes: the blunders caused by expediency, the error of relying on faulty human instruments, the belief in the gullibility of others. And at the end, dark glasses!

And Billy, who was to have lost everything, would take control of G. Carb. and, for the time being, of G.D.M. as well. The very thing which Sam had ruined himself to prevent.

Family affairs were no business of Devery's, but he was curious by nature. "That was one for the book," he said. "Billy and your stepmother. I wonder how serious that was. She'll be after him now all right, now she knows he'll be rich. Do you think he'll wed her?"

"What the devil do I care about that?"

"He's too good for her, in my opinion."

"Oh, much too good!" the prisoner snarled. "Goody goody Billy, the young Adonis. Getting into bed with his aunt."

"Tut tut tut," said Devery.

>>> If you've enjoyed this book and would like to discover more great vintage crime and thriller titles, as well as the most exciting crime and thriller authors writing today, visit: >>>

The Murder Room
Where Criminal Minds Meet

themurderroom.com

9 781471 902772